BLISS
WAS IT
IN BOHEMIA

MICHAL VIEWEGH

BLISS WAS IT IN BOHEMIA

Translated from the Czech by
DAVID SHORT

JANTAR PUBLISHING 2015

First published in London, Great Britain in 2015 by
Jantar Publishing Ltd
www.jantarpublishing.com

Czech edition first published in Prague in 1992 as
Báječná léta pod psa

Michal Viewegh
Bliss was it in Bohemia
All rights reserved

Original text © Michal Viewegh
Translation copyright © 2015 David Short
Jacket & book design by Jack Coling

The right of David Short to be identified as translator of this work has been asserted
in accordance with the Copyright, Design and Patents Act, 1988.
No part of this book may be reproduced or utilised in any form or by any
means, electronic or mechanical, including photocopying, recording or by any
information storage and retrieval system without written permission.

A CIP catalogue record for this book is available from the British Library.
ISBN 978-0-9933773-2-7

Printed and bound in the Czech Republic by EUROPRINT a.s.

This translation was made possible by a grant from the Ministry of Culture of the Czech Republic.

CONTENTS

Foreword
iii

Translator's note
ix

Bliss was it in Bohemia
1

Appendix
275

FOREWORD

If you ask a Czech reader to name a contemporary Czech author, chances are high they will choose Michal Viewegh. Having started his literary career in 1990 with his first novel *Názory na vraždu* [Opinions on a Murder] and thanks to his prolific production, Viewegh's name has become synonymous with the successes of Czech literature in the new, post-socialist era. Ten of his novels have been adapted for the screen, including *Bliss was it in Bohemia.** Directed by Petr Nikolaev in 1997, the film version of the novel has become part of the canon of comedies that look back at the period of state socialism – when

---

* The title of the screen version is translated as "The Wonderful Years of Lousy Living". See Translator's note.

the country was ruled by the Communist Party – that have shaped the collective memory of the past for many Czechs.

In 1992, when *Bliss was it in Bohemia* was first published, Viewegh was not yet the household name he is now. His position within the Czech literary field is practically unique. Born in 1962, Viewegh initially studied economics and later Czech in order to become a teacher. But by the early 1990s, after only a few years of teaching, he gave up his career and became a full-time writer, a position enabled by the huge commercial success of his works, which has earned him both condemnation from critics and a large following among readers. A number of his novels and short stories have been translated into German but his 1994 novel *Výchova dívek v Čechách* [Bringing up Girls in Bohemia] is the only other novel available in English. In December 2012, Viewegh suffered a traumatic aortic rupture and it was thought at the time that he would never write again. His many Czech readers were surprised when he published his twenty-fifth novel in 2013 called *My Life after Life*.

Bliss was it in Bohemia was the breakthrough novel of a then largely unknown young author. At that time, condemnation of the previous regime ruled public debates, and various legislative measures were introduced to deal with the crimes perpetrated during forty years of Communist Party rule. In this atmosphere, Viewegh's tackling of the socialist period with humour and detachment arrived like a breath of fresh air. Viewegh was not the first to look back upon aspects of this past with light-hearted humour; one can think of the film adaptations of Miloslav Švandrlík's *Černí baroni* [Black Barons] or Josef Škvorecký's *Tankový prapor* [The Tank Battalion], which drew crowds into cinemas in the early 1990s. These texts, however, were written earlier, at a time when their critical tone consigned them to the drawer, and their authors had to wait for the changes brought about by the Velvet Revolution of November 1989 to see them published. *Bliss was it in Bohemia* was perhaps the first novel of the 1990s to reckon with the recent past using gentle humour. The book, published when the author was thirty, was heralded as the voice of a generation that could look back at the period of its youth and adolescence with self-deprecating irony.

The partially autobiographical novel narrates how defining moments of recent Czechoslovak history touched the lives of one – rather eccentric – family. Through the characters of the mother, father, grandparents and, in particular, the incisive commentary of the narrator, Kvido, Viewegh paints a political trajectory that was not uncommon for many in Czechoslovakia. Initially, the characters place high hopes in the liberalization and reforms of the 1960s, summarised by the slogan 'socialism with a human face', only to be shocked and disillusioned by the Warsaw Pact invasion that put an end to this period of relative freedom in August 1968. In the ensuing decades of "Normalisation", many of those who had supported the progressive agenda of the "Prague Spring" were expelled from the Communist Party or forced to leave their jobs. In the novel, the father, having been a "reform economist" in the 1960s, is demoted to a job with a glass manufacturer in the provincial town of Sázava. During the following twenty years until the "Velvet Revolution", the family must make everyday political compromises – since conformity guaranteed a decent standard of living.

However, it is not this large historical narrative that is Viewegh's main focus. What enables him to look back upon these occasionally traumatic years with humour is the perspective of his narrator, Kvido, who recounts late socialism as his older self, looking back upon the times when he was a precocious child and later insecure teenager. The discrepancy between the adult and childhood view is expressed already in the Czech title of the novel, *Báječná léta pod psa*. On the one hand, the years of Kvido's childhood and adolescence are filled with pleasant memories – *báječná léta*, or *wonderful years*. On the other hand, they also took place in the difficult period of late socialism – hence *léta pod psa*, or *years that sucked*. The tension between these two positions provides the book's humour, as the juxtaposition of a narrative of the past with a retrospective present view reveals various comic incongruities. Thus, for instance, when the invading tanks come rolling into Prague in August 1968, little Kvido believes he is witnessing a film crew. Especially in the first half of the novel, Viewegh effectively exploits the gap between the wider context known to the reader and the political innocence of Kvido. For the young protagonist, knocking down the portrait of President Husák in a game of skittles at school is an unfortunate accident; for his cautious father, it is a deliberate political provocation on the part of his son. Viewegh thus set a precedent for practically all post-1989 comic depictions of socialism, which would go on to use a young protagonist to generate an indulgent view of the period.

Later, as Kvido gets older, much of the comedy of the novel focuses on the figure of the father, whose fate also contains a hefty dose of the tragic. The father realises that all the family's material troubles would be solved if he joined the Communist Party, yet he resists. When his boss at work, Comrade Šperk, enumerates to him, "You haven't registered for an evening course in Marxism-Leninism, you don't attend meetings, you hold no official positions, you simply don't show any kind of *commitment*!", he, and with him the reader, realises how many moral sacrifices are required to lead a "normal" life. Yet Viewegh treats the father's dilemmas comically and in his attempts to please Šperk has him go through a number of embarrassing situations. The portrayal of the father places Viewegh's prose within the tradition of the popular Czech hybrid genre known as "bittersweet comedy".

Through small, private episodes, Viewegh paints a picture of the joys, fear, small acts of heroism and moments of cowardice that the period afforded. What makes the description of such events particularly enjoyable is Viewegh's language, which playfully switches between registers and genres and never fails to convey subtle irony. David Short's deft translation brings to life the nuances of tone and plentiful allusions, from Kvido's prematurely intellectual observations, to Grandpa Josef's salt-of-the-earth pieces of wisdom, and the mother's frequent quotations from her theatrical roles. The English version effectively guides the reader through a novel with a complex self-referential structure, where retrospective memories are constantly interspersed with later reflections that eventually result in the main protagonist completing the manuscript of a novel also entitled *Bliss was it in Bohemia*. Light-hearted and sophisticated at once, this is a book that reminds us that comedy too can successfully tackle large historical subjects.

Veronika Pehe
London, August 2015

TRANSLATOR'S NOTE

This tale is firmly set in Central Bohemia – Prague and the glassworks town and mediaeval monastic centre of Sázava a little way to the south-west on the picturesque river of the same name. Excursions to places further afield are very much of the age – the Baltic coast of the GDR as a holiday destination, Croatia and London as places with business links, both highly exotic to the largely untravelled 'ordinary' Czechs.

Bohemia is then central, with any associated thought of 'bohemia' not beyond the realm of fantasy.

As I read it, I was put in mind of *Tristram Shandy*, though any similarity to the great English classic is probably largely fortuitous. The present, equally 'biographical' story is much more condensed (and we get the quasi-narrator's birth at the beginning, not a third of the way through), and the problems presented are of a different order of topicality (notwithstanding the tenor of the author's disclaimer), though the treatment has a whimsy not too dissimilar from Sterne's.

The actual task of translating this book was by no means as fraught as some others, not least because I had plenty of first-hand and second-hand experience of the events in the background of the narrative. The language is straightforward, with little variation in style outside the direct speech, and even the latter presents no great difficulty. The whimsical lapses into verse adopted by one character mercifully lent themselves readily to an English rendition. One minor problem proved to be the quotations from other writers: with the aid of the author's agent I did manage to trace the initially opaque line from Shakespeare, but that from Eugene O'Neill has remained as a back-translation, which is certainly close to the original, though all attempts to find the real source have failed.

The one HUGE problem was the title. The original defies any neat literal matching; an approximate version might be along the lines: 'Those fabulous years of lousy living.' However, this was found wanting and alternatives were sought – the publisher even held an open competition to invite suggestions, and these came in from all over the world. I never saw them all, but there must have been several dozen all told. The title finally agreed on takes us back to English literature, to Wordsworth.

In his 'French Revolution', as many will recall, he has the lines:

> Bliss was it in that dawn to be alive,
> But to be young was very heaven!—Oh! times,
> In which the meagre, stale, forbidding ways
> Of custom, law, and statute, took at once
> The attraction of a country in romance!

which are about changing times and perhaps hint at uncertain outcomes, as is also pinpointed in the closing lines:

> But in the very world, which is the world
> Of all of us,—the place where in the end
> We find our happiness, or not at all!

So I have adopted the Wordsworthian idea of bliss and relocated it to Bohemia and the aura of the Czechoslovak winds of change that blew in such contrary directions between the 1960s and 1980s. Any bliss is obviously contingent on change. I leave it to others to judge how far the title suits, how well it sits with the story that follows.

David Short
Windsor, July 2015

This novel – like most novels, when all's said and done – is, typically, a patchwork of what is called the truth and what is described as a fiction. Whatever the ratio between these two components might be, it cannot be claimed with certainty – notwithstanding the assertions of numerous readers – that the novel's characters are actually living persons and that the events narrated really did happen.

Nor, of course, can it be claimed – as many authors would have us believe at this point – that "the persons and events portrayed in the story that follows are entirely fictitious".

I.

1. By Zita's reckoning, Kvido should have been born during the first week of August 1962 at the Podolí maternity hospital.

By that time, his mother's acting career had seen her through twelve seasons already, though she viewed the vast majority of the children's parts she'd had, in plays by Alois Jirásek, Josef Kajetán Tyl, Pavel Kohout or Anton Semyonovich Makarenko, as ever so slightly compromising sins of her youth. As things stood, she was in the fourth year of her law degree and took being an extra at the Czechoslovak Army Theatre in Vinohrady as something she did just for fun (though that didn't prevent her from making out to her more successful fellow thespians that the largely fortuitous circumstance of the birth's coming during the summer recess was a matter of perfectly obvious professional self-discipline). However paradoxical it may sound, though, Kvido's mother – one-time star of school plays – was in fact, beneath the veneer of a keen enthusiast for amateur dramatics, an extremely shy person, and apart from Zita no one else was ever permitted to examine her. Zita, senior consultant at the Podolí maternity hospital and Grandma Líba's close friend of many years' standing, strove patiently to accommodate her whim, promising to reorganise the doctors' rota so as to ensure that there wouldn't be a single male present on the day.

"At Podolí, under Zita's reign,
  having a baby comes without pain,"

Kvido's Grandma Líba jingled at lunch, and even his father's father, Grandpa Josef, though resolutely sceptical towards anything communist – and he made no exception even for the health service – was prepared to concede that the probability of Kvido's head getting crushed with the forceps was likely to be below average on this occasion.

The one thing no one reckoned with was the bedraggled black Alsatian who showed up on the evening of August twenty-seventh in the ruddy glow of the sun on the embankment, just as Kvido's mother was hauling herself out of her taxi, and who – after taking a short, silent run-up – pinned her against the warm plaster of a house on the corner of St Anne's Square. It cannot be said that the stray dog's intentions were blatantly hostile – he didn't bite her even once; it sufficed, however, that he put his entire weight on her thin shoulders, panting straight into her face with – as his mother put it later in perhaps not the best-chosen terms – "the rank smell of a mouth that hadn't seen a toothbrush in ages".

"Eeeek!" Kvido's mother shrieked having partly got over the initial shock.

Kvido's father, waiting as arranged outside the Theatre on the Balustrade, heard the shriek and shot off towards it. He may not have been sure whose the fear-distorted voice was, but there was an instantaneous odd sensation in his gut that needed to be eliminated.

"Eeeeeek!" Kvido's mother shrieked again even more piercingly, given that the dog's front paws were literally crushing her fragile collar bones. Kvido's father's suspicions were unfortunately confirmed. For a split second, he froze, paralysed by some uncanny power, but then he broke free and ran towards the voice that, to him, was the dearest of all voices. He sprinted across the granite paving of the square, filled with a love now tainted with rage, fearing that his wife had been attacked by yet another of the string of inebriates whom she, having once played Hettie, the third waitress in Arnold Wesker's *The Kitchen*, was apt to try to talk some sense into instead of simply giving them a wide berth. Then suddenly, he saw his wife holding out against the monstrous black burden with the last fibres in her body and did something that in Kvido's eyes gave even greater stature to his five feet eight inches: he grabbed the nearest dustbin, lifted it up and whacked the dog several times with its bottom edge, killing it on the spot.

Kvido's mother would later claim that the bin had been full, though I believe it's fairly safe to say it wasn't. What's worse, though, is that a *conscious* role in the whole incident – and so the right to offer an eye-witness account – is claimed by Kvido himself:

"Obviously I don't deny that in all likelihood I was, like any other foetus, blind at the time," he said later, "but somehow I must have been taking things in because why else would I be so overcome with emotion every time I see binmen at work?"

Evidently desiring to outdo Tolstoy, whose memory allegedly went back to the very threshold of childhood, Kvido would go even further in later years as he tried, for example, to convince his younger brother, with a chilling gravity, that he could visualise perfectly that "dim Rembrandtesque image of our mother's egg clinging to the mucous membrane of her womb in the manner of a swallow's nest".

"Christ, Kvido, you don't half talk some rubbish!" Paco would rail at him.

"Discounting the incident with the dog, I have to say that for any, even slightly intelligent foetus, pregnancy is unimaginably boring," Kvido rambled on unperturbed. "I say 'intelligent' deliberately, so as to exclude all those bare, paralytic, cave salamander-like things, of which you are a prime example, as indeed you remained for several days *after* you were born, when I had the misfortune to stare willy-nilly into your ugly purple mug. But you might be able to *imagine* just how boring those roughly two hundred and seventy days are, each one exactly like the one before, when the now *active* consciousness is condemned to be staring passively out into amniotic fluid, just aiming the odd kick at the wall of the womb so that those 'up there' don't start panicking. Two hundred and seventy days without a decent book, without a single written word, if we discount the hackneyed dedication on Zita's ring! Nine months in an aquarium with the lights off! I spent the last three months praying that Mother would at last break one of those ridiculous taboos and take me out for a cross-country motorbike ride, or send me down a couple of puffs of cigarette smoke, if not a decent glass of white Cinzano. Believe me, brother: That dog was a godsend!"

Kvido first made his impatience quite plain for the first time when his mother, weeping slightly hysterically, collapsed into his father's arms. But the dead dog was itself enough to draw the attention of those who stopped to gawk, and the very idea of another scandal, this time in the form of being brought to bed prematurely, was plainly more than his mother could take. So she wiped her eyes and smiling bravely, radiantly even, she assured all the many enquirers that she was perfectly all right, really.

"My mother," Kvido recalled later, "never ever left a party to go to the toilet unless she could do so unobserved. And not to put too fine a point on it, she was always inordinately embarrassed even by the simple act of blowing her nose."

It was to her utter diffidence, which did have a certain girlish charm to it, that Kvido's mother owed protracted bouts of sinusitis and cystitis, her habitual constipation and, from the twenty-seventh of June, 1962, also her *in-theatre* delivery:

her contractions had started just as she was handing her light check coat in at the cloakroom, yet she did manage to put Kvido off – hypnotised by the imploring looks of Kvido's father – until the final curtain, though not a moment longer. For as soon as Estragon and Vladimir had exchanged their final words, followed by that familiar brief silence before the applause starts, Kvido's mother let out her first cry of anguish, followed at once by a whole string of others. Kvido's father sprang from his seat and, struggling past the row of transfixed spectators, beat a path to the foyer, thence into the night in order – as he doubtless imagined – to make, coolly and calmly, whatever arrangements he thought necessary. As luck would have it, an elderly lady sitting to Kvido's mother's right came quickly to her senses: she had her two neighbours phone for an ambulance and she herself attempted to steer the mother-soon-to-be out of the crowded, stuffy auditorium. Kvido's mother did her level best to hold on, mortified at the prospect of giving birth in the presence of so many men, but also – as she would maintain later – it struck her as rather tactless to disturb the Beckett-induced atmosphere of existential hopelessness with anything so provocatively optimistic as giving birth to a healthy child. But, despite her resolve, she collapsed at her conductress's feet just as they were proceeding along the aisle beneath the footlights, where she was later raised up by two men, almost to the very feet of Václav Sloup and Jan Libíček, who had come to take a bow, but now stood rooted to the spot in horror. The audience, apart from a handful of women, who, disregarding their evening gowns, hurtled towards the stage to give the young mother the benefit of their own experience, stayed where they were, probably in the belief that the birthing scene, which was getting closer by the second, was part of the production, if conceived somewhat untraditionally.

"Water. Fetch some hot water!" someone with initiative shouted. "And some clean sheets!"

"Clear the theatre!" one of the doctors present ordered, having finally forged a way through to the mother-to-be.

"Please go!" he demanded urgently, but no one made a move.

"Eeeeeee!" screamed Kvido's mother.

A few minutes later the auditorium echoed to the howls of a new baby of the male sex.

"It's Godot!" yelped Jan Libíček in a flash of inspiration, which might easily have proved fatal.

"Godot! Godot!" the audience chanted enthusiastically, while the two doctors modestly acknowledged the applause. (Fortunately the nickname didn't stick.)

"We're saved!" declaimed Václav Sloup.

"His name's Kvido," Kvido's mother whispered, but no one heard. From the embankment came the wailing siren of an approaching ambulance.

2. "Just so's you know," Kvido told his editor years later, "I'm in no mind to keep drawin' the entire tree o' life wi' branches all over t' place till some dead executive in construction or steward of the Thun estates falls off it an' tells me who I am, where I come from an' that Masaryk fired on the workers!"

"I think," said the editor in a conciliatory tone, "we'd best leave Masaryk out of it. Wasn't your paternal grandfather a miner?"

"Picked a right one there, you 'ave!" Kvido laughed. "Wanted to own a hotel, 'e did! You should've 'eard 'im! When a delegation arrived at Tuchlovice unannounced an' t' Comrades didn't 'ave time to change Grandad's shift, they thought it best to keep him down t' pit. While t' other miners were 'aving a session wi' t' Party delegation, Grandad were all alone deep underground, cussin' and bangin' away like crazy at t' pipes. – T' other miners called 'im Cinderella."

"All well and good," said the editor. "But how do we use that?"

"Exackly," said Kvido. "How…"

Kvido's father was born with a high IQ into lowly circumstances. Day after day for twenty-one years, they were brought home to him: the beds never made, the smell of gas and warmed-up meals, the empty bottles and the scattered bird seed. Night after night, the drunks leaving the pub next door, Banseths', would throw up right beneath the window of their one-room ground-floor flat in Sezima Street. The scruffy plaster on the wall outside was often smeared with the blood of Gypsies from Nusle. Kvido's grandfather used to leave early in the morning or right after lunch to take the miners' shuttle-bus to Kladno; whenever he was at home, he would pace the room, smoking and crushing bird seed underfoot.

"Life's a bitch," he was often heard to say.

On other occasions, he would spend hours feeding the budgies or playing records of Louis Armstrong or Ella

Fitzgerald with the volume up high. Kvido's grandmother, a furrier, was at home all the time, working away with her needle from morning till night. She would bumble around her old tailor's dummy, her mouth full of pins. The wood-block floor creaked. Kvido's father tried to kill time anywhere he could: He and his friend Zvára would go climbing the old walls at Vyšehrad. They would play hide-and-seek among the rolling stock parked in the sidings at Vršovice station. Sometimes they spent the night in the main hall of the local grammar school. Later, they would hang out in a reading room at the university, which was the whim of Kvido's father, or at the Demínka coffee house, as Zvára preferred. They would take odd jobs and Kvido's father would spend two evenings a week at night school, studying English. Coming home after nightfall and reading out of his textbook by the light of a small table lamp, the book propped against the poo-covered bird-cage, he sometimes felt he was saying the words of some mysterious prayer.

At one point early on in their eighth semester Zvára brought Kvido's father a ticket for the theatre. His expression spoke volumes: she who had been its intended beneficiary had for some reason declined.

"What's the play?" Kvido's father asked. "Who wrote it?" He was no theatregoer and could scarcely expect the play's title to mean anything to him, but he needed to have a cop-out in case the ticket was too expensive.

"Does it matter!" said Zvára, as if appealing to the understanding of the passers-by. "Shakespeare, probably, who else?"

But he was wrong. It was Lorca's *The Shoemaker's Prodigious*

Wife. During the interval they ran into a former girlfriend of Zvára's, who introduced them to her companion, a slim bespectacled girl in a dark-blue velvet dress with a white lace collar.

"And *not* covered in budgie poo," Kvido always added.

It was Kvido's mother.

Three months later, Kvido's father was taken for the first time inside the flat on Paris Commune Square. Obviously, he noted the size of the two rooms, the height of the ceilings, the gleaming piano and the many pictures, but what impressed him most was Grandpa Jiří's study: the whole length of the farther wall was taken up by a mahogany bookcase holding at least a thousand books, and in front of it there was a roll-top writing desk, also in a dark wood, concealing beneath its slatted top a typewriter and much other office paraphernalia, including sealing wax, the family seal and a letter opener.

"Come in and sit down," Grandpa Jiří indicated a leather armchair.

"Do you eat carrot spread?" Grandma Líba popped in from the kitchen to ask.

"Have done for twenty years or more," said Grandpa glumly, lighting a Dux cigarette.

"I wasn't asking you," Grandma smiled teasingly. "I'm talking to our guest."

"I eat anything," said Kvido's father truthfully. "Don't worry on my account."

"Don't you worry," said Kvido's mother somewhat enigmatically. "She won't."

Although both grandparents clung to a modicum of vigilance (Kvido's mother was their only daughter, after all), the visit exceeded all expectations. Kvido's father kept a grip on himself and weighed every word; so in the end, Grandpa took to him more than he did to most of the young actors, poets and scriptwriters who came to the flat to read their outpourings, blamed Grandpa for the horrors of the nineteen-fifties and spilled red wine on his desk.

"Come again sometime," he bade him almost casually as he left, but at that moment Kvido's mother knew that Kvido's father had stood the test.

3. "So I was born prematurely," Kvido would tell people. "Both grandmothers were totally distressed. By the age of one I weighed fourteen kilos, but they kept trying to keep me alive. And at five, they went into battle to save my skin by means of chocolate eclairs."

Kvido was the first grandchild on both sides and so became permanent flavour of the month. They all (except Grandpa Jiří) tried to outdo one another in the number of times they took Kvido to the zoo. It was some time before Kvido realised that hippos, ostriches and kangaroos are not domestic animals.

Every trip to the zoo was naturally followed by a visit to a cake shop.

"What's the lovely smell, Kvido dear?" Grandma Vera would ask.

"It's coffee!" little rotund Kvido would reply, so sweetly that all present would be overcome with a sense of barely definable nausea.

Whenever Kvido's mother introduced her son to anyone at the theatre, her voice was tinged with a kind of provocatively cautionary tone.

"Especially after one middle-ranking director of short films jokingly asked if they might borrow him for their current public-information film on the merits of hormonal contraception," Kvido would explain. "Anyway – as I realise now – that was the only time in my life when I was loved to maximum effect, while affording minimum grounds for it. They loved me for the simple reason that I *was*. Those were the days!"

Grandpa Josef used to take Kvido fishing, to football matches or to feed the seagulls.

"Sock it to 'em!" Grandpa would holler from the terrace.

"Here you are, greedy-guts," he would call to the gulls down by the river.

"Hold still, you can have the skin," he would snap at a worm resisting being hooked for bait.

All this took place at a terrible speed that Kvido could never quite fathom back then. At home, Grandpa was in a hurry to get to the match; even before half-time he'd head round to the refreshment stand for hot-dogs, which they hadn't finished before he had them careering back to their seats in case someone took them – and twenty minutes before the end of the match they'd be scrambling past the expletive-spouting spectators and heading for home. Grandpa was in a hurry to go fishing and in a hurry to get back home, he hurried to and from work, to and from the pub. Hardly had he arrived somewhere and he'd be looking to go somewhere else. It was a long time before Kvido understood what made him so unsettled: his grandfather was in such a hurry so as to outrun the bitch of life.

Kvido – unlike his father and grandfather – had been fond of the tiny flat in Sezima Street. He hadn't lived there, but Grandma Vera would often let him stay with her so that he wouldn't have to go to nursery. He could play with the soft furs and there were those three pretty blue budgies flying about. He was filled with glee at the realisation that while he was lounging around on sheepskin cushions and idly watching budgies clawing their way up smoke-imbued curtains, his coevals were being subjected to some boring programme aimed at turning them into better persons. Grandma had her budgerigars so well trained that she could leave the window open and they wouldn't fly away. They would promenade up and down the window sill and only if they were joined noisily by one of the thousands of local pigeons would they scuttle back inside and perch on their protectress's head and shoulders. In the summertime, so as not to get scratched by their little claws, Grandma would thread two empty pin cushions onto the straps of her camisole.

"When all three of the birds took up position on her," Kvido would tell people, "two on her shoulders and one on her head, Grandma achieved all the symmetry of an altar, literally."

One thing that Kvido couldn't stand though, was Grandpa's habit of sharing his food with the budgies: first he would carefully chew up whatever it was, then open his mouth wide – and the birds immediately flew down and demanded their share, pecking at his nicotine-stained false teeth.

"Never in my life, not even in any of the porn films I've seen," Kvido would tell people, "have I seen anything more revolting than those three little drool-soaked, feathered heads inserting themselves by turn into Grandpa's mouth full of sour cream sauce."

If Grandpa Jiří seemed somewhat restrained in his treatment of his grandson, it certainly wasn't for any lack of love: for one thing his work in the President's office kept him far busier than anyone else in Kvido's family, and for another he did not mean, as he put it himself, to go *competing* for the child's favour. He preferred to wait his turn, not foisting himself on the lad, and certainly not – as the two grandmothers were so keen on doing to spite each other – more or less secretly kidnapping him. But whenever the boy was entrusted to him at last, he would have a hugely detailed plan worked out for him so that Kvido never knew a moment's boredom: they might fly to Karlovy Vary, take the steamer up-river to Slapy, they climbed dozens of Prague's many towers and spires, gradually they took in all the city's museums, Petřín Hill, Vyšehrad, the planetarium and, of course, the Castle. Grandpa had a pass that opened even normally closed doors for him, so, for example, Kvido saw the Bohemian crown jewels several years earlier than any other mortals. And then Grandpa also had a fine sense for that moment when the attention of the otherwise very receptive boy was beginning to flag. At such a point, he would quickly end the visit, escaping by this alleyway or that unfamiliar street until they suddenly found themselves by a tram stop, whence they would be borne off somewhere for soft drinks and large helpings of meat but few veg.

Grandpa never said much during these outings, but there were a number of occasions when what he did say stuck fairly accurately in Kvido's memory.

"Everything matters," he once instructed his mother from the bath. "But nothing really matters that much."

"Who told you that?" she asked with a smile.

"Grandpa Jiří," said Kvido, and as he bent his head over the little red-and-white steamer bobbing on the bathwater, the ridges of three baby chins formed at his throat.

Encouraged by such evidence, Kvido's mother thought – as most mothers would – that beneath her son's folds of fat lurked an extraordinary talent, which would, sooner or later, shine forth. Which is why she would declaim to the two-year-old mite her best parts, and not only her roles as a child actress, and also not only parts that she had actually played. For example she would often recite to him:

"Elvira, my father's dead; and the first blade
With which Rodrigo fought, made him a shade.
Weep, weep, my eyes, dissolve in water!
Half of my life has entombed the other,
I must avenge myself, this fatal blow,
For one no more, on one still here below,"*

---

* Translation adapted from: poetryintranslation.com/PITBR/French/LeCidActIII.htm#_Toc168900824

not assuming, of course, that he would have any comprehension of Corneille's verse, but hoping that through it, Kvido would become at least a little different from all those other children fed on comic books and fairy-tales.

"And in the end, she succeeded," Kvido would tell people in later years. "My psychiatrist and I have never forgiven her."

The first outcomes of his mother's upbringing through art were in fact so inconclusive that she had moments of uncertainty as to whether the child might not, in the end, take after his father, so she surrounded him with other stimuli "of a technical nature", which ultimately almost cost him his life. For she gave him, amongst other things, a clapped-out old radio which, in her own words, would be "an indicator of Kvido's genius for electronics" – one gloomy Sunday afternoon, he secretly plugged the radio in, snapped the back of it off and reached inside for what was the most powerful stimulus of his entire ontogenesis. The sight of Kvido's glazed and bulging eyes as he lay on the Persian rug beneath the table, temporarily not breathing, was so unbearable to his mother that for many months thereafter she made do with entirely traditional and – as she had once described them – intellectually utterly sterile crayons and modelling clay. Kvido was, however, very pleased with the crayons: his best drawings included 'Parachutists in the Rain'.

"Just look how nicely he's captured those little mushrooms in among the fallen pine needles!" she gloried, thus unconsciously anticipating an image of many of his later dealings with publishing house editors.

But there was one talent that Kvido possessed beyond all question – his talent for reading. Without any of those around him bothering about such things at all (believing it to be too early), by the age of four he had mastered the entire alphabet. This transpired for all to behold early in September 1966, during one of the first rehearsals of Kohout's play *August, August, August*. He had previously shone a couple of times before that by reading some short headlines in *Plamen* and *Literární Noviny*, but each time his performance had got lost amid the confusion surrounding his mother's viva. And that morning, too, Kvido's mother was less intent on the few lines of her part than on sitting in the wings brushing up on business law. Meanwhile, her son was clambering about the red plush seats in the dark of the auditorium, running his hand over the gilded décor of the boxes and, with all the stopping and starting of the rehearsal, which had gone on for two hours and more, getting thoroughly bored. Finally, the wardrobe mistress, Mrs Bažant, took pity on him and brought him a pile of old theatre programmes from one of the offices. Kvido whispered a quiet thank you and moved closer to the stage in order to see the letters better. Just as he was settling down, the director, Mr Dudek, looked round and gave him a slight smile. Kvido took this smile as a cue.

"A Strange Tale, or: How Not to Marry Off One's Daughter,"* he read in a quiet voice from the green programme that lay

---

* Wolfgang Hildesheimer's 1961 adaptation of Carlo Goldoni's play *Fathers-in-Law*.

on top of the pile.

"Shh!" the director came back at once.

Pavel Kohout, who was sitting to Kvido's left, watching the rehearsal, glanced at the boy suspiciously.

"Listen, Pavel," Kvido whispered, expertly licking his forefinger the easier to turn the pages.

"Oh, mother of moths, mother of people, mother of all that lives,
 grant the moths the power to return where life so onerous is," he read fluently.

"Good grief!" Pavel Kohout cried, "The child seems to be reading!"

The rehearsal was stopped for a moment. Vlastimil Brodský and Vladimír Šmeral both looked down on the obese infant with interest.

"Sorry," Kvido's mother apologised, red in the face, in a hurry to haul her son away: "Sorry, Pavel."

"Wait," said Kohout, "Let him finish reading it."

He pointed at the relevant line in the text.

"… we need them so, for all they are so delicate, and in
 this world of ours on every side such mammoth monsters grin," Kvido finished reading.

"Well done!" Vladimír Šmeral exclaimed. Some of the actors clapped. There could be no doubt: Kvido could read.

4. *Kvido's parents' room. Evening. Kvido is asleep.*

FATHER (*setting down the Highway Code*): I hope it isn't going to be icy, seeing as it's January. That would be the death of me.

MOTHER (*ironing*): I still don't understand how you could spin the car round three times when you were only queuing for petrol.

FATHER: The instructor gets me so on edge. He's got it in for me. Before we'd even left the driving school yard, he started shouting that he'd fail me – probably because of the bagful of meat I was supposed to have popped in the boot...

MOTHER (*taken aback*): So where did you pop it?

FATHER: Under the bonnet. I was in a real state.

MOTHER (*laughing*): And when did you find out?

FATHER: On Černokostelecká Street. The cop who was sitting in the back insisted he could smell kebabs burning.

MOTHER: You never mentioned that!

FATHER: I forgot. You know I can't bear to think about passing an oncoming car when only a tiny wrist movement separates me from certain death. That's the whole problem. A few centimetres – and curtains! Or CPR at A&E – if I'm lucky. D'you know they don't let visitors into CPR departments?

MOTHER: You shouldn't take it to heart like that. You need to be more self-assured.

FATHER: I am, on one-way streets. I love one-way streets. My driving changes completely on a one-way street.

MOTHER: Like at that petrol station! Or that time on the motorway!

FATHER: A motorway's something else again. I'm never going back on one of those! I'm not an astronaut!

MOTHER: So why are you applying for a license?

FATHER: Because you wanted me to.

"Modern man," Kvido told the editor, "can't get by without a car. Incidentally, that meat reminds me of something."

5. "Grandma," Grandpa Jiří would occasionally say over lunch, "is unquestionably an expert cook. It's just a pity that nine times out of ten she squanders her undoubted expertise on meat-free dishes."

He was right: six of a week's dinners consisted of potato gnocchi, pancakes, pasta with quark, potato fritters, potato-and-egg bake, and apple crumble.

"I really can't afford to buy meat when Grandpa gives me so little housekeeping money," Grandma Líba protested on the brink of tears as she poured her exquisite dill sauce over the lamentably lonely dumplings. "I simply can't get by on so little. I can't."

However, the whole family had known for a long time that not only could Grandma get by very nicely, but that she had enough left over to be able to take an annual trip abroad with Zita and her other friends.

"The girls and I want to go to Yalta this year," Grandma had told the family in the spring of 1967, her face taking on a charming girlish flush. "Didn't I tell you?"

("Yalta!!" Grandpa Josef yelped on hearing the plan. "Yalta? She actually fancies a holiday in the very place where they finally sold us to the Bolshevik!!")

"I don't think you did," said Grandpa Jiří, for his part very politely, as, with utterly oriental composure, he finished off the last morsel of celeriac risotto.

Many years later, as he was hosing a fully dressed Jarka with ice-cold water following a three-hour marital row, Kvido had a sudden flash-back to the expression of unrivalled comprehension that was mirrored in Grandpa's face.

"Grandma Líba was an orthodox tourist," Kvido would say. "From a tender age, she would spend the holidays with the best families in England and France. Later she would spend New Year's Eve in the Swiss Alps. The life she now lived could not satisfy her: all it was was a kind of endless long-stay arrangement, whereas she adored – as she frequently remarked – themed sightseeing trips. Grandpa was an attentive guide, but sometimes, in truth, rather difficult."

From Yalta – as from all her trips – Grandma sent a monochrome postcard with a poem of her own composition:

"The beach is great,
the company too,
we swim and crochet
and think of you,"

it said, followed by the customary "Love and kisses from Yalta, Líba".

Kvido, who was in a singularly good mood that day, Grandpa having marked Grandma's departure by cramming the fridge with smoked tongue, calf's liver and pork chops, attempted a joke, likewise in verse, sort of: "Love and kisses, life pisses – me off!"

His father chuckled, but Grandpa Jiří wasn't laughing. Kvido's mother raised a hand and slapped him across the face. It was one of those unfortunate slaps that land a few seconds too late to be deemed impulsive.

Kvido winced, but he wasn't going to give in.

"Love, kissing, life pissing...," he developed his theme stubbornly and got another slap for his pains.

Then his face crinkled with the double effort of holding back his tears and trying to think of something even bolder and more telling.

His grandfather and parents stared as his chubby chin vibrated ever more violently.

"Love, kissing, but meat's missing!" he blurted out finally.

His mother compressed her lips and raised her hand a third time, but Grandpa arrested it.

"One perhaps ought not to be rude," he said to Kvido. "Perhaps not even when one is actually right. – Will you try and remember that?"

Kvido was still nodding when he was assailed by an explosion of liberating tears.

"That day," he would tell people later, "I recognised for the first – and certainly not the last – time, the terrible consequences that follow when the relentless law of artistic creativity is directed against the artist's own family."

Incidentally, the first person to draw a prophetic link between Kvido and verbal art was his father. (He was thinking ironically, in part, given that he too – though he never admitted it – was beginning to get fed up of the endless stream of poets, playwrights and lyrics writers who came to visit his wife.)

"Do you think he was interested in all those animals?" Grandma Vera complained after the first spring trip to the zoo. "Not a bit of it! The entire time he had his nose buried in the book Grandpa bought him at the entrance."

"How like him," said Kvido's father. "He's developed a craze for reading."

"And we go just so we can see the animals being fed!" Grandma was at pains to stress.

And she wasn't exaggerating. Real live animals could pounce, crawl or fly about so close that they could smell them and see their every hair, every shiny scale and every gaudy feather, but Kvido just propped his book on the rail round the enclosures and read the texts beneath the fairly shoddy photos. Grandma hadn't known what to do about it. She was so put out by his behaviour that this time – unlike last time – and despite her pedagogical principles, she was willing to show him monkeys mating, but the monkeys were all asleep.

"What kind of child is he?" Kvido's grandma now asked his father. "Tell me, what's to become of him?"

Kvido's father had a fleeting image of his son in places where yellow-and-black giraffes munch the tips of tall trees, lions tear at thirty-kilo chunks of red beef and where eagles' wings cast a larger shadow than all the sunshades in the nearby garden café... reading a book about animals.

"A writer, probably," he said cheerfully.

"Do you know what the one time was when he wasn't reading?" Grandma asked pensively. "When we were standing by the dogs."

6. The evening before Christmas Eve in 1967, Grandma Líba and Kvido's mother were making a potato salad. Kvido's father was sitting at the kitchen table, reading under his breath something in English on the back page of *Plamen*: 'We would like to call our readers' attention to the following contributions in the December edition of *Plamen* –,' he read.

"I'm wondering," said Kvido's mother, "whether it's entirely normal for a Czech reader of Czech journals to read only the English résumés."

"It's not normal," said Grandma Líba.

"Why not?" asked Kvido's father. "I like brevity. A résumé holds everything. How do you suppose I managed to get my degree?"

"So when are we going to decorate the tree?" Kvido was keen to know. "You keep putting it off. Have you any idea how depressing that is?"

"Once Daddy manages to fix the tree into the stand," his mother informed him.

"So, Dad!" the lad persisted, trying to take the journal away from him.

"Only after you read something to me!"

"Hang on," the boy's mother had remembered something;

she wiped her hands on a tea towel and flicked through the journal until she found a page with a section underlined. "Read this out to us."

"That much?" Kvido asked, feigning disappointment, but he was actually quite pleased to show off his reading skills on a more or less continuous piece of text.

"One of the intellectual symptoms of Stalinism was a constriction of the riverbed of creativity between the top-down regulated and de jure intransgressible banks of the one 'correct' and 'progressive' method, identified formulaically as Socialist Realism," Kvido was surpassing himself. "The aesthetic norms and principles of this conception were essentially derived from the Realist prose of the nineteenth century, the objective descriptions of which enabled it to depict the *entire* reality of life, especially that which was of greatest significance to the Marxist conception of the function of art, namely the movement of and conflicts between the social classes."

"Excellent, Kvido," his mother praised him. "That took some doing, eh?" she said, turning to his father.

He meanwhile had been more interested in the culinary activities of his mother-in-law. "Doesn't it need a bit of chopped salami?" he asked.

"In a potato salad?" Grandma Líba was duly horrified.

"Trust you to show no interest," said Kvido's mother. "All you're bothered about is salami in the salad."

"Salami in a salad does not bother me," said Kvido's father. "I was merely intrigued by the question of its possible *absence*."

"Salami in a potato salad!" Grandma Líba shook her head

in disbelief. "The very idea!"

"Well what about the tree then?" Kvido cried.

"Come on," said his father. Kvido grabbed the stand and his father compared the radius of the trunk with the hole in the stand. Then he asked for a knife and carefully, almost tenderly, started removing the requisite section of bark.

"Ah, that smell," he said. "I love wood."

"More than résumés?" asked Kvido's mother.

"Yes."

"But less than one-way streets?"

"Oh yes," his father laughed. "And less than you."

A key rattled in the lock.

"Grandpa," cried Kvido.

"Evening all," said Grandpa Jiří as they welcomed him into the kitchen. The crown of his hat and the shoulders of his winter coat were covered in wet snow. "I was held up by Frank – he hauled me off to have dinner."

"But I made some burgers this afternoon!" said Grandma Líba reproachfully.

"*Cabbage* burgers," Kvido's mother added, to keep the record straight.

"I'll just rinse my hands," said Grandpa, "and come and have some with you."

"One," said Kvido's mother cheerily.

"And what did he have to say?" Kvido's father was curious to know when Grandpa Jiří came back from the bathroom.

"Frank? That people trust us, for example," Grandpa replied with a mildly mysterious smile. "Do you mean the people here at Vikárka?" I ribbed him. "No," says he, "I mean people all over the country. They say we have the chance of a lifetime in our grasp."

"I believe him," said Kvido's mother. "And I'm quite fond of him. I believe you all, really. Now all you I'm fond of, go rule and heal this country of ours!"

"What did you say to him?" Kvido's father asked.

"What *can* be said on the subject of political prognoses?" said Grandpa sceptically. "Nothing. Except that for all I'm a lawyer, I personally hold no chance in *my* grasp and that therefore I don't go around making promises. Though, I'd obviously be pleased if it came off and I'd do my level best to help things along."

"Well said," said Grandma Líba. "Did he say anything about visas?"

"No," said Grandpa somewhat taken aback. "He's got nothing to do with visas."

"What do you think?" Grandma had suddenly remembered, "is there supposed to be salami in a *potato* salad?"

"Well," said Grandpa slowly, glancing quickly the length of the worktop, "that depends on the temperament of the cook."

"There shouldn't be," said Grandma Líba.

"At the Academy of Sciences," Kvido's father chipped in, "things are also happening: Do you know what Šik has had put up on his office door? FOR SALE: INDULGENCES FOR MISTAKES WITH THE ECONOMY! Zvára showed me it yesterday."

"For God's sake," Kvido cried. "Are we going to start decorating the tree then or not?"

7. When, on the twenty-first of August 1968 at half past four in the morning, Kvido's Grandpa Josef got up in the kitchen to get ready for work, he caught the sound of an odd, unfamiliar roaring noise as it entered the window, descending from somewhere high in the still dark sky. He put the kettle on the gas cooker, quietly, but his consideration was pointless, given that his good wife had also been awake some time because of the racket.

"What's that?" she asked reproachfully from the next room.

"How would I know!" snapped Grandpa. "Not the binmen, that's for sure."

He suddenly stopped, realising that he hadn't seen any of the budgerigars yet. He glanced into the room, put the light on, put it off again and came back into the kitchen, looked up at the cupboard and the picture rail, turned back the curtain – but they were nowhere.

"Where are my budgies?" he cried, staring at the open window. "They're not here."

"Are you blind?" Grandma called. "Where d'you suppose they are?"

"How would I know!" Grandpa yelled, getting riled now, as he looked all about him. "Come and help me find them, since you're that clever!"

Unfortunately, he was right. The budgies had gone.

Kvido woke up shortly before eight. In bleary-eyed surprise, he looked at his grandfather, who should have been at the pit long before then, but instead was sitting at the table in his pyjamas, listening to the radio.

"Our little sweeties have flown," Grandma said sorrowfully. "Something must have frightened them."

Kvido threw his head back to look up at the ceiling, then he leaned forward in his bed to get a view of the cage. It was empty.

"How come?"

For now, he felt no particular pity. He was slightly put out at the prospect of never again seeing the budgerigars clambering up the curtains or perching on his grandmother's head, but at the same time, he was glad that henceforth there'd be none squatting on the edge of his plate at mealtimes, poking their claws into his mashed potatoes.

"How come!!" Grandpa shrieked. "How come!! 'Cos Comrade Brezhnev has gone an' declared war on us!!"

"Stop that now!!" Grandma suddenly screamed in a way Kvido had never heard her scream before. "Stop it!... It's not war, get a grip, will you!"

She gave him a withering look and went and sat on Kvido's bed.

"Grandpa's going a bit crazy," she said and kissed the boy's cheek. He got a pleasant whiff of the almond face cream she used. "They're making a war film and Grandpa has to go thinking it's for real, would you believe?"

Kvido got up and curiosity propelled him towards the window, but he could see neither cameras nor soldiers. Grandpa sprinkled some bird seed on the window ledge.

"Have your breakfast," she bade her grandson. "There's some sponge cake on the fridge."

She cleaned out the birdcage, changed the water in the little bowl, then sat down on the kitchen bench and stared towards the vacant window. Seeing how sad his grandmother looked, Kvido felt a bit ashamed and tried to make himself miss the budgies as well: he tried to focus and all through his breakfast thought hard about what a pretty blue they were, what lovely soft feathers they had and how like little beads their eyes were until it all made him start crying.

"Don't cry," Grandma said, affected. "You can go out with Grandpa and put up some notices."

Grandpa snatched the cigarette from his lips. "What notices, for goodness sake!"

"What do you mean, what notices?" Grandma snapped back. "To say we've lost them."

"Now??" Grandpa yelled. "You want me to fuss about budgies now?"

"And when else? It's not my fault they chose to disappear now!"

"I don't mind putting some up," said Kvido. "If you'll let me…"

"Hold still, you can have the skin!" cried Grandpa Josef every time one of the scraps of paper announcing the loss of three budgerigars from No. 2 Sezima St. declined to remain in place. His eyes blazed and a lock of silvery hair kept falling across his perspiring brow.

("Even quite recently, before it eventually dawned on me what Grandma's job was," Kvido explained to the editor, "I hadn't fully appreciated the point of this favourite saying of Grandpa's…"

"I don't want to hear it," said the editor. "No porn if you please. We're going to cut this whole chapter anyway.")

First they stuck the little notices on some of the lamp-posts in their street, then some more in the square. He stuck one each on the phone box, the tobacconist's window and the tram stop.

"Why so much fuss about budgies, now, for Christ's sake!!" some man shouted after them, having read their notice. "Call yourselves patriots?"

Grandpa gave a broad sweep of his hand without turning round, and under his breath muttered some incomprehensible oath. Kvido didn't understand what the man meant, but there wasn't time to think about that now, because his eyes were roaming the sky, the trees and the window ledges of all the houses. No sign of the budgies. They crossed the stream, passed under the railway bridge and headed up the Nusle Steps.

"Shall we stick some here?" Kvido wondered aloud.

"Obviously," said Grandpa and lit a cigarette.

They stuck the last bits of paper up and sat down for a brief rest on a bench in the park on Tyl Square. There were lots of people out and about, not only on the pavements, but also in the roadways and some even between the tram tracks.

"Look!" Kvido cried suddenly: two green-and-brown low-loaders were approaching from the direction of Charles Square; compared to the cars parked around they seemed positively gigantic to the little boy. Grandpa sat rigid where he was, but Kvido, who'd always counted theatre and film actors among his best friends, jumped up and waved happily at them.

"In a nutshell, I was one of the eight or nine people in the whole of Prague who smiled on the forces of occupation," Kvido explained to the editor.

"Waste of paper," the editor shook his head. "Save trees."

Kvido's grandfather hauled him away and without offering any kind of explanation, told him not to wave at the film folk. Kvido promised not to, but that didn't stop him dying to find some more. His grandfather brushed away any such idea and said that they needed to go to the Valdek to wash away the vile taste of the sticky tape from their tongues – and he was as good as his word.

"So what do you think of it, tough guy?" an elderly, fair-haired lady disturbed Kvido, who, with mixed revulsion and fascination was watching how the surface of the beer in the pint glass magnified his grandfather's front teeth.

"Dunno," he replied. "I haven't seen it yet."

"I suppose not," the lady said. "Though we have, eh, Joe? Back in March '39."

"Right enough," said Grandpa Josef. "They should string 'em up. All of 'em. From their beloved birch trees!"

"I couldn't agree more," the lady said.

About an hour and a half later, as soon as they were back in the street, Kvido noticed that his grandfather's gait was oddly unsteady. He was old enough to know what that meant, but he politely tried to pretend he hadn't seen, and began telling him about that funny business of renaming the Prague Dynamo Sports Club to its present name of Slavia, as he'd once heard it told by Pavel Kohout at the Theatre Club.

"I'd rather not hear," Grandpa said with utter scorn, "about that Young Commie."

To Kvido's considerable surprise, they found waiting for them at the flat in Sezima Street not only Grandma Vera, but the entire family. He would scarcely have believed that they'd all fit in such a tiny space, even finding somewhere to sit, though in the case of Kvido's father this was on the laundry basket. Thanks to Grandpa Jiří and Kvido's mother's cigarettes the whole room was full of grey-blue smoke.

"They're here!" cried Grandma Líba, who'd been the first to catch her grandson's voice in the corridor outside and had run to let them in. "Where on earth have you been?" she let fire at Grandpa in the doorway.

"They've been on the razzle," said Kvido's mother in the voice of Hettie the maid. "Unless I'm very much mistaken."

"For God's sake, Dad," said Kvido's father despairingly. "We've been sitting here for three hours, worried sick!"

"Where've we been?" Grandpa Josef yelled back, sticking his chin out in the direction of Grandma Líba. "Where? We've been to give them the once over – those buddies of yours from Yalta!"

"Stop it now!" screamed Grandma Vera.

"Sorr-ee," Grandma Líba protested. "If I happen to have said what nice, sociable people they were, that is far from meaning that I agree with them all about everything. We spent long evenings together – you can ask Zita about that – arguing very hard with them for hours on end. One of them, Grigorii – I think I've told you about him before – was particularly intransigent. Just imagine, he even had it in for…"

"Vegetables?" asked Kvido's mother.

"Come on," Grandma sighed. "I didn't deserve that. I expect you're getting back at me for…"

"Let Josef get some sleep," said Grandpa Jiří. "Come on, let's all get off home. And I'd be very glad," he added with some force, "if you'd *all* stay there."

A burst of gunfire came from somewhere in the city centre.

"This is terrible!" Grandma Líba cried. "What are we going to do? Have you called Frank?"

"Do? Grieve," said Kvido's mother. "Our job now is for everyone to go into mourning. In a wall'd prison, packs and sects of great ones, that ebb and flow by the moon."

"Frank," said Grandpa Jiří irritably, "isn't going to be any help, nor Shakespeare either by the look of things!"

"String 'em up, the lot of 'em," said Grandpa Josef. "That would help!"

"Mum," Kvido's father chimed in. "Do get him to bed, will you! We're off now. He can kip in the kitchen."

"Is that Kvido's fault as well?" Kvido's mother added for good measure. "At least he's been able to tell the time ever since he was three!"

"She's jealous because of the film folk," Kvido whispered to Grandpa Jiří.

"What's that?" shrieked his mother, who'd heard what he said.

"You're jealous because of the film folk," Kvido squeaked and hid from his mother, who lashed out at him, behind his grandfather's legs.

"Dear oh dear! I always thought he was a genius," said his mother in disbelief. "But now I see he's an idiot!"

"Leave the lad alone," Grandpa Jiří thundered. "You're being very silly. How much more do you think he can take?"

"Tie 'em to a birch tree, bend it back – and launch 'em up into the sky!" Grandpa Josef hollered from the very depths of his bleak imagination.

"Just look at him!" Grandma Vera yelled. "See!"

"That's not so bad," said Kvido's father, resigned. "What's worse is hearing him as well."

"I'm sorry," his mother said suddenly. "Sorry, Kvido. All of you, I'm sorry. Honest!" And she burst into tears. "It's all been too much for me."

"No need to apologise," said Grandma Líba. "I've forgiven you already. This certainly isn't the time for private squabbling. The times ahead aren't going to be easy the way things are looking. We're all going to have to grit our teeth and start saving. Incidentally, I wonder what effect it's going to have on travelling."

"Jeepers creepers," said Grandpa Jiří, "are you going or not?"

"We're going," said Kvido's mother, quieter now. "But where to?"

II.

From Kvido's diary

20 September 1968

We're moving to some place called Sázava! Nobody can tell me in plain terms why. All they've said is that I missed the start of the school year and would be spending another year in pre-school in Sázava. Bad news all round. On top of that no one knows where Sázava is. We couldn't find it on a map of Czechoslovakia. Father said he'll get a bigger one tomorrow. He won't stop singing Katyusha. Mother's saying nothing.

21 September 1968

It's not on the bigger one either. Father said he'd get hold of an even bigger one. Mother just laughed hysterically and suggested he borrow one from the army. If they still have any, she added. I asked

Father why I was expected to break at one go all the emotional ties I've formed to Prague. Because I didn't want to wait till they sacked me, he said. He wanted to leave on his own terms. If I was really fond of Bruncvík, he'd arrange for me to go and see him at weekends. It felt as if he was having me on.

22 September 1968

My parents are going to be working at the Sázava glassworks, where they apparently make world-renowned laboratory and kitchen glassware. We're to live in a large company house with a vast conservatory, and after work we'll be able to go swimming in the river that flows right beneath our windows, Father said. We're going to see it tomorrow. Mother looked sceptical and dismissed Father as a sentimental poet. She told me that what I'd seen wasn't a film being made, but a common-or-garden military occupation. Grandma said it wasn't an occupation, but a pogrom aimed at tourists.

23 September 1968

We made our first trip to Sázava today. The monastery was sort of okay, but when I saw the surroundings, it was obvious to me that the monks had left voluntarily. Father took me to have a look round the house. I liked the little bits of coloured glass stuck in the plasterwork. Mother had stayed in the car. I told her the house was called DRÁBOVKA. *She said it was a pretty name. Then it started to rain. When I went into a shop to buy a lemonade, I was struck by the way they kept chocolates and soap and other stuff all next to each other on the shelves. Father explained that it was a general store and this was a practical solution ahead of its time in many ways, though he did concede that the furniture polish was probably in the freezer cabinet in error. Then it had to start raining in earnest, so we ran to take refuge in the nearest restaurant. We were running for nearly half an hour. Mother screamed that a driver who's scared of driving in the rain needs to see a psychiatrist. The restaurant was full of hikers. They had soup spoons stuck in their boot-tops, which I thought distinctly unhygienic. Mother and Father had an argument about whether the poster declaiming* WE BUY RABBIT SKINS *was Modernist or Functionalist. We polished off our hot-dogs and the rain stopped. I wanted to go, but Father insisted we wait until the road was dry. Mother ordered a rum. Then she joined the hikers in a sing-song, but burst into tears at the fourth number. I asked her what was wrong and she said she'd been overcome by the plaintive refrain* SO KICK THE BLOODY BARREL AWAY. *Back in Prague Father made us hang about in the park for an hour so you couldn't tell Mother had been crying. Later, she told Grandpa that the Sázava valley is a balmy region full of odd, but amiable people, but that from here on she would be thinking of it as a Czech Siberia.*

29 September 1968

We made the move this afternoon. Outside the windows of Drábovka there were crowds of strange people. Mother said the two removal men must be drunk seeing that they were taking her bed into the conservatory. Father said that her rudeness about the men completely missed the point, because the conservatory was indeed to be our temporary home. Mother ensconced herself in a wicker armchair on the path outside the house and stared at the rippling river for the best part of an hour. Then she took me by the hand and informed Father that we were leaving for Prague. Father said that he'd always wanted to marry a girl who'd see him through thick and thin, but what he'd actually got – as he could now see – was a Proud Princess. What did she suppose their friend Zvára was to do, given that he and his fiancée had been living illegally inside an electricity substation for more than two weeks? As dusk descended, Mother told me that living with Father was getting more and more like that game, Canada by Night.

30 September 1968

The conservatory is glazed on three sides. Last night Mother was too embarrassed to change into her pyjamas. She claimed that hundreds of pairs of eyes were watching her through the glass. I felt a bit sorry for her. I crept under the duvet to join her and snuggled up against her coat. Father was reading various books about glass.

1 October 1968

October's here. I asked Father what he would do when the icy North Wind blew three or four tongues of snow in on us – he said he'd hoover them up. Sometimes I wonder if he's at all up to supporting Mother and me. Either he's reading about glass, or he's whittling fancy walking sticks. An ordinary whistle, of the kind I've politely asked him for several times, is obviously beyond his capabilities. The day after tomorrow they're going to work for the first time, and me to school. Metaphor is the key to reality. I read a book about the writer's craft and help Mother. When she wants to get changed, I build her a bunker of mattresses.

2 October 1968

Today Father and I went down to the river. He said he needed some sticks to whittle. I asked what had got into him with all this whittling stuff: he said that as a working material it's got brilliant mental-hygiene properties, something that's hard to appreciate fully in an Eastern bloc country. In the evening he finally made me a whistle. At long last.

3 October 1968

Apart from Miss Havel and the quark with raspberries, my nursery school reflects the abysmal state of pre-school education in this country, and I told them as much. Miss Konečná, who came in from the baby class to see me, said that I would be an asset to the school. I sit with Jarka Macek. She's quite a nice girl, if provincial, and full of naïve prejudices against metaphorical expressions concerning obesity. Mother brought home four bagsful of papers from work. I played 'Love's Dream' on my whistle to welcome her, but she just leapt at me and tossed the whistle out of the window. I shouted that I'd jump out after it, but she voiced some doubt that, given my bulk, I could even haul myself onto a chair and thence onto the window ledge. The alienation between Mother and me is growing like a panthercap toadstool after a cloudburst. I'm giving up all sweet things from tomorrow.

4 October 1968

Last night there was a storm. I crept into bed with Mother, but

Father wedged himself between us. We watched the sky flashing blue and white. Father said that it was a better show than any feature film at the Alfa cinema. The rain pounded at the roof like a gang of savage roofers. Father kept stroking Mother, which I found distinctly tactless vis-à-vis myself.

5 October 1968

At school today I went without dessert and let Jarka Macek have it. (Yesterday it was an orange.) During our afternoon nap she returned the favour by showing me her privates.

6 October 1968

Jarka wanted to see my privates! I told her she could have my dessert tomorrow. Mother is getting more and more uptight. In the evening, Father suggested they go out somewhere, but fifteen minutes later they were back, having tumbled in the dark into the sewage outlet next to the hostel for Polish workers. They stank like polecats long estranged from soap and water. And I told them as much.

14 November 1968

I'm writing with a lot of noise in the background today, my parents having brought Mr Zvára and his fiancée home. Round my bed they erected a metre-high wall of boxes that still haven't been unpacked since our move and tried to make out that I now had a room of my own. Then they sang some Soviet war songs and drank vodka from some insulators that Mr Zvára had stolen from their sub-station.

15 November 1968

Today I asked Miss Hájek if, as an exception, I could take my afternoon nap in the morning. She said I could, but wanted to know why, so I gave her a brief account of how late into the night I'd been kept awake by a medley of mournful and vigorous Soviet 'songs'. She appeared to be fairly sympathetic, but I don't think she really believed me until I showed her my vest, which Father had used, in the dark, to wipe up some alcohol that they'd spilled. She let me sleep on the settee in the head teacher's office! So I had a lovely kip while my country cousins had to play all those infantile games!

16 November 1968

Father and Mother aren't speaking to me. I have to go to bed at seven on the dot like some bleary-eyed chicken. At the stroke of seven both my parents start whispering provocatively. Mother might as well not have bothered, because from her life on stage she was used to whispering very loud. And I told her as much.

17 November 1968
18 November 1968

I spent the entire weekend behind my boxes. Nobody's talking to me still, nor I to them. I'm reading Montaigne's Essais. A lot of the time I find myself agreeing with him 100%. But when I read that "he who would teach people to die would also be teaching them to live" I was beset by a sense that he was quite off his rocker.

19 November 1968

Father and Mother are speaking to me again. Mother only a bit, because with all that stage whispering she's given herself laryngitis. When I asked her why she whispered so loud, putting such a strain on her vocal chords, she explained that this was how she – like any other actor worth his salt – showed her solidarity with the students up there in the gods. Father claimed to have used my vest by mistake – half-blinded because Mother had scorched his cornea with her cigarette. I said I would explain things properly to Miss Hájek tomorrow. "You'll do no such thing!" Mother wheezed. Her eyes were so bulging that it crossed my mind that we could soon be hauling her off to the Bohnice asylum.

20 November 1968

I've managed to get Father two big chunks of ebony that someone had tossed, unforgivably, onto the rubbish dump at the foot of White Rock. When I got home with it, neither of them was back from work yet. They're getting in later and later. I've told them they shouldn't have taken jobs that they're clearly not up to. Everybody else comes home at two-thirty.

21 November 1968

Father maintains that it isn't ebony, but charred bakelite, but that he was grateful anyway. He was a bit standoffish, but Mother praised me and said that I was possessed of a bitty intelligence. Otherwise all they talk about is their work, though as little as two months ago they knew sod-all about laboratory glassware. And I told them as much.

22 November 1968

The school is awash with problems: this morning was sunny, so they herded us out into the garden like a bunch of calves. Miss Konečná forced me to go and play inside one of those ghastly tin play-houses. I asked her what she thought I was supposed to play there. She said I could play at receiving visitors. I told her that the absurd ritual that receiving visitors is in this country was a chapter to itself – the more so in that so-called play-house, which was more like a cramped train compartment or a burnt-out dummy on a tank firing range, and that I'd much rather – provided that was all right by her – go and finish reading my Heinrich Böll on a nearby bench. She said certainly not, because we didn't have any Böll, just games involving communication. So I asked her if she really wanted to develop my character – as per her job description – or to suppress it. She said that the only thing she wanted at that moment was to survive in peace until her retirement. She looked about to burst into tears, so I obediently went to do some communicating with Jarka Macek, just to make her happy. We did it in the red play-house. It was quite interesting to see Jarka's privates under different light conditions!

23 November 1968

We had Miss Hájek today and all was pleasantly peaceful. In the morning, while playing skittles, I knocked the picture of President Svoboda off the wall, the glass broke and cut the President's upper lip, which made him look a bit like an ageing hare. Jarka Macek found it funny. Miss Hájek asked if I intended to partner Jarka at the Christmas dance. I said I probably would, though in truth

I wouldn't want to commit myself prematurely to one particular provincial girl. When I got home, I started shivering dreadfully with the cold. I opened a window and scattered a few handfuls of wet leaves from the garden over my bed and the other furniture to get Father finally to realise that outdoors autumn was coming to an end. When he saw it in the evening, he went for me with the strip of wood that he'd got ready prior to creating a plant stand, but instead of me he clouted Mother. After they'd both calmed down, they sat down with their backs to the electric fire and started interrogating me about that picture. Father didn't believe that I hadn't done it deliberately: a picture can get knocked down during football or basketball, but not during a game of skittles. "At skittles only an idiot could knock a picture down!" he yelled. Mother urged me not to get cross with Father, because he'd had his party-political appraisal earlier in the day.

25 November 1968

Yesterday was Saturday. We were supposed to go to Český Šternberk, but instead Father spent an hour threatening me: he'd got two witnesses who would confirm that, having hit the picture, I'd shouted: "Bull's eye!" I confessed that that was indeed so, but it had only been so as to distract the other children from how useless I was at skittles. Father sighed and went off to the cellar to finish making the plant stand. Mother confided that Father needed a psychiatrist and that we'd be going to Šternberk after lunch. However, before lunch, Father ran a semi-circular chisel into his femur, so we ended up going to A&E at Uhlířské Janovice. We were taken there by Mr Zvára because Father refused to drive in his condition. For the entire time, Father kept laughing this weird laugh and going on about some chap called Šperk from the works committee. I was cold and missing Prague. I'm going to write to Grandpa.

III.

1. Kvido's mother was always convinced that Paco had been conceived on the first Saturday in June 1970, at roughly a quarter to midnight. She claims that it happened a few yards from a dying campfire, in an army sleeping bag, to the strains of Karel Kryl's song 'Salome', which was being played and sung a little way off to his brand-new wife (with whom he had finally moved from the sub-station to a married couples' hostel) by Mr Zvára. This assumption obviously provided her with an apparently rational explanation for Paco's later passion for camping out with the boys. However, from the outset, Kvido's father described such inferences as vulgar pseudo-logic, rejecting his wife's hypothesis about the conception lock, stock and barrel by appealing to his fairly sound knowledge of her menstrual cycle.

"You have to consider though," Kvido's mother objected, "that on that warm night – moreover by a campfire – I got properly warm for the first time in ten months or so of living in that freezing conservatory!"

The warmth to which she had been a stranger for so long, as she explained in earnest, had, for one thing, stirred her former vitality, thanks to which she had even agreed to that distinctly *outdoor-fiendish* way of spending a Saturday night – and for another, it might well have accelerated her ovulation.

"What bullshit!" Kvido's father had laughed.

Whatever the case, his wife's pregnancy was beyond dispute: "That's how it is, my girl," Zita told her that August at the Podolí hospital. She looked tired, but her eyes were still bright blue. "You're going to give birth out there?"

"I'm going to have to," said Kvido's mother as she put her clothes on. "You know I always wanted to have it here."

"You could have!" Zita said, feigning reproof. "But you preferred to see Dr Libíček."

"He's a bungler, I'll grant you that," said Kvido's mother. "Fancy, he didn't even know how to bite through the umbilical cord!"

"Scandalous!"

"Can you forgive me?"

"No," said Zita with a smile.

They sat down in some beige-coloured armchairs. Kvido's mother suddenly recalled being comforted by Zita in these very chairs when she'd rushed in to see her, frightened witless by her first period. Now she sensed a kind of nostalgic sorrow. What a wonderful woman, she mused.

"Zita?" she said.

"Yes?"

"Can anything be done about it still?"

The consultant took a very deep breath and raised her eyebrows ever so slightly, creating a sorry crease just above her nose. Her smile had saddened.

"In February?" she said as if dubiously. "In February '71?"

"I could be formally registered at the Nusle address," the mother said.

"That's not the issue," said Zita. "It's too late, my child."

"Late?" Kvido's mother didn't get it.

Zita leaned across to her and pushed the hair from her brow with one finger. Then she took her head in the palm of her hand and patted her cheek. Kvido's mother noted the damp glint in her eyes.

"By February I'll be an usherette at the Realist Theatre," she said. "You see?"

"She was wrong," said Kvido. "She became a cloakroom attendant at the Yalta cinema."

"Grandpa!" Kvido cried.

"Hi there, Kvido!" Grandpa Jiří called back, delighted, but this time he didn't take his grandson up into his arms, because he hadn't been feeling too well for some while. He'd had to leave his long-term job in the presidential office, but although, fortunately, he hadn't had to change his profession, he was having a hard time getting used to his new position. Not even the brilliant dill sauce with actual meat in it – so not just the usual egg – that Grandma Líba had prepared for the guests could restore him fully to his previous mood.

"What's Frank doing?" Kvido's father asked out of quite sincere interest once they were all settled in the kitchen.

"I'm not entirely sure," Grandpa said. "Something with the Parks and Gardens department."

"But that's awful," said Kvido's mother.

"Not really," said Grandpa with a tone of sceptical resignation. "He's out in the open, in the fresh air… Others have come off worse."

"They wouldn't let Karla go to Switzerland," said Grandma Líba. "Can you believe that?"

"You must be joking!" said Kvido's mother. "Seriously?"

Kvido's mother having declined a cigarette with her coffee and finally told Grandpa Jiří her big news, he did show a spark of life.

"Are you sure?" he enquired with a smile.

"I've been to see Zita," Kvido's mother said, blushing, since she could never put anything to do with gynaecology into words even among her nearest and dearest. "I think it's going to be a boy."

"A boy!" Grandpa shouted, jubilantly. "And what are you going to call him?"

"Paco," said Kvido's mother. "After his dad here," she pointed at Kvido's father.

"Really?" Grandpa queried in a neutral tone.

"My name's always been Josef," said Kvido's father stiffly.

"Not in all my life have I ever heard of anyone being called Paco," said Grandma Líba.

"Nor me," said Kvido's father with hope in his voice. "As if Kvido here wasn't enough!"

"Do you mind!" Kvido protested

"Kvido's a lovely name," Grandpa chipped in.

"And Paco's interesting," said Kvido's mother. "At least as interesting as 'Drábovka.'"

"How on earth does that come into it?" Father protested.

"Simple!"

"Paco," Grandpa Jiří repeated the name intently. "Paco. It doesn't sound all that bad. Paco."

"And there's nothing un-Czech about it; it works well in the language, fully declinable."

"Just like Kvido," said Grandpa. "So that's good."

"If you go about choosing names based on how easily they decline, you might as well call him Filé," said Kvido. "That doesn't inflect at all."

"So you see," Kvido told the editor, "I was well ahead in grammar."

"Another child?" Grandpa Josef said disapprovingly. "Now?"

As he paced the room, scattered bird seed crunched under his slippered feet. Once more, three budgerigars were perched on the picture rail, green ones this time. Kvido noted that the window was closed.

"A baby at a time like this!" Grandpa ranted. "Do you want to get him shot dead by one of those Bolsheviks?"

"Stop it!" shrieked Grandma Vera. "Stop it right now!"

"Me? Me stop it? And they can carry on just shooting at folk?"

"Come on, Dad, keep your voice down," Kvido's father urged him. "Shouting won't help."

Grandpa took a furious drag on his cigarette.

"All right, I'm done," he said struggling to control himself. "So what *will* help?"

"How would I know, Dad?" said Kvido's father helplessly.

"I'll tell you something," said Grandpa Josef, raising his voice again. "Hang the lot of 'em – that'd help!!"

"No, it wouldn't," said Kvido's father. "What you need is a psychiatrist."

2. In the months that followed, he often had the feeling that he rather needed one himself, given that despite every promise, he still had no flat for his wife and son. That September, he was to have been assigned a three-room flat on the first floor of the Drábovka, but in the end it went to an entirely different family. At the time, Kvido's father came close to a breakdown. The previous winter, spent in the conservatory, had been an experience that he wouldn't want to repeat. On days at or below freezing, the indoor thermometer rarely rose above 13 degrees, even with both their heating appliances going full blast. The chairs, table and beds were unpleasantly cold to the touch, and at night, when the outdoor temperature sank to its lowest, human breath turned at once into a white vapour. Kvido and his mother fell victim to countless colds and he himself, though he never confessed, suffered with rheumatic pains in his joints.

"I promised to stay by you for better, for worse," his wife had told him at the end of summer, "but I'm not putting up with anything under eighteen degrees this year. So do what you have to."

Kvido's father had tried: He added his wife's pregnancy to his application for a flat, took a close personal interest in how the waiting list was moving, chased up their case orally and in writing, responded to several dozen small ads and finally drafted a formal complaint, in his own fair hand, but nothing came of any of it. October was coming to a close, the river was awash with fallen leaves and each morning an ever clammier mist rose from its surface. Having come in from work, Kvido's mother would crawl straight into bed and he would immediately point one of the heaters directly at the bulge beneath the duvet where he guessed her belly must be. Seeing that little mound where Paco lay snug, Kvido could only look on in envy and deliberately make his teeth chatter. In mid-November he caught – as expected – the flu and his mother had to stay at home to nurse him. For ten days they both lay in bed, made cups of hot tea and munched on vitamins. When Kvido's temperature fell back, his mother permitted him to read Dürrenmatt's plays to her – and in return she read Hans Christian Andersen's fairy tales to him. At other times they just lay there in silence, watching the manifold shapes and colours of the clouds through the sixty small panes of glass that surrounded them on three sides – and dreamed.

During one such interlude, Kvido started to imagine some strange, exotic landscape. While the focal point was obviously Prague Castle and the Old Town, the whole scene became a cascade of white cliffs descending gradually towards the sea. The sand on the beaches was hot and silvery-gold. In the shade of the nearby palm trees sat Miss Hájek, Grandpa Jiří, Pavel Kohout and Mrs Bažant from the costume workshop. They were reading plays and laughing and drinking the milk straight from coconuts. Azure-blue budgerigars fluttered in the air or came to perch on Kvido and Jarka Macek's suntanned shoulders, but instead of claws they had tiny velvety suckers on their little feet, so neither of them felt a single scratch. Together they collected sea-shells or went for a swim, and when they were tired, they basked in the sunlight on huge beaver and mink pelts. Whenever Kvido so desired, Jarka would show him her privates. – The vision of this landscape so captivated him that Kvido would summon it up quite often and let it expand over successive days. But he worried in case he wouldn't remember all the fabulous things that he had shaped in his landscape. So one evening he resolved to record it once and for all: he got into bed with a notebook and pen and while it was all still crystal clear, he carefully jotted down everything that he could see the moment he half-closed his eyes.

"They wouldn't pass it for publication today, obviously," the editor said sarcastically. "Not even if you deleted Kohout. It's all surrealism and child pornography, and that group under the palm trees cuts right across how class relations are structured."

"The lad's dreaming of warmth!" Kvido's mother told his father, having sneaked a read of her son's little work. "Do something!"

"Do something!" his father exploded, not having said a word since he got in from work – for which, truth to tell, he had plenty of good reasons. "You really are something! But do what? Tell me one single thing that I might have done and haven't done so far! If you can," he added in a huff, "apart from joining the Communist Party!"

"Don't shout!" Kvido's mother looked round towards her sleeping son. "You haven't been to see Šperk, for one thing. Everybody says that's what matters most."

"I *have* – and twice at that. It's not my fault he refused to see me both times."

"But he did see Zvára, didn't he?"

"Yes. He did," Kvido's father said. "I expect Zvára had something worthwhile to tell him…"

"What?" Kvido's mother sat bolt upright in bed. "Do you mean to say that Zvára – ?"

"Yes," said Kvido's father with an odd kind of forbearance.

"Well I never… who'd have thought…"

"They say he's had enough of people who're suffering," the father said. "He's worked it out that what's needed for spreading the truth is guile. That's the nature of the times. 'They' are our competitors – and with competitors you have to employ tactics, otherwise it's just tilting at windmills. An animal survives by merging with its environment. All that red is just protective coloration. A chap must simply march with the times – even more so having collected a kidney problem from the cold in that sub-station."

"Aha," said Kvido's mother.

"He says I don't have even the smidgen of an instinct for self-preservation."

"That's true."

Suddenly something dawned on her. "So, even though they're expecting only their *first* child, they're going to get a flat!"

Kvido's father faltered briefly.

"Not going to," he said and looked away. "They've got one already."

Kvido's mother gave a short laugh. She lay back down and stared in silence at the cracks in the ceiling.

"And their room at the hostel –?" she asked shortly, in a low voice.

"Already assigned…"

"To the Havelkas?"

"No."

"The Tondls?"

"No."

"We're third," said Kvido's mother.

"The ones who got it weren't even on the waiting list."

"Vile," said Kvido's mother. "It's so vile, vile, vile."

"Yes. It is vile."

"And you're not doing anything about it! How on earth am I supposed to respect you?"

"Let me read to you," Kvido said to the editor, "what professor Michal Bědný says: 'A girl who marries should bear in mind that the fast route to widowhood and the orphaning of her children is to keep badgering her husband: You're a man, you have to do things. I'm a weak woman, I don't have to. Psychologists know that generally it is these weak women who are the most demanding.' What do you say to that?"

"That we're wasting time. We'd agreed on a comic novel, and instead you're going on and on about how cold you were as a child, not to mention the fact that, for no apparent reason, you keep blaming members of the Party."

"And I know why," said Kvido. "God and I, we both know."

"So stop bothering me with it!" the editor was getting irritated. "Most of the chapters you've brought me so far are never going to be seen in print. Don't you get it? If you really can't write two paragraphs without taking five swipes at the Communists, just say so and we can move on. Forget about me, write for your drawer, and for all I care send it to Sixty-Eight Publishers. This is getting us nowhere."

3. December 1969 wasn't particularly cold, but Kvido's mother spent every weekend and, of course, the Christmas holidays at her parents' in Prague anyway. Kvido's father, who, given the circumstances, was rather troubled by these visits, had to remind himself, rather to his own amazement, that his wife uttered not a word of complaint; on the contrary, she was buoyant and kept quoting from various plays and in the end, he believed he was the only one to have noticed how often she pressed her back against the huge tiled stove in Grandfather's study.

Early in the New Year they returned to Sázava and the first snowfall. There wasn't much of it and it was the wet sort, but it was enough for sledging and the local Lark Hill regularly came out in a rash of children after school. Kvido and Jarka among them. Kvido wanted Jarka to sit *in front of* him, since he was the slightly taller of the two, but Jarka was afraid to watch the trees at the foot of the hill rushing headlong towards them and so sat *behind* him. During the descent she laughed as she pressed her face against Kvido's shoulders, also closing her eyes in her blind faith in Kvido's actually unremarkable steering skills.

"The worst thing is," Kvido would tell people after his marriage in a strange mixture of pride and horror, "that that's exactly how she lives with me."

Back then Jarka used to wear, as Kvido recalled, a white, woollen roll-neck sweater, black leggings and red boots handed down from her elder sister. They were slightly too big for her, so now and again she'd lose one on the way. He also liked the feel of her hot breath on his neck, though equally it worried him that she had to touch his tub-of-lard belly – and in the days that followed he would encase himself tight in an elastic bandage before going out. Then he was totally untroubled and could stay out sledging until dusk fell.

The following Saturday, however, Kvido came back from Lark Hill surprisingly early. He was soaked through and shivering. His mother put him to bed, made him some tea and took his temperature: this was exactly 39°C. Kvido fell asleep, but when he came round later that evening, he was feverish. This time the thermometer showed almost 40°C, but what probably frightened his mother even more was his laborious, irregular breathing. Kvido's father got his coat and went out to phone for an ambulance.

"Did you get through?" she asked in a panic the moment he got back.

"They'll be here within the hour," her husband sought to reassure her.

Kvido's mother, rendered almost immobile by her ninth month of pregnancy and the four jumpers she was wearing, settled awkwardly into an armchair opposite Kvido's bed and gnawed desperately at the knuckles of her right hand. The boy's father slung a chequered blanket round her.

"We're all going to die here one by one," she told him. "You can't say I haven't warned you often enough."

About forty minutes later, the wheels of an ambulance screeched on the gravel track outside the Drábovka. Kvido's father trotted out and led the doctor – to the latter's amazement – all the way to the conservatory.

"Now I've seen everything," the doctor remarked, having first taken the whole room in with a single glance, but then he quickly bent down over the boy where he lay.

"It might be pneumonia," he said finally. "In any event," he said, taking another disbelieving look round, "we'd better be getting him out of *here*."

"If you wouldn't mind," Kvido's mother said, "I'd like to go with you. I'm due there in a day or so anyway, so I could…"

"What? Already?" Kvido's father exclaimed.

"Of course," the doctor assured her, shivering himself. "Would you like to come too?" he turned amiably to Kvido's father. "We'll sort something out for you."

"That's not really on," the father laughed, but you could tell that he had wavered for a split second.

Kvido's mother fetched her leather bag from the wardrobe and began gathering up the essentials. The ambulance driver came in.

"The mother's coming too," the doctor told him.

"Right," said the driver, pleased. "Two birds with one stone!"

"Now there's a fine comparison," said Kvido's mother and snapped her bag shut.

The wings in which they put Kvido and his mother were separated by about thirty metres of snow-covered garden. By coincidence, their wards were almost directly opposite each other, though on different floors (Kvido's on the third, his mother's on the second), but the single clump of decorative conifers growing there unfortunately blocked their view of one another. So one of the kinder nurses at least arranged for them to have a daily exchange of letters, but when Kvido later wanted to see his mother as well, he had to go to the window of the adjacent ward.

"Hello," he would say to the adults present, "would you mind if I gave a quick wave to my mother?"

"Waving," Kvido explained later, "always played an important part in our family life."

"Of course, young man, of course," a Mr Hlavatý, an asthmatic pensioner, would croak back, enchanted by the boy's good manners.

So Kvido said thank you and somewhat lumberingly clambered up onto the radiator, because he wouldn't have been able to see through the whitewashed lower half of the window. At first, he sometimes had to wait quite a time in this somewhat awkward position before his mother glanced in the right direction, but they quickly agreed by letter on 10 a.m. and 4 p.m. and for several days it worked a treat.

But one morning Kvido's mother failed to show – and she didn't show up that afternoon either. The nurse who had been their letter-carrier happened to be off that day, so Kvido was left guessing what might have occasioned his mother's absence. He couldn't believe that she could have suddenly forgotten their arrangement.

The next day he was already in the neighbouring ward by nine-thirty and under the transparent pretext of having a chat with Mr Hlavatý, he managed to stick it out on the radiator for a whole hour, but without a glimpse of his mother. He returned to his bed disappointed only to flick absently through Karel Plicka's coffee-table book of photos of Prague Castle that his Grandfather Jiří had sent him via his father. When a nurse entered, he asked her if his mother hadn't perhaps sent him a message.

"Mother? Message? Where?" the nurse snapped impatiently.

Kvido realised that she must be in a hurry. He didn't want to risk losing her good will, so he put his entire mind into describing his predicament in one single, logically and stylistically unbelievably neat sentence. As he uttered it, his expression was so grave that the nurse took pity on him. For a brief moment, she even sat on the edge of his bed.

"If your mum's over there," she said, pointing to the maternity wing, "it's quite possible she's got other things to worry about than exchanging letters with you. Do you understand?"

Only then did Kvido understand.

The nurse was right. When that afternoon, shortly before four, his mother appeared, to Kvido's indescribable delight, at the window, she was holding what looked like a pillow in her arms.

"What's she showing me that pillow for?" Kvido cried, completely at a loss to grasp what he was seeing.

"What pillow now?" croaked Mr Hlavatý, who was beginning to tire of Kvido's constant visits. The doctor who happened to be there examining the old boy, walked over to Kvido and looked where the boy was pointing.

"That's not a pillow, you silly," he said. "That's a baby. Is there something wrong with your eyesight?"

And so it was. Paco had entered the world and Kvido had to start wearing glasses.

4. *Two days later in the garden outside the maternity wing. Nighttime.*

FATHER (*throwing stones at the window*): Psst! Psst!
(*Behind the glass can be seen the whitish shadows of nightdresses and the faces of laughing women. Then the shades vanish, the window opens and Kvido's mother appears.*)
MOTHER: What man art thou, that, thus bescreen'd in night, so stumblest on my counsel?
FATHER: Stop being silly!
MOTHER: If they do see thee they will murder thee. How cam'st thou hither, tell me, and wherefore.
FATHER (*proudly*): I have indeed come. By car.
MOTHER (*surprised*): What?? In the dark? You? And where've you parked it?
FATHER: I left it at the edge of town. You know I can't cope with car parks.
MOTHER: So you drove here in the dark? You always told me you suffered from night blindness.
FATHER: I just decided to risk it. It's a bright night. (*Above the conifers a huge luminous moon looms.*)
MOTHER (*flattered*): And all for my sake?
FATHER: My biggest worry was wild animals. Imagine what it would be like if a hundredweight hind came leaping out of the forest and landed on the bonnet! The utter carnage! Doesn't bear thinking about. So, to play safe, I kept my hand on the horn the whole way.
MOTHER (*surprised*): You drove through a forest? Which

way did you come??

FATHER: No, I didn't. But who's to say deer might not be in a field somewhere. I'm pretty sure gamekeepers don't keep them tethered in the forest.

MOTHER: I suppose you're right. You're my hero. I mean it. Honest.

FATHER: I reckon driving schools don't pay enough attention to night driving. And yet night driving has so many specific –

MOTHER (*interrupting*): I love thee.

FATHER (*taken aback*): I was –

MOTHER: Dost thou love me? (*Recites wistfully*)
I know thou wilt say 'Ay';
And I will take thy word; yet if thou swear'st,
Thou mayst prove false; at lovers' perjuries,
They say, Jove laughs. O gentle Romeo!
If thou dost love, pronounce it faithfully.
Dost thou love me?

FATHER: You're crazy. How's your urine?

MOTHER (*embarrassed*): Keep your voice down. (*Whispers*) Not now. Someone might be listening.

FATHER: Who?

MOTHER (*pointing to the floor above*): The guys in urology.

FATHER: What about them? Surely there's nothing wrong with me asking whether your urine's okay, is there?

MOTHER (*blushing*): Ssh! (*Whispering barely audibly*) My urine is fine.

FATHER: What's that? I can't understand a word!

MOTHER (*blushing ever more deeply, still in a whisper*): My urine's fine.

FATHER: What? I can't understand a word, dammit!

MOTHER (*erupts*): So stop asking me about such things with other people present!

FATHER: And your blood? I suppose I *can* ask you about your blood.

MOTHER: It's fine.

FATHER: Really?

MOTHER: Really. It's fine now.

FATHER (*in a whisper*): And your urine?

MOTHER (*erupts*): For God's sake man! I've told you not to…

FATHER (*soothingly*): All right, all right, take it easy… And what's Paco up to?

MOTHER: Right now? He's asleep.

FATHER: And Kvido?

MOTHER: I expect he's asleep as well. (*Tongue in cheek*) Does that surprise you?

FATHER: Did he clean his teeth at bedtime?

MOTHER (*tongue in cheek*): Unfortunately, I don't know. I'll ask the consultant in the morning.

FATHER: Let's hope he did. You know what he's like.

MOTHER (*still tongue in cheek*): Let's hope so.

(*Both fall silent.*)

MOTHER (*deliberately loud*): So am I to understand that you've driven thirty-five kilometres at night through whole herds of deer just to ask after your elder son's dental hygiene?

If so, the school dentist ought to buy you a box of chocolates.

(*Peals of laughter from inside the ward*)

FATHER (*smiling*): No, that wasn't the reason. (*Now gravely*) I've come to tell you something very important.

MOTHER: What's happened. (*Fearful*) Has one of the heaters given up?

FATHER: No, no. I don't want to make it sound at all dramatic, but you'd better sit down anyway.

MOTHER (*in terror*): Oh my goodness! (*She goes and sits down, no longer able to see her baby's father*) You haven't gone and joined the Party, have you? (*In a low tone to the women on her ward*) That man's going to stop me lactating! (*Aloud*) Are you there?

FATHER (*aloud*): Yep.

MOTHER (*standing up sharply*): Have you joined the Party?

FATHER: No! You're mad! What is it with you and the Party?

MOTHER: So what then, for heaven's sake?

FATHER (*solemnly*): I've registered for an evening course in Marxism-Leninism.

MOTHER: Have you gone mad? Why that?

FATHER (*taking out a bunch of keys with a smile*): So they'd give us a flat.

MOTHER (*amazed*): A flat??

FATHER (*no less amazed*): A flat!!

(*Curtain*)

"Come in, Comrade," Šperk had greeted Kvido's father that

memorable afternoon in his office. "Welcome to Sázava!"

Kvido's father crossed the red carpet rather awkwardly to shake the hand that the smiling Šperk had extended towards him.

"I've been living here for over a year now," he pointed out. "Or freezing more like."

"Even in the summer?" Šperk jested.

"No, not in the summer," said Kvido's father.

He looked up at all the awards on the wall, then let his gaze slip down to the dark, highly polished bookcase, whose shelves supported a handful of booklets bound in red, but mostly a huge range of specimens of laboratory glassware. He waited. Šperk was watching him.

"I've decided," he said finally, "that we should give you one more chance. That's why I sent for you."

"One more? When did I have one before?" Kvido's father was puzzled.

"You mean you haven't? Didn't you get a job in the sales department?" Šperk was smiling.

"Yes, but – "

"But?"

"But given that I studied commerce for five years and then worked for three more at the Academy of Sciences, it strikes me that being given a *desk-job* in the sales department is merely logical – at least more logical than a getting a similar job in accounts."

"Even though a certain Mr Šik worked at the Academy?" Šperk smirked.

"Good God!" Kvido's father sighed. "Was that any fault of mine?"

"And is it any fault of mine that that Kohout fellow has a country cottage hereabouts?" Šperk laughed. "And that Prague knows all about it? I'm answerable for that as well, you know. Do you know him?

"Me?" said Kvido's father, caught somewhat on the hop. "No. Not in person. I've seen him on TV," he lied.

"A rightist to the core, he is. But he didn't used to be – as I recall. The kids in my wife's playgroup used to recite him. But she tells me your lad is good at recitation. A good lad, obviously, not to be overlooked."

"Kvido?" said the boy's father, flattered. "Well, he does try."

"But you're easily overlooked!"

"Me? You can find me sitting on the same chair in the same office for ten hours a day. Twelve even. Look in sometime, you couldn't overlook me then."

"That's not the point," Šperk smirked. "I didn't mean in the office, but beyond, among other people, where you'd be *politically* visible."

"Politically?" Kvido's father queried cautiously.

"You haven't registered for an evening course in Marxism-Leninism, you don't attend meetings, you hold no official positions, you simply don't show any kind of *commitment*!"

Kvido's father just shrugged.

"I'm not asking for miracles, Comrade," said Šperk. "It would be enough if you joined the National Front. How about the volunteer fire brigade?"

"Fire brigade??"

"Right, the fire brigade – you're not afraid of fire, are you?"

"Depends how high the flames are," said Kvido's father.

"Hurrumph," said Šperk. "And what about football? Do you play? Our B team's been relegated. Did you know?"

"I did hear something," Kvido's father lied. "But I don't play football. Goodness, no. In all honesty, I'm not really the sporty type."

"So not football?"

"No."

"And you're not even a member of the Friends of the Armed Forces?"

"No."

"All right. Look here," said Šperk abruptly. "Get yourself onto an evening course in Marxism-Leninism and I'll let you have that flat."

Kvido's father felt a weak pricking sensation beneath his breastbone.

"Fine," he said. "We really are freezing to death in that conservatory."

"And you realise when. I mean right now!" Šperk laughed and took a bunch of keys from his desk drawer. "Catch – they're for the company's house at the foot of Lark Hill. – Get along there right away and put the heating on, otherwise the pipes'll burst! Since we moved Pitora out, there's been no heating on. And it's been a week or more now."

"House?" said Kvido's father in disbelief.

"That's right, a house." Šperk was still laughing. "With a

garden. But I'm only loaning it to you."

"I wasn't expecting anything like this," Kvido's father confessed. "Thank you."

"I hope you won't disappoint us. But woe betide if you don't put flags out – we pass the place on our torchlight parades."

"Flags?" Kvido's father queried foolishly.

Only now was Šperk's news beginning to sink in. He was over the moon and profoundly relieved and couldn't focus properly.

"Flags!" Šperk guffawed. "Not to forget to put them out!"

"Today?"

"Don't be daft. That would be taken as a provocation. No, I meant in principle, as and when – not right away."

"Oh, I will." Kvido's father had come back to reality. When all's said and done, there was nothing wrong with putting a few flags out.

"Pitora said the same thing," Šperk grinned. "And where is he now?"

"And one more thing," he said to Kvido's father finally, "you'll be needing a dog – now you've got a garden."

"A dog? Oh, but –"

"I'll sell you a puppy," said Šperk in a voice that brooked no objection. "Complete with full documentation. I breed them. Did you know?"

"Yes, but I – "

"Three thousand crowns. Stop by one time."

"Can't be done," Kvido's father tried to protest. "I don't mean the money, but it would drive my wife mad. She's terrified of dogs."

"She'll get used to it," said Šperk. "Mine did. And they're whopping great Alsatians!"

"Alsatians?" Kvido's father was horrified. "Not likely! The fright will bring the wife to an early grave. Years back she had a nasty encounter with an Alsatian. No, no, she and dogs don't mix!"

"Who's talking about dogs?" asked Šperk with a smile. "I told you, it's only a puppy."

IV.

1. The house at the foot of Lark Hill, which the family finally moved into on the mother's return from hospital, reminded Grandma Líba of a dear little boarding house for girls in Lausanne, where she'd stayed a number of times in the distant past. The same red sandstone underpinning, the same ochre-coloured window frames, the very similar veranda covered in Virginia creeper, and the almost identically distributed spruces and thujas in the garden left her drowning in nostalgia.

That spring, she had gone with two friends on an excursion to the German Democratic Republic. For almost a week they had lived amid the glorious countryside of the Harz as it came back to life – which only increased her dismay at the prospect of returning to the filthy, smog-filled city. For, of late, she had been suffering certain problems with her breathing, which she blamed in their entirety on the Prague air, and, like her two friends, had not completely excluded the possibility of lung cancer.

"We're in a café atop the Brocken,
   enjoying a coffee and scrumptious cakes.
   Our bliss and rapture to betoken
   a brief *Noch einmal* is all it takes!"

she'd written in her traditional poetic way on the black-and-white postcard, but this was followed by an uncustomary and distinctly weird addendum in prose: "We're stocking up on oxygen – let's hope it keeps us going in Prague," it said.

"What do you reckon?" Kvido's mother asked her husband, the postcard in one hand and little Paco in the other.

Kvido's father re-read the message.

"Codswallop," he declared.

"Let's hope that's all," said his wife, though she was smiling.

The April sun so warmed the tiles on the patio that you could not merely sit on them, but it was actually extremely pleasant to do so. Bees buzzed and in the crown of the nearest apple tree the coming summer's fruit could clearly be seen forming beneath the pinkish blossom.

Kvido's mother radiated her great joy – but with it a great wariness.

And properly so, though in the end it let her down: Grandma Líba turned up in the middle of May, with two suitcases and an indomitable determination to help Kvido's mother with little Paco. She arrived one Friday afternoon quite without warning, though that didn't stop her having a go at Kvido's father for not meeting her at the station.

"You mean to leave Daddy all alone in Prague?" Kvido's mother was concerned.

"He's not a child, you know," Grandma argued. "At least he knows how to buy meat."

She insisted that she couldn't have remained in Prague a moment longer, because she was literally suffocated by the smog, and as evidence to back her up she showed the family a mucus-soaked filter from the handy inhaler she'd grown accustomed to using at all the busiest crossroads.

"Smog," she declaimed, "is carcinogenic!"

She uttered the word 'carcinogenic' with a kind of reverence.

"As you will," said Kvido's mother in a tone of resignation. "As you will."

Kvido's father had to call on all his carpentry skills and furnish his mother-in-law with a *cosy summer maisonette* in the previously unoccupied attic.

"Despite the desperate emphasis he laid on the word 'summer'," Kvido went on, "Grandma stayed in Sázava not only through the following winter, but right up to her death in eighty-seven."

"In winter, it's practically impossible to heat it," Kvido's father had warned Grandma.

"You should believe him for once, Mummy," Kvido's mother tried to persuade her. "He's had plenty of experience with unheatable rooms."

However, Grandma wasn't to be put off and, to Kvido's father's dismay, she took possession of both the old heaters from the Drábovka conservatory, making out that no winter was going to catch her unprepared. As Kvido's father was aware, the two heaters together set the electricity metre spinning like a gramophone record – and the thought of paying a small fortune for electricity on top of the expensive central heating oil rendered him quite dizzy.

On freezing winter nights, he would often get up to check the metre by torchlight.

"He looked like a penny-pinching version of the ghost of Hamlet's father," was the somewhat wacky simile Kvido's mother used to describe it later.

Amazingly, Grandma's sudden fear of cancer was not dispelled by the healthier air in Sázava. At first she refused to cook in aluminium pans, eat the carcinogenic chicken that Kvido's father persisted in buying despite her admonitions, or use detergent-based washing-up liquid, with the consequence that all the plates, pots and pans were so greasy that they slipped from everyone's grasp; the range of taboos declared by Grandma just grew and grew.

On May twenty-eighth, the family celebrated Kvido's father's thirtieth birthday. The sun was blazing away, but the periwinkle-covered arch over the veranda afforded the requisite shade, so Kvido decided to lay the dinner table out there. He had a set of chisels for his father and he couldn't wait for the chance to hand his gift over.

"Dinner!" he called impatiently.

The first to show was his father himself, bearing a bottle of bubbly. His mother, who followed him, brought a huge pan of piping hot soup and a copy of the previous day's newspaper under her arm.

"Just listen to this," she said, laughing. "I'll read it to you – they can't be serious!"

She set the soup down on the table and spread out the paper.

"Surely not," said Kvido's father. "Not on my birthday."

Grandma Vera pointed at Grandpa's glass. "Don't pour him any!" she commanded.

"Listen to her! Did you hear that?" Grandpa Josef yelped, appealing for sympathy from the others. "Now I can't even clink a glass with my own son!"

"I'll only read a bit of it," said Kvido's mother. "You'll see it's worth it."

"Not now, please," his father begged. "And you, Dad, take it easy."

He started to free the cork of its wire cage.

"Do take your places!" Kvido cried. "Grandpa!"

"Coming," Grandpa Jiří called from his obligatory tour of Grandma Líba's vegetable beds, now heading back somewhat out of breath. Kvido noticed that his grandfather had shed a few inches.

"So what did you think of it?" cried Grandma Líba.

"Wonderful!" said Grandpa, but his gaze had swept all the way to the wooded slopes of the river valley, so it wasn't entirely clear whether his admiration wasn't for more than the celeriac, cauliflower, pumpkins and rhubarb.

"I should say so," said Kvido's mother. "Sázava," she went on, bizarrely, in Russian, "is one of the most popular areas with tourists."

"Show-off!" said Grandpa Josef scornfully. "Speaks Russian, she does…"

"Stop that!" said Grandma Vera. "It really is a fabulous house, lass. Seriously…"

"Except for the garage; it's unbelievably narrow," said Kvido's father. "Whoever put it up must have been a total idiot. I can scarcely reverse our Octavia into it."

"We're trying to swap it for a hangar," said Kvido's mother. "If we don't manage, he'll have to learn how to reverse with the driver's door closed."

"She's exaggerating," said her husband. "Come on now, let's raise our glasses."

"Don't wake Paco. Please!"

The family gathered round the table. Kvido's father popped the cork and began pouring the champagne into their glasses.

"What's this?" Grandma Líba shrieked. "Cut glass? Are you trying to poison us all? Don't you know it's got lead in it!"

"Course I'm not," Kvido's father smiled. "I can assure that as long as my wife refrains from reading *Rudé Právo,* we'll survive the toast."

"I refuse to let lead anywhere near my lips!" Grandma went on shrieking and squeamishly put some distance between her and the glass.

All the rest bent with some distrust over their glasses.

"What's all this nonsense?" Grandpa Jiří was seriously puzzled.

"The lead in cut glass," said Kvido's father, slowly and with an air of superiority, "is bound at the *molecular* level. So I believe there's not the remotest possibility that even a microgram of lead would come – as you put it – anywhere near your lips."

"Guess who I met yesterday," said Kvido's mother, seeking to change the subject. "Pavel Kohout."

Grandma Líba padded her glass round with a paper napkin.

"Your health," she said truculently.

"And *yours*," Kvido's father raised his own glass. "And yours."

"Ecology – and originally put," said the editor. "I'll have that. Though without Kohout, obviously. So you see, it can be done if you put your mind to it…"

2. It has already been noted that Kvido could read fluently long before he started attending the first grade in Sázava. Thus, it was only to be expected that he would find the primitive simple sentences in the Primer boring – often the case with children like him, though with him the problem was slightly different. Because like any experienced reader he combined syllables automatically, subconsciously, he couldn't appreciate the purpose of words that were only there for the purpose of practising those combinations. Kvido couldn't bring himself to believe that all those words had been printed just for their own sake, with no aim or purpose, and so as he read them he tried really hard to grasp the point of them. He knew that the words in books and plays were definitely not chosen at random and he couldn't concede that things might be in any way different with the words on the early pages of the Primer. Thus words like PUSSY, COLA or MILKY as uttered by Kvido took on an urgent, dramatic tone that anyone who heard him spotted at once, but could scarcely account for.

"An utterly banal sentence like, say, MARY IS MAKING MEATBALLS," Kvido was to explain later, "sounded, in my rendering, like an evocative statement about life and death, or a sample drawn from some unknown Gothic horror. It had everyone agog!"

Kvido's renown soon reached Mrs Šperk, the teacher who ran the school's recitation circle and who at once came to hear him.

"All stand, children!" cried Comrade Mrs Jelínek when her colleague from the junior school appeared at the classroom door.

"Sit down, children," said Comrade Mrs Šperk with a smile. "I've only popped in to hear how nicely you read."

When, as if by chance, it was Kvido's turn, he was faced with three short sentences about a little green pea. Unconsciously imitating Vladimír Šmeral in the role of Pius XII, he read them intently.

The two teachers exchanged glances.

"Would you like to join the bigger children in reciting some nice poems?" Comrade Mrs Šperk asked him.

"In all honesty, I don't know," said Kvido. "When all's said and done, it's only art in reproduction; I think I'd rather try writing something of my own."

"You could do that anyway, once the performances are over," Comrade Mrs Šperk said, surprised. She'd already heard all sorts about Kvido, but actually meeting him like this, well, that was something else.

"I don't know," said Kvido. "I'll have to think about it."

"Well," said Comrade Mrs Šperk rather primly, "all right."

Her colleague gave her a conspiratorial wink.

"You and Jarka could recite something together," she suggested to Kvido. "Jarka reads nicely as well."

Kvido's interest in recitation – as his teacher had rightly surmised – rose a fraction.

"But she might not want to," he said.

"Far from it!" the teacher laughed, beaming at her pedagogical success. "Jarka, come here!"

Jarka trotted obediently to the front and stood before the two teachers. It was a moment before her pigtails stopped swinging. Kvido wanted to give her a smile, but she wasn't looking his way.

"Would you like to say some pretty poems, Jarka?"

Jarka gave a slight, shy nod and dropped her gaze.

"Although the engagement of two first year kids was unprecedented in the history of the circle, Comrade Mrs Šperk did not hesitate," Kvido explained. "Jarka and I were taken on that very day."

When – while they were still living in the conservatory – Kvido first donned, slightly awkwardly, the blue shirt with the badge of the infant arm of the Young Pioneers on it, his mother didn't even smile; on the contrary, she wore a rather grave expression.

"Is it going to be in school?"

"At a meeting," Kvido informed her.

"I see."

Kvido's father entered the room with an armful of lengths of wood that he meant to turn into a shoe cupboard.

"Hail to the Red Flag," he said, having noticed Kvido.

His wife shot him a brief, meaningful look.

"And what will you all be reciting, dear?" she enquired.

"Various things," said Kvido not very helpfully.

"Naturally, at the time, I hadn't fully appreciated the essence of the problem," he would explain years later, "but even back then, I sensed there was something not quite right about the recitation."

"And you?" his mother enquired further.

"Me, 'And you can be proud.'"

"And you can be proud that you haven't defiled your lips or your breast with falsehood?" Kvido's mother was recalling her own childhood, half of which was spent in the Disman Radio Ensemble.

"You know it?" said Kvido in surprise.

"Mm," his mother said pensively. "And who says 'Lenin – a beacon, Lenin – a bell'?"

"Jarka," said Kvido, blushing.

For those in attendance at the meeting – and not just the Party members – the preliminary sing-song and recitation by Young Pioneers was as much a matter of course as the soft drinks on the table, but little Kvido, who saw as little sense in the revolutionary verse of Stanislav Kostka Neumann or Ivan Skála as he had in the simple sentences in his Primer – and so read them with that same fervour of a seeker after truth – was something they hadn't encountered before.

"Who's the little nutcase?"

"He's the son of that lawyer woman and her engineer husband."

"It's like his life depended on it!"

"Isn't he keen!"

"Just look at the little guy!"

"The little bastard's really got stuck into it!"

No matter how caustic some of these remarks, one thing was without doubt: people had noticed the fervour of his recitation and remembered it.

"And they remembered me from *meetings*," Kvido would explain to Paco. "That's to say, in a favourable context. Favourable to our father! They were both as indulgent as could be, just like true parents when their child chooses a tasteless toy that they don't care for in the slightest, but since it was the child's own choice, they don't want to deprive him of it. Except it suited Father's plans, and so he didn't try to prevent it – and that's the very word for it, they simply didn't try to *prevent* me from doing it. I, my dear little brother, I did their dirty work for them: one round of 'And you can be proud' for the Party members at the glassworks, and two rounds of 'Ode to Peace' for the street committee – and Dad could fly to London.

"You're exaggerating," said the editor. "As usual, you're exaggerating. Is there any point at all our going on with this?" he added.

"Of course I'm exaggerating," said Kvido. "I only want to show you what might have *contributed* alongside all the other stuff. It might sound stupid to you, but I'm still convinced that my recitations for the Communists, the purchase of Šperk's dog and my father's playing football were, so to say, the three sources and three conditions of his subsequent short career."

3. "So, how's the new house, Comrade?" Šperk asked jovially as he came and sat for a second next to Kvido's father in the works canteen.

"Very good, thank you," said Kvido's father. "There's no comparison – the conservatory and where we are now."

While he was genuinely grateful to Šperk, he was ill at ease at having people see him chatting amiably to the man.

"You did put the flags out, saw it for myself," Šperk said with a grin.

"Yes, I did," said Kvido's father.

"But you're still not visible!" Šperk rebuked him. "Don't you ever play football? We need someone on the B team."

"I've already told you, I've never played," Kvido's father said with a shrug. "Only when I was on military service, and that's something I'd rather forget."

"Ah well," Šperk was grinning. "So not football."

"No. God forbid!"

"Never mind," said Šperk. "Never mind. But there is one more thing: I've got that dog for you, you know, like we agreed?"

"That's crazy!" Kvido's father got scared. "I told you, my wife's scared to death of dogs!"

"Get away with you!" Šperk chortled. "An Alsatian like this one for only three thousand! No hurry, don't worry!"

"That's not the point, honestly. My wife is simply scared of dogs. She was bitten by one once and had to go to hospital, dreadful, it was!" Kvido's father was improvising out of desperation. "No, no dog!"

"But like I said, it isn't a dog!" said Šperk, a bit grumpier now. "It's a puppy. Pop by tomorrow."

"So, once again," Kvido's mother said to her husband that evening, "you think that I, whose periods are triggered prematurely by the sight of any untethered dog, of any breed… that I'm just longing to have a dog in the house, and an *Alsatian* at that!"

"No," said Kvido's father dispiritedly.

"So do you think Kvido is dying for us a get a dog? Our Kvido, who pees and craps himself whenever a dog barks without warning?"

"No," said Kvido's father with a sigh.

"Or does little Paco long for a sturdy Alsatian? Has he found some way of getting his wish across to you?"

"No!"

"So it's only you who wants a dog in the house!"

"I don't, though," her husband tried to disabuse her. "All I want is to land a decent job."

"Hang on," his wife marvelled, "just explain: you *don't want* a dog? *You* don't want one either? So actually no one wants one – and yet we're to have one?? And so you're going to bring one home, tomorrow?? Why??"

"That's what I've been trying to explain: so I can do my proper job."

"And for that you have to buy a hairy work permit from Šperk for three thousand crowns!"

"Oh, my dear God!" he wailed. "It's not as if I can help it!"

It was instantly obvious that something had dawned on the editor.

"Good grief!" he yelped. "I've got it at last!"

He slapped his thighs and rose smartly out of his chair.

"Here's me forever blaming you for doing so little in the way of self-censorship, getting excited because you set yourself so few limits – yet really it's quite different!" He laughed sardonically. "You haven't set yourself *any* limits! So far you've been carrying out no self-censorship *at all*!"

"Well," Kvido had to admit, "so far that's pretty much right, but – "

"So," the editor cut in, "you just set it all down as it is, warts an' all, as they say, the plain truth, with no regard for anyone or anything, and you're more or less reckoning – because you're not totally naïve, that *afterwards* I, like some wicked Jesuit, will *just* cross the odd thing out, right? Is that it?"

"Pretty much," Kvido said, resigned.

"Brilliant!" exclaimed the editor, lowering his voice dramatically. "Except that *afterwards*, afterwards it'll be too late to start deleting things!"

"Really?" Kvido feigned shock. "Well there's a howdy-do! What shall we do? Here's me slogging away over a true story, and in the end it turns out it can't have bits deleted"

"Are you finding this funny?" the editor asked coldly. "I thought you wanted to get this novel *published*. In which case, you'd have to do quite a bit of deleting. But that doesn't look possible, because you've been structuring the entire thing in such a way that if you were to start cutting bits out, it would come down on your head. The whole edifice would come tumbling down."

The editor crossed triumphantly to the open window, drummed his fingers on the sill and looked absently out into the street. A tram passed along National Avenue.

"Too bad," said Kvido. "It had better come tumbling down then."

Having paid Šperk the three thousand crowns, Kvido's father took possession of a six-month-old bitch called Tera. From the very outset he loathed the name. It had a sharp, cold sound, but more than anything else it reminded him of the war film *Tora! Tora! Tora!*. All the way back from Šperk's place he was thinking about having a different, softer, more tender name for the animal, something more in tune with its – as he hoped – placid, trustworthy and affectionate nature, something that would have an immediate, unequivocally reassuring effect on his wife and Kvido. He fully appreciated that renaming a dog who'd had several months in which to grow used to the name he'd been given was probably a grave sin in dog-loving circles, on the other hand he was genuinely worried by the family's likely reaction to the name Tera – and he also derived some small satisfaction from the idea that if he hadn't been able to decide on the names of his sons, he could at least determine what the dog was to be called. He was briefly tempted to give the dog the feminine equivalent of his own name and so call after her 'Josephine!', but then wisely set aside that idea, born, as it was, of vanity. Yet he was still beset by the idea of renaming the dog.

"Milly. Fay. Vanilla," he tried under his breath. "Lulu? Lulu perhaps?" he wondered, but oddly that put him in mind of canine intercourse, so he scrapped that idea too.

As he mused thus, the journey was quickly behind him and suddenly there he was, with the dog, still called Tera, by the red sandstone posts of his garden gate. Summoning the totality of his nous, wit and invention, Kvido's father strode towards the house. In the space of ten to twenty seconds a good fifty female names flashed through his brain, but not one, he felt, cut the mustard. Then he rounded the last corner and saw his wife on the veranda, sweeping up periwinkle leaves. Poking out of her cream-coloured jumper was her little white collar. He'd got it.

His wife still hadn't noticed him.

"I've got her!" he called out gaily. "She's called Sweetie!"

Surprisingly, Sweetie was accorded the best reception among the entire household by Kvido. His movements still evinced a measure of circumspection, but he cradled her, played with her and generally danced attendance on her. Grandma Líba merely took her for yet another meat-eating mouth to feed – and Paco was still too small to gain any special pleasure from a puppy. Kvido's mother resolved to ignore it altogether, so there was a serious danger that in her constant to-ing and fro-ing she might step on it at any moment. After this had gone on for two hours and more, Kvido's father could stick it no longer.

"You're giving a lousy performance," he pulled her up short. "It's just not believable. Look at Kvido. Doesn't it strike you as a bit ridiculous to pretend you're scared of a puppy?"

"I'm not scared of it. For now," she said. "But I was against having it, and you knew."

For now, Kvido's father was happy enough that she wasn't scared.

"Come, come!" he said, relieved. "How could anybody be scared of such a playful, affectionate, trusting ball of fluff? Why do you suppose I called her Sweetie?"

"Where I'm concerned," Kvido's mother returned, "it will always be a black, evil, long-fanged, fearsome, foul-smelling hound! – And I couldn't care less if she was called Miroslava!"

"Get away with you!" Kvido's father said with a laugh. "Just come and stroke her, you'll see how beautifully soft she is."

"Never! And you can tie her up somewhere!"

"Are you crazy? Nobody ties puppies up!" Kvido's father shook his head in disbelief and bent to pick Sweetie up. She raised her muzzle and stared at him with her dark, shining eyes. "Do stroke her. Please."

Kvido's mother wavered.

Then she stretched out a hand and laid her palm on Sweetie's head.

Sweetie turned to see her.

Kvido's mother withdrew her hand.

"See!" Kvido's father laughed contentedly. "What was it like?" Only then did Kvido's mother open her eyes.

"Like stroking a dead rat." she said.

"As long as Sweetie was a puppy, there were no major snags. Naturally, she gnawed the odd table leg and a few books and peed on the carpet, but there were no *real* problems," said Kvido. Though as she grew, so did the problems. Kvido's father, who had attempted to train her according to Hegendorf, that classic of German kynology, discovered that though a bitch was supposed to be "calmer, more willing and more amenable than a male", the reality was almost the reverse: Sweetie was wild, stubborn and extremely disobedient. Later, he read in another manual that she was probably "a hard case with a dominant leadership instinct, which, in the dog-man pack, leaves any leadership to man only with the greatest reluctance."

"Damn me!" Kvido's father vented his alarm.

He read on to learn that a reliable criterion by which to tell a hard dog from a meek one was how it reacted to a spiked collar: a hard dog puts up with one. So he could have ascertained fairly easily which kind of dog Sweetie was, but in the face of his awful certainty he preferred to remain blissfully ignorant and kept postponing the purchase of said collar. Instead he put even more effort into training.

For a long time, he vacillated between the *coercive* method, as recommended by Hegendorf in the case of hard dogs, and the *imitative* method, which was better suited to his own character.

"Imitative method?" his wife queried? "Am I hearing right? Do you have a single quality, aptitude or skill that a dog might be supposed to imitate?"

However, Kvido's father had long been immune to his wife's invective and so he continued patiently with his training programme, a combination of both methods. He'd long given up on the idea of getting the dog to crawl, let alone retrieve things; he'd have been in seventh heaven if Sweetie would at least sit or lie down at his command, if she wouldn't tug on the leash so much and, especially, if, having been let off the lead, she would come back when called. But sometimes all of these goals seemed too high and his zest for getting the dog trained gradually abandoned him.

So he took it all the more badly when anyone – even in all innocence – scuppered his periodic successes.

"Really, what kind of instruction is that you're giving her?" he once launched into his wife, after hearing a whole string of her 'commands'. "Your 'Now you lie down!' or 'Plonk yourself here!' What's that for God's sake? I've told you *a thousand times over*, the command is 'Down!'"

"So will you kindly tell your monster to stop taking bites

out of my face!" she screamed back.

"She's never bitten you! It's just licking!" Kvido's father argued back with passion. "You should count yourself lucky, because that's her showing obedience to you! If only you'd get round to reading Hegendorf yourself, you'd know. 'Members of the pack evince their subordination by licking the muzzle of the pack leader,'" he quoted.

"Well, she's not licking *my* muzzle!" his wife yelled back. "I don't give a damn for your idea of obedience. For me, an obedient dog is one that doesn't lick me!"

"Oh dear," he sighed.

He'd have loved to teach Sweetie not to go licking his wife's face – along with many of her other bad habits – but he was far from certain of success. His confidence as a dog-trainer shrank by the day.

After several months he finally did what he had long been loath to: on a business trip to Prague, he bought a spiked collar. As he fitted it on Sweetie that evening, he tested the sharpness of the spikes with his thumb and felt confident that this time he wouldn't feel her pulling on the lead. But as soon as took the first steps off the patio onto the stone path into the garden, Sweetie shot forward, indifferent both to his confidence and the spikes, and for the entire walk jerked and strained just as before.

"I'm afraid it's now clear," he told his wife that evening, completely knackered. "She *is* what they call a hard dog."

"And what follows from that?"

"Not sure. She probably won't always obey. She'll probably

try to get her own way."

"Not always," his wife repeated. "Where do you get these euphemisms? This animal was *never* going to obey us – I knew that from the outset, even without Hegendorf!"

"Obviously, I'll keep up with the training," Kvido's father assured her.

"What? You?" his wife was surprised. "You with your instinct for subordination, you want to train a dog whose instinct is to lead? Doesn't that strike you as absurd?"

"Yes, it does," Kvido's father admitted his defeat.

4. Kvido's father sank back into pessimism, though his failure with Sweetie obviously wasn't the only reason; on the contrary, the number of grounds for it seemed only to grow.

The job of deputy manager of the sales division went to his friend, Mr Zvára, which Kvido's father had expected, yet couldn't understand. Outwardly, they still got on well together, but both preferred not to think too much about the past, least of all which of them had a degree in two languages, or which of them had written the other's dissertation. The only – however oblique – reference to these remarkable circumstances was made by Zvára himself sometime in October 1972, when he was to be sent to the West – to the industry trade fair in Frankfurt.

A week before the flight, Zvára spent his time doing nothing more than counting the German marks that he been allotted officially or acquired by other, illicit, means, toying with his plane ticket, unfolding and refolding his map of Frankfurt, and vainly trying to dredge up the words of German that he'd long forgotten.

"Do you know how to say 'Are you married?'?" he asked, without taking his eyes off his phrase-book.

"Sind Sie verheiratet," said Kvido's father.

"And 'Take your clothes off!'?" Zvára winked towards his secretary.

"Ziehen Sie sich aus."

"And 'Open your mouth'?" Zvára asked with a lecherous grin.

"Offen Sie den Mund," Kvido's father said with a sigh. "And do you know what this means: 'Ich habe einen Ausschlag, Herr Doctor. Es juckt'?"

"No, what is it?"

"I've got a rash. It itches."

The secretary tittered.

"Don't worry about me!" Zvára laughed. "I can take care of myself!"

"Daran zweifle ich nicht."

"What's that?"

"I don't doubt it," Kvido's father translated, by now rather irritated.

He didn't envy him, at least not in the usual sense of the word, and he didn't want Zvára to think that he did, but he was finding it harder and harder to share his glee at the prospect of the trip. And his expression threatened to betray him. So he turned to his desk and pretended to be snowed under with important work that had to be shifted. Of course, Zvára saw through it.

"I know you're better," he said unexpectedly.

Kvido's father pretended not to understand. "What?"

"Do you know why it's not you going, even though you're better?"

Kvido's father got that familiar pricking sensation beneath his breastbone.

"Give over," he said with as much indifference as he could muster.

"Seriously," said Zvára, "D'you know why?"

"No, I don't, boss. Would you mind explaining?" Kvido's father attempted to lighten the tone, but it did nothing to release the sudden tension in the office.

"Because you're an idiot!"

"Well I never!" said Kvido's father in a slightly strangled voice, "and all the time there was silly me thinking it was because I hadn't joined the Communist Party."

"And you were thinking right. And that's what makes you an idiot."

The secretary was watching them in horror.

For a fraction of a second, Kvido's father was tempted to lash out at his friend, but instead he took a number of deep breaths and a wave of something deep inside him washed his anger away.

"You know what, boss?" he said in a now conciliatory tone. His vision had cleared. "Bugger this for a game of soldiers!"

"Oh, sir!" the secretary feigned shock.

"As you will...," said Zvára in the same instant.

"Sergeant Zvára!" Kvido's father called across about fifteen minutes later.

"Sir!" Zvára responded as prescribed. It looked as if he'd long forgotten the previous altercation.

"Mind you don't go doing anything silly out there in the West!"

"Will do!" Zvára saluted as prescribed.

All three had a good laugh.

"And that's the way it always was," Kvido explained. "My father's antipathy to conflict and his physical incapacity to cope with it, they usually won the day. The thought of having to spend forty hours a week in the same room as someone he was at odds with was so unbearable that he may never have actually had a proper row with Zvára. The moment it looked as if an argument was brewing, he drew back. Few truths were worth ruining his nerves over."

"And you're never once going to tell him," his wife would badger him, "exactly what you think of him?"

"Why bother? We'd just end up scrapping. Or do you suppose it would open his eyes and make him change?" Kvido's father objected. "I'm no good at training dogs, let alone people."

"True," Kvido's mother agreed with him, exceptionally. "And doesn't it worry you that you're living a lie?" she went on.

"Yes it does," said he. "But it worries me rather less than having someone in the office creating a shindig because he's taken offence. It scares the wits out of me. It brings me out in a rash."

"So you live a lie because of a rash."

"And you're not living a lie?"

"Of course I am. We all are. Only I try to fight against it! In my own way, not perhaps very obviously, but I do."

"Following the law," Kvido's father commented.

"Yes, following the *law*. I'm a lawyer, so I'm for the law."

"In a land without the rule of law," he added. "Don't you find that something of a quandary?"

He seemed to have touched a nerve, since Kvido's mother reacted quite tetchily: "Whereas you fight for right over your carpentry bench!"

"No I don't," said Kvido's father with a sigh. "And I've never claimed to. I work to calm my nerves. You wouldn't believe how soothing it can be. Before I'm even finished making a single shelf, the world has ceased to exist."

"A shelf!" said Kvido's mother scornfully. "Get yourself some LSD. That way you'd forget about the world much sooner, and there'd be a bit of *style* about it."

"LSD's a doddle, but try getting hold of some wood!"

Kvido's father knew what he was talking about: some time before he'd managed to get hold of a second-hand treadle lathe that was going cheap, but he couldn't – just when he'd thus extended his creative options – lay his hands on the right materials, and so for weeks on end he had to make do with off-cuts. These he turned into fishing floats, though he himself was no angler, or various pendants that nobody wore, and all simply because it allowed him to keep escaping to his workshop.

"Once he had nothing left to mount on his lathe, he started whittling all manner of trinkets with conspicuous symbolical meanings," Kvido explained. "His best known work from this period will probably prove to be his miniature version of the barrier across the road at the Rozvadov border crossing."

"Come on now, are you taking the piss here?" said the editor. "Living a lie, a state without the rule of law... Had we made an agreement about this kind of thing, or not...?"

"But it's true," said Kvido obstinately. "What'll be the point of it – if it isn't the truth?"

"Point!" said the editor. "You really are still a child! I ask you, since when have we been able to ask, in this country, whether literature has a point? That's a luxury we've never been able to afford. The only question we've ever asked is whether the country even exists. Whether it *is*! Don't you get it?"

"No," said Kvido. "I don't."

As soon as his father did get hold of the necessary materials and the palettes in his workshop could boast of neat piles of pine and spruce planks, some balks of oak, sheets of plywood, laths of varying length and some reddish stumps of wild plum trees, his father had gone to work on them with a zeal that he'd had to suppress for so long. To get his hand in, he turned a number of bowls and candle sticks and a new frame for the big mirror – then he set about the curtain rails that Kvido's mother wanted, and he made the promised box to go round the radiator in the boys' room. For Kvido he made a simple, practical bookcase and polished and painted the bench on the patio. But he still sensed that his DIY endeavours lacked something. Anything he brought out of the workshop into the light of day invariably had a couple of minor flaws, which, though mostly visible to him alone, gave his jobs what he saw as a hallmark of amateurism. It might be a slight gap round a joint, a few tiny bubbles in some paintwork, angles that weren't spot on. At other times, the product might be rendered with perfect craftsmanship while lacking something on the aesthetic front.

"That was the case of the magazine rack," Kvido explained. "Father gave it a lot of time and effort, but it turned out to be so big and bulky that every visitor's first question was why did we have a manger in the living room."

Kvido's father couldn't abide amateurism. He had spent his entire childhood and adolescence amid things that creaked, wobbled, pealed and collapsed, repaired by his keenly amateurish, or rather dilettantish father, Grandpa Josef. Even now, when he recalled all those cupboard doors chocked up with bits of folded cardboard, the flexes taped round with sticking plaster and the loose parquet flooring sealed with chewing gum, he was seized with a strange, at times even hysterical attack of nerves. He believed that if his often meaningless work in the sales division couldn't be in any sense professional, at least his work with wood could be to a professional standard. And yet no matter how focussed he was, no matter how good his materials and how sharp his chisels, nothing was ever quite right. He understood that he probably lacked some unlearnable, innate sense for woodwork, while believing that he could compensate for this shortcoming by upping the number of hours he spent in the workshop.

"My father," Kvido explained, "was trying to get one over on his genes."

Around that time, one major, if, to say the least, peculiar, commission came from Grandma Líba, whose preventive measures against carcinogens had led from messing about with all manner of herbs to the very brink of mysticism: a certain diviner, whose advice she'd sought, confirmed, for a small consideration, her surmise that the electromagnetic currents that are everywhere crossed her attic room *diagonally*, and he easily persuaded her that her bed should definitely respect that direction. Thus the classical rectangular bedding chest became immediately unusable, owing to the consequent need for one of a completely different shape – *three-sided*.

"I know about *corner* sofas," said Kvido's father, having become acquainted with Grandma's requirement, "but a corner bedding box will probably be the only one in the entire country. – One day I'm going to find myself knocking up a bed of nails for her!" he said in gloomy anticipation to his wife, but at heart, he was quite glad to have an entirely legitimate reason for staying in his workshop till all hours of the night.

Possibly even stronger than her faith in electromagnetic currents was Grandma's sudden lunatic conviction that by walking in an easterly direction during her tours with her friend, that is, against the earth's rotation, she was growing physically younger. Kvido's father tried repeatedly – at the last attempt by summoning to his aid the round shade from the kitchen light, some coloured felt-tip pens and a torch – to prove to her that this theory was, to put it mildly, highly irrational, but to no avail, and to make things worse he pulled the kitchen light from its fitting. With an obstinacy worthy of Galileo,

Grandma stood her ground, claiming that the moment a road or footpath bent directly eastwards, she could feel *unequivocally* her feet making the earth rotate, like a circus bear rotating a huge roller or sphere.

"So I'm actually walking against time," she explained.

Kvido's mother didn't believe her. She thought Grandma was just playing a silly game with them, the point of which was to boost the family's sympathy for her advancing age. However, one day Zita unfortunately confirmed that Grandma did believe the things she said.

"She goes a few paces ahead of us, compass in hand, and suddenly, out of the blue, she darts forward like a mad thing," she described the case with some sorrow.

"Where are you going, Líba?" the ladies call out after her, but she doesn't hear them. The varicose veins vanish from her calves, her flabby muscles fill out, and each step is lighter and springier than the last. Her hunched shoulders unbend and her firm, full breasts stretch the material of her check shirt tight. Her grey hair regains its colour and sheen, thickens, slips out of her chignon and explodes at every step around her smooth, young face. The air is pure and fresh and to breathe is sheer delight. The trees just skim past her and there ahead, where the forest ends, some nice, bright stripling may be waiting for her, certainly more congenial than the old biddies shouting to her from behind. She can sense the calm, steady beating of her heart and she smiles upon the world with her lily-white teeth. It's 1930 and Grandma is eighteen.

"We'll catch up with her round the next bend," Zita reassures her breathless companions.

"Indeed so: where the path turns northwards, there's Grandma Líba waiting for them. Slumped against a tree, she's fighting to get her breath back and her eyes radiate a kind of ethereal weariness.

"It's all right now, lass," Zita says not without emotion and hands her a drink to wash down the requisite pill. "We're here now."

5. Christmas came. Grandpa Jiří had to go in for some operation so couldn't be with us. Kvido, his mother and Grandma Líba took him his presents a day earlier, to hospital. Grandpa was a little pale, but he wore a smile. On the bedside table, Kvido spotted a small, fairly thick book; it had no jacket, so he couldn't detect either title or author.

"What are you reading?" Kvido asked his grandfather, his curiosity about the book growing.

"Don't ask! Shakespeare's sonnets!" Grandpa laughed. "I'm going nuts. D'you know what it means when a lawyer starts reading Shakespeare?" he said, turning chirpily to Kvido's mother.

"No, I don't," she replied.

"Claims not to know!" said Grandpa. "And what's Paco doing?"

Right from first thing, Christmas Eve passed in an atmosphere of calm. Unspoiled even by Sweetie, who had managed by lunchtime to gobble up half the turkey meant for the evening meal, or by Kvido's mother, who turned the rest into schnitzels and fried them on a carcinogenic Teflon frying pan, and not even by Grandma Líba, who subsequently flushed them with revulsion down the toilet; Grandpa Jiří's uncustomary absence had made everyone extraordinarily tolerant. It took Kvido to spoil things a little.

"What on earth's *this*?" he asked without beating about the bush, having failed to find in the last parcel in his pile of presents the longed-for black, broad-brimmed hat, but only a black-and-white football. He made no effort to disguise his disappointment, let alone feign anything like pleasure.

His parents were smiling mysteriously. Little Paco was playing happily with his presents.

"You really bought that thing for *me*?" Kvido asked, his voice showing signs of starting to break. "Is it supposed to be a joke? If so, it's a bad one."

"Wait –," said his mother, clearing her throat, but Kvido wouldn't let her get a word in.

"Having refused to take part in the sorry business of pretending to write to Santa Claus and expressed myself *unambiguously* on my urgent need of a black, broad-brimmed hat, I would have expected my wishes to be respected!" he went on irritably.

"Kvido," said his father reproachfully.

"I would quite understand," Kvido's voice rose, "if I hadn't received anything – God is my witness that I have always taken your economic situation fully into account – and of course, I would have forgiven you if I'd received a dark-blue, or even brown, hat, even though I'd never have set foot out of doors in such colours in my right mind, because at least there would have been a visible sign of your trying to oblige, but this *football*, I'm not forgiving you for *that*!"

Paco looked up at his brother, startled.

"In Celetná St. I've seen oceans of black hats," said Grandma Líba. "And cheap ones at that."

"Hush, Mum," said Kvido's mother.

"Wait, Kvido –," said his father.

"I won't wait!" Kvido wailed. "I *know*, get this, I *know* that I'm unathletic, bespectacled, gawky, fat and introverted, but there's no point at all in making such expensive jibes at it!"

Silence reigned, broken only by Kvido's fuming aloud. His father looked up at the wooden ceiling and from the box behind his back withdrew a black, broad-brimmed hat. He flung his arms wide. "It really was meant as a joke," he said.

"Where's your sense of humour?" Kvido's mother asked. "Grandma also laughed when we gave her that orienteering compass."

"Stupid compass thing!" said Grandma Líba.

"But you liked it!" Kvido's mother remonstrated.

"Not any more!" Grandma declared resolutely.

Kvido's mother shrugged.

"So who's the ball for?" Kvido asked mistrustfully.

His father bent down and scooped the ball up into his palm. "Me," he said.

He held out his arm and stared at the ball in a very odd way.

"What?" said Kvido.

"Really," said his mother. "He's not lying. You've probably forgotten that when he was at Opatovice on military service it was because of football that he had to run the assault course at night in his pyjamas."

She'd known since the evening before that Kvido's father really had bought the football for himself, but she was still puzzled.

"*Without* pyjamas," he clarified matters and his gaze wandered off somewhere into a dismal past.

"Without? You poor thing," Kvido's mother laughed. "You never told me that!"

"Why?" Kvido asked diffidently. He was ashamed now of the scene he'd created.

"Handball," said his father with remarkable brevity.

"And now tell us," Kvido's mother was enjoying herself, "how the boys in your platoon pinched your specs and after a practice session on the firing range wired them to one of the target figures…"

"*Before* the session," he said apparently reluctantly. "But fortunately everybody missed. So they had to run over them with the field kitchen instead."

"You never told me that either!" she laughed. "You've obviously been keeping heaps of things from me!"

"Handball?" Kvido asked, with some sympathy.

"That too. And an own goal."

"So," said Kvido's mother, her eyes streaming, "so now you've bought yourself a football for a spot of nostalgia! Though, from the nature of the events, I'm afraid it's going to be more like psychoanalysis."

"The compass was definitely better," said Grandma Líba, coming round for a moment from dozing.

Kvido's father raised the ball level with his face. "Perhaps it isn't even a ball," he said rather enigmatically.

"Dead right!" his wife exclaimed. "It's the key to your personality!"

"No, no. D'you know what it really is? It's my last sacrifice to the gods of careers."

"What?"

"Reality is a cipher. Appearances can be deceptive. You mustn't be misled by size," said Kvido's father, unsmiling. "It could be the right marble to fit the Golem."

"Could be!" his wife conceded with a laugh. "Unless it's the spirit of your unit commander."

Kvido's father lifted the ball even higher. The Christmas tree candle flames leaned away from the stir in the air.

"Accept my libation, ye gods," he said.

Kvido and his mother exchanged glances. Grandma Líba was asleep.

"I beseech ye," said Kvido's father urgently.

"Enough," said his mother. "We know that Granny dragged the supernatural into the house. But I wouldn't have expected our greatest family rationalist to be the first to be fired by it."

"What else can he do?" said Kvido's father. "He's been here five years, doing a job that doesn't require a degree and makes 1,200 a month."

Paco stood up from playing with his new toys. "Give me

ball!" he begged.

His father tossed it to him.

"I've got a degree 'with distinction', having graduated in English and German, a commendation from the Academy of Sciences, I've had five years' practice, an evening course in Marxism-Leninism, a dog and a son who does recitations," he said. "Now I'll learn how to play this team game with a ball and I'll be done."

"I think he really must have got hold of some LSD!" Kvido's mother exclaimed.

Kvido's father ignored the remark.

"Do you know the rules at least?" he asked his elder son. "I need to clarify a thing or two – handball, the offside rule and suchlike."

"Pretty much," said Kvido. He looked slightly bemused, but realised that his father was, for whatever reason, in earnest, and he wanted to help. "I've watched the boys at school."

"Great! Could you find me a moment tomorrow sometime?"

Kvido nodded enthusiastically: "Sure," he said.

"In the afternoon on Christmas Day, we went for our first training session," Kvido explained. "One problem was that my father – much as at any time in his life, except possibly when he was at school or in the army – possessed neither tracksuit, nor appropriate footwear, so he had to wear a sweater, jeans and some old shoes, the heels of which keep sinking into the soft lawn."

Another problem arose as they sought an appropriate place

to train: for obvious reasons, Kvido's father was keen that this should be as far away as possible – which happened to be the same spot as where he'd once tried in vain to train Sweetie and to which he was loath to return – some kind of superstition. In the end they found another spot, a little way above their garden, at the very foot of Lark Hill.

First, Kvido's father wanted to practice elementary passes at close quarters, but although he and Kvido stood ever closer together, they still spent most of the time looking for the ball in the adjacent hazel bushes.

"So many molehills," Kvido's father declared, as if apologising to some third party. "Of course, there wouldn't be any on a real pitch." He brought the ball back and spent a long time setting it down on an imaginary spot.

"Catch!" he cried finally.

He attempted to give it a sharp kick, but it got bogged down in the matted grass way before it got anywhere near Kvido.

"The grass is too long," he called by way of explanation.

"It won't be at a real game!" Kvido called back by way of encouragement.

Both, of course, sensed that even on a level, neatly mown pitch things wouldn't be much better.

In the course of this and later training sessions, Kvido's father was able to verify the familiar truth that movements that look so easy, fluid and natural when made by players on television are by no means so easy in practice: his own were forced, jerky and barely coordinated. His running looked unnatural and lumbering and, after two hundred yards or so, lamentably like someone who's totally exhausted. When running with the ball, Kvido's father would either kick it too far ahead of him, or trip over it. Dribbling past an opponent, selflessly represented by his son, only worked if Kvido remained stock-still; the minute he moved to the same side that his father had chosen for his attack, it would end in what looked like a pretty dangerous collision. He approached ground-level passes in a manner usually reserved for stamping out burning matches or wasps, not much use for just stopping the ball. Consequently, the ball usually ran straight under the leg raised in readiness – or he might stop it, but in such a violent manner that he slipped on it ignominiously. Airborne balls he eventually stopped trying to do anything with at all (much as he had given up on training Sweetie to retrieve): he couldn't use his head because of his glasses, his hands because of the rules, and trying to kill the ball with his chest entailed a serious risk of winding himself. His shots lacked both power and, unfortunately, precision, so mostly they looked like sloppy passes. Probably worst of all was that whenever the ball came anywhere near him, the sheer effort of doing anything with it caused him to poke his tongue out, leaving him looking like a half-wit.

"Great shot!" Kvido praised him notwithstanding.

"A man's movements do not suit him *a priori*," Kvido maintained. "For this or that motion to be truly becoming, it must first be thoroughly lived, absorbed. For example, it well became my father, who had spent tens of thousands of hours at his desk, when he reached towards the bookshelf with his left hand for some title he suddenly needed while his right hand continued, with an impressive independence, to make notes or tap away at his calculator. That apart, like every one of us, he performed a million other movements, more or less decent, but then also a number that were downright embarrassing: like when during a trade-union-sponsored holiday in the mountains, he slipped on some wet steps having been obliged to pretend to be a polar bear. Or whenever he played football in Sázava."

Although, in the case of Kvido's father, progress could only be measured as the incomplete elimination of the most blatant shortcomings, he did train several times a week right through the winter. He purchased a sober black tracksuit and some yellow-and-black canvas football boots, which at last allowed him to leave the cover of the hazel bushes and go for a run round the immediate environs without anyone registering surprise at his outfit.

He practically abandoned his workshop in the cellar, took a cold shower every morning, and started reading the sports pages. He also read Bican's *Five Thousand Goals* and Ota Pavel's *Dukla Among the Skyscrapers*. Of course, none of this was reflected in his performance and Kvido, who usually accompanied his father, was chiefly concerned that someone might see them.

"It was terrible, but it did do me some good," he recounted later. "Firstly, I lost a few kilos, and secondly, I realised once and for all that if ever I was to impress Jarka with anything, it certainly wouldn't be my dedication to the setting up of rapid counter-attacks."

Early in March, Kvido's father showed up, sort of accidentally, at the first training session of the Sázava B team. Comrade Šperk, who by tradition always attended the start of the spring season, welcomed him with unfeigned delight – unlike the players, who received this newcomer who went on endlessly about Josef Bican with some mistrust.

The next two hours merely confirmed how right they were: Kvido's father wasn't up to the task either technically or physically. As soon as he got the ball, he lost it again, and, broadly speaking, he carried on repeating all his previous errors. This time, too, he fell twice; each time the nearest opponent being so far from him that there could be no suggestion of the latter being to blame. His two shots at goal, which were, unusually, on target, were deflected by the keeper with his fist and obvious disdain.

"Might have a degree, but he's full of shit!" he remarked loud enough to be heard.

"So there you have me, for what it's worth," Kvido's father said after the session.

"Why the fuss!" Šperk laughed. "You made yourself visible!"

Shortly after midday on the twentieth of May, Kvido's father was finishing off his beef and rice in the works canteen. He was about to leave when Šperk, bearing his aluminium tray, came and sat at his table.

"Hi," he chortled. "You didn't have the dumplings?"

"Hello. I prefer rice," said Kvido's father.

Šperk set about his dumplings.

"How's Tera getting on?" he asked with his mouth full.

"Tera?" Kvido's father was momentarily confused. "Oh, yes... She's getting on fine."

However, Šperk didn't appear particularly interested in the reply.

"They're off to England – have you heard?" he asked.

Plenty, Kvido's father thought to himself.

"Yeah," he said.

"So, I've been thinking whether our lot oughtn't to have somebody with them who knows the business and speaks the language," Šperk said, smiling across his plate.

In the first instant, Kvido's father found the cynicism of such a frank admission perversely pleasing and was about to laugh out loud when he suddenly wondered whether Šperk mightn't have meant what he said.

"Probably a good idea," he said cautiously.

"You bet," Šperk was grinning. "And I've been thinking about suitable candidates."

Kvido's father got that pricking sensation beneath his breastbone.

"Yes?" he said, with a hint that he found it funny.

"I reckon it could be you," Šperk said. "Youth first, right? But I've had to vouch for you myself."

V.

1. Kvido's father was due to fly to England in early July. Grandma Líba, who, thanks to her regular cycle of bread pudding, pumpkin fritters, kale rissoles, carrot croquettes, potato gnocchi, green beans with rice and salsify bake as the family's weekly menu, had finally saved up enough to go on her dream tour round Italy, was flying there at the end of May.

The fact that she was to go abroad before Kvido's father filled her with a glee that was nothing short of infantile. She took no less delight in drawing teasing comparisons between the two countries. Obviously, Italy came off the better by far: she went on about the damp London fog, the cold sea and the superciliousness of the English – and her eyes sparkled merrily. Kvido's father, affected whether he would or not by Grandma

Líba's enthusiasm, though at first he did try to stop himself, adduced in turn the stifling heat of Italy, its pickpockets and the cuisine, with most meals cooked in aluminium or Teflon vessels. She, who had hitherto argued with him practically non-stop, now responded to his provocation almost magnanimously, even forgiving him his passing inanity on what the Italian for 'malignant tumour' might be. Kvido's mother, who, like Kvido, had never been further than the High Tatras, listened to their good-natured chaffing with growing aversion, though she was sincerely happy for each of them to have the chance to travel. Sometimes she was a bit slow to clear the dinner table before the two travellers started spreading out their maps and brochures right there among the dirty plates.

"I do wish you'd stop!" she fussed. "I think we've all heard enough of it."

On May 20th, Grandma left for Prague and Grandpa Jiří saw her as far as the airport. Nine days later, a black-and-white postcard arrived in Sázava showing the interior of S. MARIA GLORIOSA DEI FRARI in Venice.

> "We're taken around by coach and bus,
> quite a harem, the lot of us,
> then we walk miles on our feet,
> blue sky above, in all that heat!
> But if we really start to tire,
> there's always gondolas for hire."

it said and, as usual, there was an addendum in prose:

"I'm making huge progress with my Italian and English! Love to all, Your Líba," she wrote.

"So they might have," Kvido's father remarked. "But her versifying's not getting any better. What's this 'we walk on our feet'? I suppose they walk on their hands some of the time!"

"Someone at the post office has pealed the stamp off again!" Kvido voiced his annoyance.

"Well I'll be…," said Kvido's mother. "She's making huge progress with her Italian and English. I'd very much like to know what that means exactly."

As the date of Grandma Líba's return approached, there was a rising edginess in the household: Grandma's thriftiness had only grown with her advancing years and she found even the cheapest souvenirs inordinately expensive. Hence, she would acquire these indispensable little gifts for the family in manners uniquely hers, sometimes quite startling. So each of her returns constituted a bigger faux pas than the last. Kvido's parents had learned to accept all those lovely vases and tablecloths bearing the names of hotels where she had stayed with a kind of sympathetic good humour, but for Kvido these circumstances were a pain. Usually – like that time when she had come back from the GDR and given him a hunting knife with the scratched-out dedication 'From Helga P to Günter K.' still visible – he managed to stutter a single thank you, flushed bright red and disappeared to his room for several hours.

"I wonder what she'll bring us," Kvido's father mused caustically during the last dinner without her. "I really do."

Kvido chortled.

His mother administered a more or less automatic rebuke to the pair of them, though in fact, she saw in Kvido's laugh some guarantee that this time he would cope better with his grandmother's homecoming.

She was right: next day, when Grandma Líba unlocked her famous grey suitcase and with the guilty expression of an incorrigible spendthrift gave Paco a melting bar of chocolate and Kvido a dead crab, the latter didn't bat an eyelid.

"Grazie," he said gravely. "Just the one I needed."

"Good, that's over," his mother said to herself with relief. But this time, she was wrong: the worst was yet to come.

"Now listen carefully," said Kvido to the editor, "this is key: here I make my first compromises with adults – instead of *socking* it to them!

"First, but by no means last," said the editor meaningfully. "All right, read on."

Yes, Grandma's broadly traditional problems with returning to everyday life burgeoned into something more serious this time. She began – like a child who's finished off her own sweeties and is now enviously watching others who've still got some – envying Kvido's father his trip to London.

During the first few days, she was content to make the odd joke about London fog, but nobody laughed at them and she felt she was on the wrong tack; any fog in London is, after all, better than sunshine in a miserable dump like Sázava. Having also failed with the cockroaches supposedly infesting all the hotels on the left bank of the Thames, she took herself off to her attic in a huff, surfacing only in the night to pinch something to eat from the fridge, for when Kvido's mother had called her down for lunch or dinner, she had resolutely refused.

"It's all right for him, he's going, and I can't!" she added plaintively.

"Mum!" Kvido's mother chided her. "You're behaving like a silly little girl!"

And so she was: Grandma Líba was regressing to childhood. Everything pointed to a relapse into her first period of *recalcitrance*.

"It's not fair!" you could sometimes hear coming from her room. "It's not, it's not, it's not!"

Whatever the rest of the family happened to be engaged in at such moments, they became rooted them to the spot and would stare up at the ceiling in fascination. Seeing how the ceiling sometimes shook, Kvido was prepared to bet that his grandmother was throwing a tantrum and stamping her foot.

"Good God!" Kvido's father whispered, "perhaps I should think of going somewhere else."

Grandma having spent over two days stubbornly alone in her garret, Kvido's mother summoned up the courage to make one last desperate attempt "to sort things out sensibly". Before lunch, she lit a cigarette, made some coffee and took it with her up to the attic. Kvido's father hoped to spare the children the likely row and under the pretext of a spot of football practice, he took them out in the garden, though his good intention was ultimately thwarted, since they could hear every last word through their grandmother's open window:

"It's not fair, it isn't!"

"But, Mum, you've *had* your trip!"

"So what, I don't care!"

"Pass!" Kvido's father called to his elder son.

"Okay, but lock the dog inside!" Kvido cried. "I'm not having my leg chewed because you want to play football!"

"What do you know about negotiating contracts? Be reasonable, Mum!"

"Pass!"

"Shut the dog in first, for God's sake!"

"I know you know Germanic languages, dammit!"

"Ball, ball!" Paco wailed.

"I'm going with him!" Grandma yelled.

"Pass the ball!!!" Kvido's father bellowed like a real lunatic.

"Come up here, will you," Kvido's mother shouted down, leaning in resignation out of the window. "Come and explain to her why you can't take her with you."

"With me!!" said his father, storming into the attic room. "True, I've heard of presidents' wives accompanying their husbands sometimes. But –," his voice was rising, "I've never heard of a president, let alone some petty Czech clerical worker, taking his aged mother-in-law with him on a trip abroad."

"Stop arguing!" Kvido called up from the garden. "I refuse to grow up in this kind of environment!"

"Did you hear what he said?" his grandmother screamed. "Right! This *aged mother-in-law* won't stay here a moment longer!"

At this point Kvido's father's self-control abandoned him

completely: "You shouldn't go nourishing people's false hopes!"

"I'm leaving! I refuse to live alongside such a selfish individual!"

"So you're simply going to pack up and go?" Kvido's father shouted. "First you do your damnedest to turn us into pumpkin fritter junkies, and now you're going to leave? How low is that! I bet you won't even leave us the recipe!"

"Mummy!" Paco was crying, having been bowled over by Sweetie.

"I'm leaving! This very minute!"

"Of course I needn't say how much you'll be missed," said Kvido's father, glancing at the array of the old lady's sources of heat: the radiator, two-bar electric fire and room heater had been joined that winter by an electric blanket and foot-warmer. "Not to mention how you'll be missed by the power company. Do you realise your leaving's going to put people out of work?"

"Pleb!" the old lady cried venomously. "Primitive pleb!"

Kvido's father suppressed the urge to go and grab her by her suntanned throat and hold on to it for a few minutes.

"Mummy!" Paco was crying hysterically.

"Come down and eat," Kvido's mother pleaded. "Coming, dear!" she called.

"I'll go to him," said Kvido's father. He shook his head, heaved a sigh and smiled.

Kvido's mother caught up with him on the stairs. "She's not evil," she said, "she's just reached that age."

Something about his wife's voice made Kvido's father look up. His wife had tears in her eyes.

"If I could afford it, I'd even buy her a round-the-world trip!" she said.

2. Like many before him and since, Kvido's father was shocked by the West.

"He was a bit like the mother in Erben's 'Treasure'," Kvido was to tell Pavel Kohout later.

Although he was applauded for this jocular comparison, it wasn't really accurate: his father had also been astounded by the colourfulness and cleanliness of the streets, the magnificence of the architecture old and new, the abundance of the wares displayed in shop windows and much else besides, but he wasn't blinded by it all, even for a moment, unlike that poor woman in Erben's poem. Moreover, the comparison failed to capture what had fascinated Kvido's father most in the West: the respect – not overblown, but widespread and apparently entirely natural – for his education, work and knowledge.

He sensed it at all the negotiations that he conducted, but it came to him even more when they sent a company car to collect him, when they had a dedicated phone line put in his hotel room, when he was invited on a tour of London and for dinner – even though a provisional deal had already been done. At the end they'd asked him if he had any special requests.

"Yes," said Kvido's father in English. "Ask me that same question again."

Doors would open automatically on his approach. Where they weren't so fitted, someone else opened them: a hotel porter, liftboy or commissionaire. Phone boxes worked. When, one afternoon his English colleague raised one arm in Kensington High Street, a taxi pulled up immediately. Policemen smiled. The drivers of even the poshest cars stopped at zebra crossings for him. Toilets smelled nice. The post office biro, which no one had stolen yet, didn't leak. People blithely offered him newspapers, tickets for the races, the chance to join some church or the army, five-coloured ice cream, houses for sale, massages, shoes and a trip to the Philippines. Women in Soho amiably offered him their love. All the things on which he stood, sat, wrote or lay were sparkling clean and didn't wobble (nor were they covered in budgerigar poo). The shampoo he bought didn't leak into his briefcase. And having used it twice, he was suddenly rid of the dandruff that had been showering from his head for thirty years. So for the first time in his life he could go uninhibited to the barber's and for the first time in his life have a haircut that matched the shape of his face. He suddenly felt more suave.

He felt more successful.

The assistant in the pet shop where he'd asked about a flea and tick collar for dogs, didn't laugh at him; instead, he showed him four different ones. The food in restaurants was neither half-desiccated, nor cold. The waiters were extremely obliging.

"No vegetables, please," he would ask them.

The grovelling servility he adopted with waiters back home, thanks to which he was enabled to consume a cake with the cream gone off and look grateful for such a boon, was a thing of the past. He bore himself with more energy and greater confidence. When he tossed 5p to a beggar in Park Lane, he no longer remembered that in a recent match with Bělokozly FC he'd been taken off after eight minutes.

But the contentment he experienced as the hotel porter took care of his luggage, or when he stood outside the Houses of Parliament for the first time, was not born of vanity. It was the joy of a patient over a nicely healing wound.

"As Grandma tramped eastwards when she wanted to feel younger," Kvido told the editor, "our father – so as to feel like a human being – had to travel to the West. "They had it neatly shared out between them."

It had been agreed that because of the lateness of Kvido's father's flight, the family would wait for him at home in Sázava, and so the British Airways arrival at Ruzyně Airport was awaited by only the driver of the company car.

When, about an hour later, he was dropped off by the red sandstone gateposts, it was almost dark. Kvido's father opened the gate quietly in order not to draw premature attention to himself, crossed the darkened garden, stepped onto the grill that protected the cellar skylight, grabbed the sill of the kitchen window and hauled himself up. His forehead collided gently with the flimsy, blackened string to which his wife tied lumps of suet for the blue tits in winter. The first thing he saw was an old Arab lady, her face covered up to the eyes with a black scarf. She was doing a crossword puzzle. In a second, he realized that it was his mother-in-law. There was no one else in the kitchen.

"*Well,*" he sniggered under his breath in English. "*Let's go.*"

The moment he opened the door into the hallway, Sweetie came hurtling down from the landing to greet him. She jumped in the air, whined and licked his face. He was pleasantly surprised. He gave her a friendly pat or two and stroked her. Then he looked her straight in the eye.

"*Down!*" he commanded experimentally.

Sweetie obediently lay flat on the floor, her head between her front paws and her tail joyfully sweeping the tiles.

"Well, I never," Kvido's father thought and magnanimously let her out into the garden. The handle of the living room door dipped and the door jerked half-open. Kvido's father smiled into the broadening gap, its lowest part eventually revealing little Paco.

"Peep-o!" he said.

"Daddy!" Paco shouted.

His father bent down and threw wide his arms. The little lad flung himself into his embrace.

The sound of hurried footsteps came from the living room.

"Hi, Father," said Kvido hoarsely. He looked at his father in surprise: "You look like Josef Abrhám."

"Hello," said Kvido's mother, likewise slightly surprised. "Where's the dog?"

"*Hallo, boys. Hallo everybody.*" Kvido's father was smiling broadly. "The dog's in the garden. I haven't brought you anything, boys, *I'm sorry*. I just couldn't bring myself to kill that crab – you wouldn't believe the admonishment in his eyes. Good evening!" he called loudly to Grandma Líba in the kitchen. "How are you?"

No answer came the stern reply. He set Paco back down on the floor and clasped his wife to him. She gave him a kiss.

"Hi," she said. "It suits you."

"Has our Islamic separatist still got the sulks?" he whispered.

"Just ignore her." Kvido's mother closed the kitchen door. "She doesn't want to inhale the dangerous fumes from the colourless varnish I did the skirting boards with," she explained with mock seriousness. She looked her husband up and down a second time: the soles of the new light-coloured loafers that he'd bought in Prague before the trip to London weren't worn down yet, which made him stand unusually straight. She didn't recognise his jacket, but it did seem to fit him somehow better that day.

"That was two years ago! How stupid can she get!" he marvelled.

She shrugged. There was a merry sparkle in her eyes and despite the first wrinkles that had begun to settle about her eyes and across her forehead since she hit thirty, there was still something of the little girl about her.

"I know…," she said. "But she knows someone who *also* gave his floorboards a coat of colourless varnish. And when they opened him up, they found a tumour in his belly as big as a coconut."

"When they open me up, they'll find a tumour the size of a pumpkin fritter!"

"Don't be naughty!" she pretended to be cross. "Oh, you've got a new watch!" she registered.

"Show me! Show me!" cried Paco.

"A present from the company," his father told his mother. "Later on, I'll show you how it glows in the dark."

He hung his arm down so that the boys could have a proper look. Paco covered the watch with his little hand. "It's not glowing," he cried, disappointed.

Kvido's father glanced at his wife and grinned: "It only glows under a duvet."

"Goodness me!" she exclaimed. "Since when have you taken to making saucy innuendos? Did you get seduced by an air hostess?"

"*Never mind, boy!* There are some things that should be talked about quite openly."

"But not in my hearing!" Kvido's mother requested. "Did you go to Soho? You seem a bit sure of yourself. Remember, that's the first stage on the way to crashing the car!"

"*Take it easy!*" he laughed. "Shouldn't we go and eat? I could eat a horse. The last time I ate was over the Channel. I mean the English Channel, obviously," he added, anticipating a question from Paco. Kvido will show you where it is on the map. What are we having?"

"Salsify soup and watercress omelettes," Kvido's mother replied diffidently.

"You're joking!"

"Sorry, no."

"Do you want to force me to emigrate?"

"No," she laughed. "Of course it was a joke. I've done you some schnitzels and a salad."

"I didn't doubt you for a minute," said Kvido's father happily. "But what are we going to do with the dried meat I bought from some Laplanders on the plane, just in case?"

"Give it to the dog," she tinkled. "Come and eat."

She linked arms with her husband with an unwonted devotion.

"I'm so glad you're back," she added. "I've been scared witless by the bitch you call Sweetie."

3. After his trip to London, Kvido's father had indeed changed a bit. Kvido and his mother weren't the only ones to notice. Some of the people at his work who'd got to know him thought him more dynamic and resolute than previously. He appeared more eloquent and even shared the odd joke with several of them. Also, his frequent interventions at meetings were now more critical, with more bite, but also more well founded. This generally got him nowhere, of course, and so he continued to withdraw after every lost argument into a kind of defiant silence, though without the previous air of defeatism. Those present were surprised on a couple of occasions to discover that he was even capable of raising his voice. Indeed, his voice, gait and body language had all acquired an assurance that was hard to put into words.

"*Take it easy*," he often repeated, smiling.

Understandably, there were also some tiny changes at home as well. The sales division, corseted by a thousand and one regulations, didn't offer much space for Kvido's father's more vital new self, so he now tried to apply some of his ideas, or the useable modicum of them, within his own household.

"Surely *different* laws don't apply here, do they?" he would ask. "What else is a good family but a well functioning crew? Isn't then a good family first and foremost a good team of well coordinated professionals?" he proclaimed.

"He'd stopped being a father," Kvido explained. "He'd become the family manager."

One day, Kvido's father came home bearing a large IBM desk calendar. Each page had seven columns corresponding to the days of the week. Each column also had four rectangular fields in varying densities of green – and it was this number that had fired his imagination. That Sunday evening he headed the Monday rectangles with the names of the members of the family (though missing out Grandma Líba, obviously), followed by the jobs lined up for them: tidy away toys and water plants (Paco); wash dishes, empty bin, and do a number of specified assignments in the *Compendium of Mathematical Exercises* (Kvido); and weed the rockery below the patio (Mother). He set himself the task of having dinner with the Belgian delegation that were on an official visit to the glassworks, appending the phone number on which he could be reached in the event of an *emergency*.

"It might strike you as pedantic, but as time passes, you'll realise what a useful aid it is," he sought to convince his wife on Tuesday morning as he laboriously rubbed out her own insertion 'have Sweetie put down (Father)', "so please don't make fun of it."

"You smell of some Belgian hooch," she replied. "Unless it's a Belgian perfume."

"No," said Kvido's father. "It's perfectly ordinary Russian vodka."

"I see," said Kvido's mother. "That explains it. It was puzzling me all night."

"What was?"

"Why you were going at me all night like Alexander Vasilyevich Suvorov."

"Was I?" Kvido's father was surprised. "Seriously? In which case I apologise. Sorry. I don't know what must have got into me. These Belgians also drink like fish!"

"I like the choice of simile," said Kvido's mother.

Another innovation was the notice board that Kvido's father put up in the hall. On it was gradually assembled all the information that he deemed indispensable to the household: telephone numbers for ambulance, fire and police services, numbers for the junior and infants' schools, opening hours at the health centre, an overview of the opening times at various shops and services, Kvido's school timetable and the rail and bus timetables between Sázava and Prague. One section of the board was for Finances, on which he immediately pinned up some outstanding bills and invoices, one was for Lost & Found, one was Sundries, which so far had just a calendar of family birthdays and anniversaries hanging from it, and finally there was one for Long-term Tasks, where – unlike what went onto the IBM calendar – tasks with a remoter horizon were spelled out: To study *English for Language Schools I* (Kvido),

To revise ahead of solicitors' exams (Mother), or To fix a layer of tongue-and-groove to the kitchen ceiling (Father).

This innovation also couldn't fail to provoke Kvido and his mother into making sundry facetious amendments and additions: the opening times were expanded to include the dog training centre, the timetables to include that of Czechoslovak Airlines, and the long-term tasks were supplemented by such things as: To learn not to play football (Father).

On another occasion, having read some leader in the paper, Kvido's mother added to the same column: To continue to be involved in the successful normalisation of the country (everybody).

"Is that a jibe at me?" Kvido's father asked. As the notice board's progenitor, he had begun to take this constant sniping too much to heart.

"No, at us," said Kvido's mother. "Can't you read? It says 'everybody'?"

"But I'm not involved in any kind of normalisation," her husband went on, mildly aggressively.

Kvido's mother sighed: "No?"

"No. My desk is clean. I've never tried to fiddle anything politically in my life!"

His wife frowned gloomily. She now regretted yielding to the momentary impulse to write those words; it had been an expression of her momentary depression at life in this land, and she didn't want to make things worse by going on about it – she knew all too well the feelings that such debates left one with. But she was niggled by Kvido's father's supposed self-assurance.

"And you've never stopped such things going on. You haven't even tried," she said.

"But I don't know about any!" he said.

"So there are none going on then," she said, slowly. "If you don't know about them. Everything's all right. Nothing's happening to anyone. My father wasn't chucked out of his job. Lawyers aren't working as gardeners. Female hospital consultants aren't acting as usherettes in cinemas. History is proceeding as usual. Farmers are getting in the harvest as usual, the wheels of industry are turning as usual, and promising engineers blithely fly to the other side of the so-called iron curtain to secure us a brilliant future on the basis of brilliant contracts."

"Stop bugging me! Obviously, I mean I don't know about anything that I might have prevented and failed to. As for arguing over whether our history has stopped or not, I leave that to your Prague intellectual friends. I'm afraid that any view I might have could be distorted by the fact that at work I have to clock in and out, and a time clock, like any clock, never stops, unfortunately."

"Let's leave it," she begged him.

"What do you actually want from me? Tell me what, *specifically*, I could have done and didn't! Should I have scrawled some protest graffiti? Taken photos of the Interior Ministry? Written a letter to the UN? Or taken a bow and arrow to the Soviet base at Milovice and shot the commanding officer? – If there's one thing I can't stand, it's abstract moralisers!"

"Enough!" Kvido's wife shrieked. "You're kidding yourself!"

"Oh shit!" Kvido's father bellowed. "Now it looks as if we're heading for a row!"

The long-serving head of the sales division retired at the year's end on health grounds. The man named as his replacement from January 1 was Mr Zvára, with Kvido's father becoming his deputy.

"We'll show the peasants what's what!" Zvára shouted as they celebrated together.

A few months later, in April, they were due to be sent to the Pula glassworks in Yugoslavia. Having discovered that they weren't flying, but taking a company car and sharing the driving, Kvido's father was somewhat disconcerted.

"Will we be going on motorways?" he wanted to know.

"How else?" said Zvára. "What kind of a question's that?"

"It would be more romantic if we stuck to ordinary roads," Kvido's father hazarded.

"Come off it!" Zvára appealed to him.

As it happened, Kvido's father proved equally competent on motorways and on the roads across the Alps, with their rocky precipices just yards the other side of the crash barriers. However, they experienced two unplanned-for delays, and as twilight descended he recalled, with some concern, his supposed night-blindness.

"I should warn you that I can't see in the dark!" he advised Zvára as he took over for the last hundred kilometres.

"Nor me, it's normal," said Zvára. "You need to put the

headlights on."

He turned the car radio down and at once fell asleep.

Not quite two hours later, Kvido's father woke him. They were parked at the end of kind of wide, concrete pier. The sea could be heard washing against the piles beneath them.

"We're in Pula!" Kvido's father shouted as he tried to shake his colleague awake. "We're in Pula!"

"And where might we be supposed to be?" said Zvára half-asleep and squinted to his right, where, in the glow of the lights of the coastal motorway, several dozen yachts and cabin cruisers were bobbing on the sea. "Where's this, you ass? Is parking allowed here?"

"Have you any idea how far I drove that week? Eleven hundred kilometres!" Kvido's father boasted. "Not bad, eh?"

"Not bad, eh?" he would also say every time he got a pay rise.

And "Not bad, eh?" he would say as he described the furnishings of some hotel room.

"The point is," Kvido later told the editor, "this was his way of assuring himself that he *really* had progressed from a world covered in budgerigar poo to a world where it wasn't that bad. A world where they send cars to collect you and where you can eat steak on aeroplanes. He was assuring himself of the irrevocability of his transcendence."

It was practically impossible now for Kvido's father to be the least bit offended by any of Kvido's or his mother's snide comments in the Long-term Tasks box. He rose above them with a smile.

The success of his second business trip meant as much to him as the success of a second book means to a fledgling writer – self-corroboration. He sparkled with wit and brimmed with vitality. Life was a long, but simple arithmetical problem that could be solved, as he was finding, quite elegantly. Whatever he turned his hand to, he did well at it. He didn't even read 'Instructions for Use', let alone manuals of any kind. He trusted himself and his intuition.

"The worst possible risk is on a par with cleaning your teeth with shaving cream," he proclaimed.

It had become unthinkable that, on putting the car in the garage, he would get out and take his folding rule to see how many centimetres leeway he had. He solved most problems over the phone. He begged less and demanded more. And it worked.

"*Take it easy!*" he repeated constantly.

He'd learned how to be hard, remorseless. He stopped keeping a watch on himself, no longer taking his pulse and lubricating his foreskin with a neomycin-based cream. Kvido's mother had her first orgasm. His father understood for the first time that the books she read were largely based on deception, and he proved their authors guilty of vagueness, sentimentality and being totally cut off from real life.

"That's codswallop," he would say now, with no needless deference.

He also had a number of successes on the football pitch. He

still lacked fitness and technique, but he had gained something equally important: detachment. He wore a permanent, nicely ironic smirk that cut all his shortcomings as a player, indeed the whole of football, down to size.

"Someone who's dabbled his hands in the fountain in Piccadilly Circus and rested his limbs against the wall of Westminster Abbey, isn't going to get worked up over a match against the B team of Slavoj Čerčany," Kvido explained.

4. Kvido's father's dazzling excursions required a constant admiring audience. But that wasn't easy: Kvido and his mother had stopped listening to him, Paco was too small, Grandma Líba was out of the question for reasons that are by now familiar, and Grandpa Jiří, who sometimes came to visit and whose appreciation Kvido's father would dearly have liked to win, was now too tired of life to become a fitting audience for tales from the West. That left Grandpa Josef, whose uncritical admiration for that part of the world was widely known, and Grandma Vera.

They would come to Sázava one Saturday in the month, taking the direct train from Vršovice. Grandpa Josef was banned from reading the paper on the train so as not to get over-excited, but since he couldn't even smoke, he remained edgy anyway, snapping back at Grandma Vera any time she said something.

"Hark at her! Just hark at her!" he would say, appealing for some sympathy from his terror-stricken fellow-passengers and crunching the stem of his unlit pipe, like an epileptic crunching his tongue depressor.

"Stop that!" his wife would cry in her wretchedness.

Sooner or later, she would utter one or other fatal remark that would lift him irrevocably from his green leatherette seat and drive him through the gangway connection between the carriages to get as far from her as he could, like a real-life fugitive. His stumbling stampede over the luggage of the outraged citizenry only came to a halt at the very first or last carriage, where – his gaze flitting wildly between the buffers of the engine or, conversely, from one rushing sleeper to the next – he would be left panting furiously and seeking to drive away the "wind from the wings of madness" like a troublesome fly.

This explains why, on arrival at Sázava, each of them would alight from a different carriage. This was confusing to Sweetie, who always went along with Kvido's father to welcome them and who would pull on her spiked collar now this way, now that, howling in indecision.

"Dad," Kvido's father would start reproachfully, "what on earth have you been up to again?"

Kvido, who preferred to observe their arrival, or the final part of it, from behind the curtain in his room, duly spotted, at the bend in the road, first his grandfather, striding along like some kind of angry advance guard and mouthing unintelligible oaths. Then thirty yards behind him came Grandma Vera, his father and Sweetie. His father would be carrying Grandma's bag and smiling like the attentive, successful son he was.

"They're here," Kvido announced, which amounted to an oblique signal for his mother to dowse her cigarette.

"So be it!" she declared.

By this time, Grandpa Josef was already retired and worked as a doorman at one of the large foreign trade organisations in Prague. He spent a considerable part of the working day comparing the salaries and status of Communist Party members employed there with those of the non-Party members.

"The result of this comparison seemed to leave Grandma in the unpleasant condition of being constantly surprised, though by the mid-1970s the facts as presented were scarcely an eye-opener," Kvido explained.

That didn't stop Grandpa venting his outrage at the injustice inflicted on non-Party members as often as he felt like it.

"When the time comes and things change, we'll hang the lot of 'em!" he would vow over lunch.

"Who?" Paco wanted to know. He alone didn't know the answer.

"Eat your lunch," said Kvido's mother. "Grandpa's only joking."

"Hark at him!" Grandma cried out. "Just hark at him!"

"Don't go getting excited, Dad," Kvido's father sought smilingly to calm his father down. "Let me show you something," he added, slightly mysteriously, being used to quietening the kids down by distracting them – and from his breast pocket he withdrew a silver ballpoint pen with an integrated digital time display.

The trick worked: Grandpa, who a moment earlier had been brought to a state bordering on religious ecstasy by a plastic knife and fork bearing the legend British Airways, removed his pipe from his mouth: "English?"

"Italian," said Kvido's father casually.

"Wow," said Grandpa appreciatively. "That's quite something!"

He laid his pipe down on the table and cautiously, perhaps so as not to damage the pen by some careless movement, took it in his tobacco-stained fingers and slowly examined it.

Kvido's father looked round the faces of the others at the table. However, they all seemed fully engaged in stirring their coffees and therefore not to have noticed his pedagogical triumph.

"What a beautiful thing!" said Grandpa Josef authoritatively. "What a beautiful thing indeed!"

"It's just a trinket really," Kvido's father objected, flattered.

"Trinket?" said Grandpa Josef, his voice rising. "Trinket? So tell me why those Commie bastards won't import such beautiful trinkets!"

5. Early in September, a three-man trade delegation arrived in Sázava from Pula, or rather two men and one young woman, to continue the negotiations begun successfully the previous spring.

Kvido's father obviously knew all three well, and if he couldn't provide them with conditions comparable to his own stay in Pula, he pulled out all the stops to ensure for them the best he could. He made a personal inspection of the two rooms that had been set aside for the guests at the company hostel and despaired at their cheerlessness.

"The single room is particularly ghastly," he later told his wife. "That wardrobe, and the carpet! You'd have to see it for yourself – it's horrendous!"

"And what about cockroaches?" Kvido's mother asked with a smile, beginning to sense where all this was leading. "Are there any cockroaches?"

"Cockroaches?" Kvido's father wavered, wondering whether he might mention them too. "Who knows? And one wall is covered in mildew!"

"Mildew! I'm not surprised. And bedbugs? What's the *single* room like as regards bedbugs?"

Now Kvido's father knew he'd been rumbled.

"Seriously though," he said. "It would be an international disgrace if poor Mirjana had to stay there."

Then, appealing to the tradition of Slav hospitality by which he said he felt bound, he came out with the expected question as to whether the young Yugoslav technician might not be offered Grandma's cosy garret for a few days.

"And Grandma?" Kvido's mother enquired. "I know, she can be put in with the kids, right?"

"She's lived in private lodgings often enough," Kvido's father argued, "when she's been abroad… I'm sure she'll understand our predicament."

"One day it's a playroom," Grandma declared, hearing of the proposed arrangement, "and the next it'll be a concentration camp for the elderly!"

Despite being upset, she did submit to being relocated, and

Mirjana could move in.

The very first evening, she cooked for the whole family (except Grandma, who refused to leave the playroom), some Balkan version of a piperada. In taste terms it was slightly unusual, and little Paco promptly threw up, but Kvido's father, despite his lukewarm attitude to vegetables, kept helping himself to more and asking Mirjana for the recipe. They were speaking in English, which reminded Kvido and his mother, who could barely understood a word, about his father and grandmother's discussions on the geography of the British Isles.

After dinner, the talk first turned to work.

"Mirjana says that what she likes about international trade is the chance it gives her to meet interesting people," Kvido's father interpreted for his wife.

"Yes," she said and smiled amiably at Mirjana.

"Well? What do you say to that?" he smiled nervously. "I need something to translate back."

"There's nothing to say to it."

"What d'you mean, nothing?"

"Just nothing. *Nothing.*"

Mirjana bared her snow-white teeth and raised her eyebrows quizzically.

Kvido's father swore to himself and said something in English. Kvido seemed to think he heard the word 'interesting'.

"He's talking drivel," he scoffed to his mother.

"The opposite would surprise me more," she said.

"Mirjana would like you to tell her something about yourself," Kvido's father began again. "You strike her as having great depths of wisdom and composure."

"Tell her she can put it down to old age and apathy."

Kvido's father looked daggers at her.

"And? What you do, what you've done in the past... Just say something!" he persisted.

"I'm having my work cut out to master my own surprise – that's what I'm doing right now," she replied with a broad grin. "And what I've done in the past? I've done the best I could. Mostly so as to stay warm. And I've made children. But I've never done languages. – My father told me to do languages, but I disobeyed him. I went to the ballet and the theatre and I went boating and to the cinema, but language-learning, no, no! If I'd done as bidden –"

"Oh, do give up," Kvido's father interrupted, then translated something or other to Mirjana.

"– I wouldn't be feeling such a stupid cow right now," she finished her sentence.

"She should learn Czech," said Kvido to his mother. "If she wants to understand us."

"What things do you like?" his father asked next on Mirjana's behalf.

"Stuff that!" his mother returned.

"What's wrong with telling Mirjana the kind of things you like?"

"If I must. Sour cherry jam. The theatre. Warm breezes. Privacy. Charles' Bridge. Blue tie-dyed bed linen. The family. Jakub Schikaneder. Good taste, intelligence and tolerance. American toothpaste for smokers. And you. Some of the time.

Now translate, loser!"

"Kvido could say something as well," his father smiled towards Mirjana. "He's been studying it for two years."

"I'm not saying anything," said Kvido.

"If you don't have languages, Europe," his father pointed to Mirjana, "won't ever open up to you."

"My, there *is* a fine metaphor," said Kvido's mother with a smile, and she yawned. "I'm going to bed," she turned to her husband. "And I'd be grateful if this week Europe didn't *open up* to those who do have languages either. *Good night, everybody.*"

Half an hour later, Kvido entered his mother's bedroom. She was reading.

"Are you going to leave them together like that?" he asked, bewildered. "Don't you mind?"

His mother pushed his curls away from his forehead. "To love," she said, "doesn't mean to possess. Don't be so old-fashioned, Kvido. You're fourteen now!"

Neither of them thought this sounded particularly convincing.

"What's at home, leave well alone...," Mr Zvára warned Kvido's father with an unmistakable hint of envy in his voice. "That, me old mucker, is the wisdom of the ancients."

"Don't worry about me!" the latter laughed. "I'm not one to stray!"

"Oh, sir...," his secretary marvelled. "You do surprise me!"

Kvido's father made no attempt to hide the fact that he and Mirjana were *good friends*; now and again he was apparently quite happy to make a point of their friendship himself. Just as in April in Pula, he had still taken no greater liberty than to kiss Mirjana a few times in a state of stupefaction, but he was probably less excited by her than by the idea that his colleagues treated the beautiful and single Yugoslav girl as his secret mistress. He responded to all questions with ostentatiously shocked smiles, and the whispered comments that occasionally reached his hearing could only please him. His prestige was rising and the secretaries took more notice of him.

"*Take it easy!*" he was wont to say, smiling.

After two fairly warm, but rainy days, a glorious Indian summer broke forth. Kvido's father, much anguished by the notion that the landscape around Sázava couldn't offer Mirjana nearly so much as Pula had given him, glanced joyfully up at the cloudless sky and suggested they might take a trip in the family canoe.

"I'll take Paco with us," he told his wife.

"No, you *won't!*" she replied flatly. "He can't swim. He might fall out and I don't imagine you'd even notice."

Their eyes met. Kvido's father looked away first.

"So we can take Kvido!" he said.

"Have you gone completely crazy?" said Kvido. "Do you think I'm a Jack London? Playing football with you is quite enough, thank you!"

"You'd like it… And you did say once that you'd give it a go."

"Sure – but not with Tito's granddaughter!"

"Don't talk rubbish! Are you coming or not?"

A certain tension descended.

"Go on, Kvido. You can," said the boy's mother.

Kvido suddenly understood that her nonchalance was costing her some effort.

"Shall I then?"

His mother smiled at him.

"I'm rather keen on water sports, actually," said Kvido. "*Let's go.*"

"Make sure you're back before dark," his mother finally enjoined his father. "Don't forget your night blindness!"

"If my mother thought that my presence was an adequate guarantee of the moral probity of the event, she was wrong," Kvido explained later. As soon as his mother was out of sight, Kvido's father started putting his arm round Mirjana with ever greater frequency, winking conspiratorially at Kvido. Kvido reddened.

"Come on, now!" his father said, laughing. "We're both blokes, aren't we?"

Mirjana glanced at them cheerfully, then ran off into a meadow to pick some flowers.

When they reached the wooden boat-house, Kvido's father, the veins on his neck stretched taut to breaking point, carried the canoe down to the water unaided. Kvido wondered whether he should borrow not just a life jacket, but also one of the yellow safety helmets he'd spotted on a shelf, but quickly decided that in a place where there was neither ripple nor rock it would look a bit outlandish. Mirjana removed her linen skirt and shoes and tiptoed in her striped panties and T-shirt to join his father on the bank. The latter, whose body language following her arrival took on all the charm of a dancing master, helped her settle down in the boat, accidentally brushing against her breasts twice as he did so. Then he hopped aboard himself, causing the boat to bob alarmingly.

"*Oh, my God!*" Mirjana laughed.

Kvido looked on glumly and cursed his weakness for not turning the boat trip down.

His father leaned overboard so unbelievably far and held the paddle in such a way that it looked as if he meant to dredge the river bottom.

"*Come on, boy!*" he ordered Kvido. "Get in!"

"Stick your tongue in – you look stupid," said Kvido, but, before he climbed in, he considered whether it was more bearable to watch his lusting father, or his potential Yugoslav mistress; he finally settled on Mirjana, though he'd rather have sat with his back to both of them.

"Hold your hats, we're off!" his father cried.

But before he started paddling properly, he first showed his colleague the technique behind the three basic strokes, the proper way to hold one's torso, and a pair of mallard on an uprooted alder.

"*What a nice day!*" he rejoiced and made several solid strokes.

"What a nice day," said Kvido peevishly, but partly also to show his father that there were some things that he actually understood.

The weather was a treat: a fresh breeze was blowing, the reeds rustled quietly and the sun beat down with all the power still left to it. When they got round the first bend, Mirjana, probably wishing to treat herself to something only foreign tourists could do back in Pula, took her T-shirt off. She put her paddle down, turned carefully and settled down in the bows, facing the sun and both other members of the crew. She bent her head back to catch the full sun, half-closed her eyes and started singing quietly some tune whose words – given the circumstances – Kvido never forgot thereafter.

"Procvale su rože i vijole,
procvala je trava i murava,
procvala je lika i zelenika,
procvale su višnje i čerišnje...,"

Mirjana sang quietly.

To the extent that all Kvido felt at the sight of her huge naked breasts was a sudden confusion that quickly ended in an unstoppable urge to press his face into the wooden bottom of the boat, the same sight hurled his father to the very bottom of the abyss of hysteria.

"Not bad, eh?" he squawked at Kvido like a madman. He kept nudging him knowingly and pointing at Mirjana, laughing crazily, speaking in two languages and spinning the boat in circles.

"*Are you crazy?*" Mirjana laughed and whooped with delight.

"*Yes, I am!*" chortled Kvido's father, whose joy would have been complete if only a river steamer had come past, packed to the gunwales with all the employees of the Kavalier Sázava enterprise.

"You'll tip us out!" squealed Kvido. "Pull yourself together!"
"*Take it easy!*" his father shouted.

In the very next instant, the paddle dug deep beneath the canoe, which with a single smooth motion turned upside down. In the split second before his body broke the curvature of the surface, Kvido just had time to consider that his father's action might have been deliberate.

"*Help me!*" Mirjana spluttered with laughter and water, having first established that her feet could reach the stony bottom quite easily. Kvido's father meanwhile turned the canoe back over; all he had achieved was that it had sprung a leak. Now he hurled himself towards Mirjana.

Kvido, borne safely aloft by his life jacket, gazed stoically as the family canoe rapidly filled with water. A paddle floated past them unobserved.

Kvido's father's help tickled Mirjana.

The boat sank for good.

Kvido saw the way the current of greenish-yellow water turned it slightly, then he lost sight of it completely.

He tipped his head back into the broad collar of the life jacket, half-closed his eyes and let himself be borne gently along by the current.

His father shouted something to him, but he didn't understand what.

"Procvale su rože i vijole," he repeated to himself. "Procvala je trava i murava..."

To suppress with immediate effect any leaning towards polygamy (Father) appeared next day in the relevant field of the IBM calendar.

"And buy a boat," Kvido prompted his mother.

6. Kvido had started the eighth grade and tricky times lay ahead. Jarka had outgrown him by a good three centimetres and at break-time only chatted – as it seemed to Kvido – with a handful of classmates who were mature beyond their age and taller than Kvido by a head. He had now shed almost all his previous corpulence (a little superfluous fat round the hips had become a permanent feature) and his mother had secured him some glasses with smart, thin golden metallic frames to replace his old horn-rimmed ones, but he still thought himself small and ugly. He spent many a long minute in front of the mirror, and his father's "*Take it easy!*" wasn't much help at all. Talking to Jarka became fraught with unprecedented difficulty.

"Shall we go sledging again?" he once forced himself to ask, his voice creaking.

"Don't be daft!" Jarka shook her head. "Aren't you asking a bit early? It's only September!"

"I meant when the s-..."

"What?" she said.

Kvido thought she was making fun of him. He was crushed.

Snow, he had wanted to say, but his voice had died on him.

On top of everything else, his parents wanted him to start at the Benešov grammar school the following year.

"We're not letting you waste a year!" his father said, trying to reassure him it was a good thing. He believed the entire primary education system was just an absurd hurdle on Kvido's way to a career. "You'll have your MA by twenty-two, giving you a year's head-start over the others."

All that bothered Kvido for now was that after the holidays Jarka, who wanted to stay on through grade nine, would be sharing her desk with one of those classroom hunks. He developed this idea mentally in every conceivable direction until it became the source of unbearable torment. Well in advance, he hated all those strong, swaggering, acne-pitted lads with their incipient moustaches. At the same time, whenever he compared involuntarily his rare nocturnal emissions, easily overlooked on his patterned pyjamas, with the daily deluges allegedly experienced by them, he was put wrathfully in mind of his grandmother's meat-free and therefore – as he thought – *deficient* culinary practices.

"Love, kissing, meat's missing!" he raged in secret.

"Thank your lucky stars that Jarka actually wants to go to the grammar school," his mother was consoling. "You'll meet up again after the year… What would you do if she was going to college to start a course in nursing?"

"Dunno," Kvido admitted in his misery.

As the deadline for applications approached, Kvido's father upped his pedagogical strivings. He believed that his undoubted, and widely admired, successes at work, recently crowned by his being sent on a business trip to exotic Japan, lent him all the prerequisites for applying the method of *imitation* – except that Kvido, after his pubertal critical manner, refused to recognise such obvious and proven truths as that a man's happiness is in direct proportion to the length of his business trips, stated in kilometres, and so he was obliged on occasion to resort, however reluctantly, to the unpopular method of *coercion*.

"Bow-wow!" Kvido would bark provocatively, whenever his father came in to help him study – and when the day came that his father brought the application form, already filled in, Kvido registered his protest by putting the spiked dog-collar round his neck.

There can be no doubting that Kvido's father meant well by his son, indeed he meant the very best he could muster. After all, his prime concern wasn't that Kvido should start secondary school a year early, let alone that he might need extra coaching in chemistry or maths. No, much more was at stake: he wanted to spare him at least part of the toilsome, winding road to the Knowledge of Life by describing it to him, with an accuracy that Kvido could not yet rise to himself, from some barely accessible vantage point far ahead that afforded a good view of it and that he, the boy's father, had finally reached after many long years. Given that he meant to describe that Knowledge to him absolutely free of charge, out of pure parental good will, he couldn't fathom why Kvido was so resistant to such a *Good Thing*.

"Many's the time he ranted on against such ignorance," Kvido explained years later. "Having failed *on land*, he flew us to Bulgaria and kept on at me *in the air* on the plane and *in water* in the sea, as if he were looking for the optimum physical conditions in which to communicate his experience."

It was around that time that Kvido wrote his first story. He called it 'The Convenience Store of Cruelty'.

The action took place inside a fictional shop, the low, but spacious shelves of which bore but a single item: real, live boys in transparent, half-open boxes. Their right hands were tagged with their name, price and measurements. They were unable to speak.

The customers were, by contrast, all girls; one of them was Jarka. They had huge trolleys that they pushed along the aisles, choosing carefully: they would make a close inspection not only of the boys' clothes, but also of their eyes, mouths and teeth, they considered the colour of their hair and the clarity of their complexion, the depth of their subcutaneous fat and the size of their muscles, their height and the turn of their legs, and finally they examined their genitals, noting in particular whether these were or were not yet covered in hair. Naturally, they compared the quality of the boys on display and were loud in their evaluations. They were occasionally assisted with their purchases by the staff, who were older women with lashings of make-up and huge bosoms.

"Have you sold out of tall, tanned, black-haired ones?" Jarka asked one of them.

"Only untanned ones. We had some tanned ones this morning," the assistant replied amiably. "They sold like hot cakes."

Obviously, one of the boxes contained Kvido. The girls, including Jarka, passed him by with barely a flicker of interest. Some did make the odd comment: "Why don't you buy that little guy in specs!" they teased.

"No thanks! You have him!"

Kvido copied the story out in his fairest hand and one day took it to Jarka.

"It's weird," she said, having read it. "Weird and rude."

Kvido blushed and his face twisted into a wry smile.

"But that's how you choose," he said defiantly.

"Not me!" said Jarka. "And I'd thank you not to write about me!"

VI.

1. Kvido's father's career ended in late 1977, just as abruptly as it had begun.

The previous autumn had already seen one apparently trivial occurrence, in which anyone with a sense for such things might have discerned a prelude, an early symptom of the future crisis: little Paco – exactly like his brother before him – knocked the glazed portrait of the president off the wall while playing a game of skittles, though this time it wasn't Ludvík Svoboda, but Gustáv Husák.

The falling frame with its long sharp shards didn't injure anyone this time either. Yet unfortunately, it cannot be asserted unequivocally that the fate of the picture hurt no one: one of the older teachers recalled at once the same incident with

Kvido and went around telling all and sundry what an *incredible coincidence* it was. The episode became common knowledge and not everyone found it merely funny.

"Be careful about this kind of thing," Šperk advised Kvido's father. "People might see a connection."

"He's a child...," Kvido's father excused the younger boy awkwardly.

"And they could be right!" said Šperk. "Don't underestimate it."

"I'd bet a dollar to a matchstick that the silly chump did it on purpose, just to match up to Kvido!" Kvido's father ranted at home, his chosen phraseology betraying a subconscious longing to add the United States to his business destinations.

"And why are you shouting at me?" Kvido's mother asked with some justification.

"Normal kids don't knock pictures off the wall while skittling *at* floor level when those pictures are eight feet *above* floor level," he went on shouting anyway. "Not normal kids!"

"So now you're blaming me for giving birth to two unbelievably bad skittle-players?" Kvido's mother asked calmly.

"No, I'm not!" his father bellowed and in fit of blind rage he slapped Paco. "It's this little brat's fault!"

Paco burst into tears.

Kvido went and stood in front of his little brother to protect him with his own body.

"Are you crazy?" their mother cried in outrage. "Why are you hitting him? You're acting like a lunatic."

With an effort she took Paco up into her arms.

Kvido's father apparently felt himself that he should at least attempt to justify his temper.

"It was for his mum and dad for arguing about him," he offered uncertainly. Kvido's mother dried Paco's tears and sent him out of the room.

"You should have given him another one," she said derisively. "For Husák."

"That was the first *political* slap that Paco got," Kvido explained.

2. So Kvido's father tried *to be careful*. This was by no means easy, because, amongst other things, Pavel Kohout, a signatory of Charta 77 since January, having been expelled from Prague, had moved permanently into his villa in Sázava. While he and Kvido's mother had seen him only from time to time, during his sporadic visits to the town, it was now highly improbable that they wouldn't meet.

It happened one Saturday morning while they were shopping at the local department store. Later, following a reprise, they failed to agree who had seen the persecuted playwright first and so should have given the signal to retreat in time: Kvido's mother maintained that she had spotted him just as – *facing her way* – he had bent down to the blue crates of milk, and because at that instant she was heading, as his father doubtless recalled, for the freezer section to get some chips and butter, there was no way – without doing an embarrassing about-turn with her trolley – that a meeting could be avoided.

Kvido's father conceded that she might have first noticed him by the milk crates, but he insisted that Kohout was *facing the crates* – the logical direction to be looking anyway – and therefore *with his back to her*, so she had plenty of time to turn her trolley round calmly, like someone who's suddenly realised that they've forgotten to get something from an earlier shelf, like – for the sake of argument – oat flakes.

"So your claim that you couldn't prevent the meeting is somewhat problematical," Kvido's father concluded.

"No less problematical than your claim to have spent the entire time at issue reading the best-before date on a tin of pork luncheon meat, though that's not something you do, given your unbelievable aptitude for consuming meat that's well and truly past it with no ill effects, as you've proved to me many times, like last year when we went canoeing on the Lužnice."

"Pure demagogy!" he defended himself. "If that time I ate some salami that in the dull light of the morning seemed a bit green to you, it wasn't because I was convinced of my alleged immunity to botulism, which is downright stupid anyway, but because there *are reasons* why I prefer even aging meat products to fresh vegetables!"

"Except Yugoslavian piperada," Kvido's mother noted pointedly.

"But since you've brought up our canoeing history," his father pursued his case, ignoring her comment, "I should remind you, though it's a bit embarrassing to go into such trivial details, that even the least experienced stern paddler can estimate which way the boat is going to go next from the movement of the *nose end* – and that, in the case of your supermarket trolley, it was *not* heading towards the freezer cabinet, but *straight* for the milk crates!"

"Would someone mind telling me what the hell this is all about?" Kvido begged.

"Don't worry," his mother brushed the question aside. "It's nothing."

"I'm sorry," Kvido's father retorted like some soothsayer: "It's everything."

"In a sense, he was quite right," Kvido explained later.

"Hi, Pavel," Kvido's mother had said back then, smiling radiantly at Pavel Kohout, giving the staff, the purchasing public and, last but not least, herself to know that she wasn't afraid to speak to such a controversial dissident in such a busy place.

Kvido's father, who had paled a shade, decided to appear tickled by the situation.

Pavel Kohout couldn't fail to recognise the erstwhile Jana of his comedy in verse, *A Good Song*, later one of his friends at the theatre – and anyway it wasn't even two years since they'd last met in Sázava – and his eyes betrayed a flash of unfeigned delight:

"Hi!"

Almost at once he checked himself and lapsed into the tone of restrained affability that he had long adopted for meetings of this kind and which had no other purpose than to evince a specific kind of consideration for whoever he was talking to. The radiant smile on Kvido's mother's face showed no sign of fading even after several minutes, so eventually he decided to utter the social cliché that he had rarely uttered of late, well aware that, coming from him, it exposed the addressee to crude psychological pressure.

"So stop by sometime – when you have a moment," he said rather guardedly.

He had no wish to be impolite and skip the invitation altogether – but at the same time he meant, as you could tell, to leave them room to wriggle out of it (which he would have understood).

"And there it was. The fateful moment," Kvido told the editor.

Though no one knew it, of course. Not Kvido's father, nor his mother, nor their fellow citizens streaming past them, nor even the flies flitting above the stinking cheeses. Kvido's parents – like most married couples who have a busy social calendar – had unwittingly built up an entire system of non-language communication, from familiar random head or eye movements to such subtly expressive signs as the speed of an intake of breath, a barely audible click of the tongue or an easily missed shifting of weight from one foot to the other – but even this well functioning system now let them down, and rather unexpectedly, given that previously they had successfully fended off (with even a degree of elegance) some quite aggressive invitations.

"If the invite had been in writing, I'm a hundred per cent certain they'd have turned it down," Kvido asserted. "They'd have countless arguments to draw on. But the way it was, face to face… It was a bit much. They were simply too polite."

"How about this evening?" Kvido's mother had suggested enthusiastically, turning to her husband with her unseeing eyes.
"I'd go for that!" Kvido's father rejoiced, then he felt that sharp pricking sensation beneath his breastbone.
"Today?" Pavel Kohout was caught pleasantly off guard by such a spontaneous response. "Excellent!"
"How about grilling a chicken?" Kvido's father asked courageously, fighting back the pain and nodding towards the freezer cabinet. "I could get two right now."
Kvido's mother was full of admiration for him.
"One," said Pavel Kohout brightly. "I'll get the other one."

3. "To fight off storms, distress and wrong,
    may life take off like a bird and fly,
    may love become a brand new song
    with which to fly to the clouds on high!"

declaimed Kvido's mother with a mixture of irony and sentimentality as she dressed that afternoon ready for the planned barbecue.
"If I wanted to cosy up to enemies of the regime, I could have stayed in Prague," Kvido's father lamented for appearance's sake, but somewhat in thrall to his own civic pluck. "I didn't

escape to the country to go barbecuing chickens with them!"

"The chicken thing was your idea," Kvido's mother noted with a grin without looking away from the mirror.

"I can easily explain the chickens away, but I wonder how you're going to explain the enemies of the regime!"

"Chicken or Kohout, makes little odds," she punned, given that a *kohout* is a rooster. "But we still don't have to go…"

"Oh but we do," Kvido's father moaned. "Because of your chips and butter!"

"Because of your pork luncheon meat!"

Kvido's mother cast a last look at the mirror and asked: "How do I look?"

"God almighty! She has the gall to ask me how she looks!"

"Oughtn't we to take the kids with us?" Kvido's mother asked suddenly. "Kvido could read his story to him."

Her suggestion – as Kvido's father correctly spotted – contained a mixture of healthy motherly pride and some less healthy back-covering: with not only poultry, but also children present, the get-together couldn't look remotely like a conspiracy, was her line of thought.

"Hm, why not?" said Kvido's father.

Only after Pavel Kohout and his wife Jelena had enlightened their guests on the latest goings-on on the domestic political stage, including the fact that they were frequently tailed by the secret police, Kvido's father realised what a sombre drama he'd got himself into, if only as a spectator. To keep his hands occupied, he took charge of turning the spit, but the gastronomic enthusiasm he was simulating could not completely conceal his jitters. His lip-smacking commentary on the crunchy golden skin fooled no one, even less so for his constant glancing at his watch and the sky, as if impatient for darkness to fall, and for the fact that the only bit of breast that he helped himself to in defiance of everything he'd said wound up shortly in the bushes, where he threw up, offering only the paltriest of excuses.

Kvido's mother now realised that the possible risks attached to such a visit were slightly greater than she'd been prepared to admit an hour earlier. Ultimately, however, her fears of the possible consequences were overshadowed by her terror at the Kohouts' dachshund. Every time it rubbed against her legs in the dark, she let out a fearful scream that scared their hosts witless.

"I don't mind a woman being afraid of dogs, spiders or mice...," Pavel Kohout said half in jest and half in earnest. It had begun to get on his nerves, but then he had no inkling of the depth of her phobia, "... but I can't stand it when she makes a virtue of it..."

The day was saved by Paco and Kvido: not being scared of either the little dachshund or the secret police, they carried on completely naturally. Pavel Kohout did have some initial doubts as to whether Kvido might not be one of those young people who, after a couple of glasses of his wine, would be scathing about his Communist juvenilia, but the years of Kvido's period of ringing recitation, of which he was now not a little ashamed and which were not very dissimilar to a

Kohoutian 'intellectual malfunction', were an adequate guarantee that at this point there would be no taunting recitation of his lines on Stalin. He liked both the lads and was happy to lark about with them.

When the time for a reading of Kvido's story came round, the playwright was slightly taken aback and got ready to decline gently, if with some fitting words of encouragement. But the story – albeit the work of a complete novice – came as a pleasant surprise to him, though he had reservations about its pessimistic conclusion, the artificial cause of which he saw, correctly, in the fact that the boys for sale couldn't speak.

"But we *can* speak – that's our only redeeming feature!" he told Kvido and laughingly showed him the layer of *his own* subcutaneous fat. "You'll discover that any woman can be brought round, fortunately."

"Do you think so?" Kvido asked with interest.

Shortly after nine, they heard a car draw up on the drive.

"Aha," Pavel Kohout said under his breath. "Our security guards!"

He walked round the garage and looked over the gate.

Kvido's father felt a sharp pricking sensation beneath his breastbone.

"They're local," said Kohout. "You'll have to round the back, across the railway track. They'd recognise you."

The visit came to an end.

Kvido and Paco were ordered to be silent.

The family rapidly took its leave.

They crossed the garden to the far end. Carefully they

avoided the branches of the apple trees. The grass was damp. They squeezed through a hole in the fence.

"Hang in there!" Kvido's mother whispered.

"Bye," Kvido's father whispered.

The darkness mercifully concealed how pale he'd become.

They scrambled down the narrow path to the railway line. A few metres on, the eyes of a dog gleamed out of the darkness.

Kvido's mother let out a last piercing yell.

"Good evening," someone said. "Your ID cards, please!"

"What's happened?" Pavel Kohout called out fearfully, having come running to the fence.

No one answered.

"Been visiting?" asked Šperk with an unpleasant smile. "It's all right," he assured the two men by his side.

Kvido's father was lost for words.

Kvido's mother grabbed her two sons by the hand.

"It's all right. You can go," said Šperk. "Go on, go on."

VII.

1. Usually, when he got to musing what could have so broken his father that, when it came to his re-assignment to another job, he chose, among the five offered, three of which were clerical, that of security guard, Kvido wasn't thinking about the slightly mysterious interrogation at the secret police HQ, of which his father refused to say anything specific, nor about the thing on the radio called The Kohout Case, during which the organised gatherings of enemies of socialism held at the playwright's current abode were discussed by a number of people, including Comrade Šperk; no, he was thinking about Mr Zvára.

"I'm in the shit now!" Kvido's father told Mr Zvára the very next day after the Šperk incident.

"I'm in the shit now, I'm in deep shit!" he said again, having come back from being interrogated by the secret police in St Bartholomew Street in Prague.

Each time, there was actually a faint interrogative inflection to his voice, suggesting the hope that his colleague would tell him to stop being silly, stop exaggerating, that he couldn't really be in the shit since he hadn't done anything bad and that nothing could happen to him. Except that Zvára didn't.

Nor did he when Kvido's father came into the office one day bearing that list of five options in writing and said with a slight choke in his voice and the same detectable, underlying question:

"Looks as if I might end up as the porter!"

"Porter?" Now Zvára really did reveal his dismay.

"Yeah, I've got the offer here, in black and white…," Kvido's father laughed, his pale features contrasting sharply with his feigned jocularity. He was glad that his friend was equally surprised, which could have been why he was hoping that Zvára would bang his fist on the desk and charge off to see the deputy head of HR to ask what this crackpot idea was, since when had engineers fluent in two major languages and with valuable trading contacts in London, Pula, Düsseldorf and Tokyo – since when were such people made janitors! Except that Zvára didn't bang his fist on the desk and didn't get up to go, merely noting that anything of the kind could only happen in Czechoslovakia.

"And that's what made his mind up," Kvido maintained.

Later, Dr Liehr did not discount Kvido's hypothesis, but at the same time he remained convinced that Kvido's father had voluntarily gone for the *lowest* place in the hierarchy of five options in an attempt – consciously or otherwise – to ingratiate himself with the powers that punished, or that he was afraid of putting their backs up by electing to drop, say, only a couple of clerical grades; in this regard he pointed up the considerable symbolism of verticality in the whole business: since Kvido's father had begun with an office on the *ninth floor* and the porter's lodge was, naturally, on the *ground floor*, this was a *social descent* with knobs on, which sat perfectly with his martyrdom complex.

Kvido's mother – despite all such explanatory theorising – never understood her husband's decision, or more precisely, she refused to understand it.

"But for God's sake, why porter?" she screamed at Kvido's father that historic Monday morning. "Why didn't you take the office job? – Are you telling me you're now spending eight hours a day in that lousy glass cage??"

"Porters," Kvido's father sighed, "spend their working hours in a porter's lodge. Whether or not there are lice there, I don't know, though I doubt it."

"So in a nutshell, you'll take off that tweed jacket and the cream shirt and don some ringmaster outfit with silver buttons the size of a small powder puff and hang about by the entrance!"

"That's probably about right."

Kvido's mother's agitation rose in proportion as all the various consequences to follow from this big change gradually dawned on her.

"And with a cap and badge on your head?"

"Yes."

"And one of those ghastly red armbands?"

"Yes," Kvido's father admitted absently as he wondered in vain how he would secure his locker in the cloakroom because he had failed to lay his hands on a single padlock.

"Christ," his mother bleated. "You really must be out of your mind!"

Thus did Kvido's father become a porter. His leather briefcase, so recently crammed with his copiously filled diaries, minutes of meetings, all manner of reports, appraisals, foreign journals, address books and dozens of business cards, now held just a little pot of ground coffee, a piece of cake, a biro and two or three crosswords clipped out of newspapers.

If he was on mornings, he would be at his post as early as five to relieve his colleague who was on nights. He would get changed, sign for the pistol they had to carry as members of the works militia, carefully rule all four columns in the Daily Reports book and take up his regulation position by the main entrance. His movements and expression revealed nothing more than the businesslike focus of the novice he was – though perhaps also an air of apology for causing a shock, so early in the day, to people who were barely awake by appearing before them in an unexpected role, an ill-fitting, grey-blue militia uniform and a cap that kept slipping down to the rims of his spectacles. He would cast the occasional glance towards his commander to check that the latter was satisfied with the manner in which he was greeting and vetting arrivals – and the commander, who seems to have been slightly embarrassed, nodded his approval excessively.

On that Monday morning, Kvido's parents arrived at work simultaneously; by the porter's lodge, his mother hurriedly parted from his father without even saying good-bye. Having reached her office and lit a cigarette, it dawned on her that from the Tuesday onwards she, like any other employee, would have to show him her company ID card. She couldn't stop thinking about it all day, and after four-thirty, as she made ready to leave, she knew that the fifteen to twenty paces associated with reaching into her handbag could well prove to be the toughest walk-on part of her entire career in theatre.

Tuesday morning proved that her fears were well founded. The first rehearsal ended in fiasco: eyes agape, the hand gripping her ID card stretched out ahead of her as if her uniformed husband was a kind of supernatural apparition that could only be banished by showing it one's ID, Kvido's mother passed by the porter's lodge, lurching into the red railing as she went.

"She'll soon get used to it," Kvido's father's commander tried to be reassuring.

Fortunately, Kvido's father was sometimes on nights instead, thus sparing his wife fifty per cent of such encounters, while he himself was spared encounters with his former colleagues, whose morning wisecracks, uttered as they passed through at an unusually rapid pace, and so sometimes left only half-said, he found peculiarly depressing. On nights, he also had more time for reading, though in the circumstances he was not always able to concentrate fully on what he was reading; on days like that, he would kill the hours and minutes by repeatedly, and in terms of his job description, pointlessly, doing the rounds of the entire admin block: he would shuffle along the dark corridors, read the names on all the doors, look inside familiar offices and run his torch over the framed family photos on people's desks. Sometimes he would amuse himself by entering his own old office and scrutinising the notes in the diaries of his two successors – Zvára and his new deputy. "Idiots," he sniggered to himself. "What idiots."

2. While at work, Kvido's father gave every appearance of being resigned to his new placement and enjoying the unprecedented peace and quiet, but at home he soon abandoned all pretence and completely gave in to his defeat. He became taciturn and his responses were either apathetic or irritable. He plodded wearily about the house, indifferent now to the obsolete messages on both the IBM desk calendar and the board in the hallway.

"At this stage, it was my mother who ran things at home," Kvido explained. "The patriarchate had collapsed."

Kvido's father was now spending most of his time in his cellar workshop: as in other times of stress, he had returned to his woodworking. With something approaching sentimentality he surveyed the dust-covered, but still sweet-smelling sawn timber, meekly stroked the smooth pinewood veneers, picked up the pale-coloured lengths of squared lime wood and the dark boards of plum wood, as if mentally apologising to them for having forgotten them in favour of something as ridiculous as business trips. He tidied up and swept out, sharpened all his Swedish chisels on his circular grinder and with the aid of a little paraffin whetted them on his Arkansas oilstone. And gradually he went back to work: sawing, sanding, turning, gluing and varnishing. He would often forget about the time, and so it could happen that, Kvido, staggering half-asleep to the toilet while it was still dark, would spot him through the slit beneath his puffy eyelids, in the bathroom before going to bed, washing the last bits of fine sawdust from the hairs on his wrists. Or late into the evening, Kvido and his mother, watching television together, might suddenly be disturbed by the loud-pitched whine of his father's broach cutter, rising from the bowels of the house. Both jumped. A short while later, Kvido noticed the tears in his mother's eyes.

"Mum?" he asked.

She shook her head with a helpless smile. Even in the weak glimmer of the television you could see her wrinkles.

"My father," explained Kvido, "was treating my mother the way he treated wood – and bringing out the grain of her years."

It wasn't surprising: either he was in his porter's lodge, or in the cellar, surfacing only to go to bed or get a bite to eat, or perhaps to watch the television news, though that got him more and more upset and he would often leave before the end and go and do a spot of chip-carving on a piece of walnut to calm himself down, at least up to a point.

It was all getting a bit much for Kvido's mother: the company's legal agenda, which fell almost exclusively to her, kept her so busy that she often came home quite late. The house was a mess and there was nobody to do a spot of cleaning and tidying. Kvido divided his time between story-writing and the study of sex manuals; Paco's original, and naturally boyish interest in games of cowboys and Indians had evolved into a strange lack of interest in anything else, and now he spent days on end wandering in the woods with his friend Bearskin; Grandma Líba, who continued to breathe through wet hankies and therefore spread water through every room, was merely disgusted by the mess and refused to live in it and, like Kvido, kept to her room. And the house was getting quite dilapidated.

Dilapidated, because what it needed far more than some neatly turned banisters was everyday cleaning and maintenance. The garden had become overgrown with grass and weeds. The garden gate, fence and window frames urgently needed a fresh coat of paint. There was a cold draught blowing through the kitchen from the window that Paco had broken with his leather lasso. Some of the coal, which no one had cleared away, got rain-soaked. The house-plants that Kvido's mother couldn't reach had wilted away, and in the food processor, which she'd been unable to unscrew, the remnants of some kind of milk shake had been putrefying for months. The hall door had been scratched terribly on both sides by the dog, whom Kvido's father frequently forgot. All the taps dripped and the ice forming inside the fridge had reached such a thickness that its door wouldn't shut. The mirror in the bathroom was so spattered with toothpaste as to render it unusable, and the toilet surround, always gleaming white, was now bespattered with the yellow stains of dried urine.

"I couldn't write," Kvido explained. "The sheer chaos! I love order and symmetry!"

3. *A Friday evening. The kitchen. Kvido's mother, alone. With difficulty she is stacking empty plates on the work-top, already laden with dirty dishes, leftover food, old newspapers and magazines, football shin-pads, tins of varnish, off-cuts of fibreboard and pine bark. She switches off the stove and goes and stands in the middle of the kitchen. A long pause.*

> MOTHER (*aloud, wearily*): Dinner.
> (*No response*)
> MOTHER (*louder*): Dinner!
> KVIDO (*from his room*): Coming!
> FATHER (*from his workshop*): Coming!
> GRANDMA (*from her room, muffled by her wet hankie*): Where's the fire! (*They arrive one by one*)
> FATHER (*to Grandma*): Have you seen one of my chisels anywhere?
> GRANDMA (*raising the hankie from her face*): Me!! (*Replaces her hankie*)
> FATHER: A half-round paring gouge?
> GRANDMA (*Raising the hankie from her face*): Now what

would I be doing with one of those? (*Replaces her hankie*)

KVIDO: A half-round bread roll more like.

MOTHER (*to Kvido*): Where's Paco this time?

KVIDO: He wasn't in my room.

MOTHER (*to Father*): Where's Paco?

FATHER: He wasn't in the workshop.

MOTHER (*angrily*): Aha… Do you even remember when you saw him last?

GRANDMA (*raising the hankie from her face*): Not recently, I'll warrant! (*Removes the hankie from her face*)

FATHER (*nettled, to Grandma*): I don't have time to keep an eye on my son when I have to check the electric meter every hour because of you!

MOTHER (*with a sigh*): Stop it now. How many frankfurters do you all want?

KVIDO (*leafing through a newspaper*): Four.

FATHER: I'll have just one. I'm not that hungry today. I had a bite at work.

MOTHER (*mocking*): Have people been tossing you sweets?

FATHER (*aggrieved*): My boss gave me a whole pepperoni!

GRANDMA: Have you taken the skins off. They're out of a tin, aren't they?

MOTHER: They *are* out of a tin, but they're not the kind that needs skinning. (*Impatiently*) How many do you want?

GRANDMA (*suspiciously*): Really? Believe me, those artificial skins don't do your stomach any favours…

MOTHER (*fighting to control herself*): Definitely.

GRANDMA (*looking into the pan*): They don't look skinned...

MOTHER (*raising her voice*): They don't *look* skinned, because they aren't the sort that *needs* skinning!

GRANDMA: Please don't shout at me! I'm still your mother.

MOTHER: Sorry! I thought you were the district health inspector.

KVIDO (*showing his father the paper with a photo of Vladimír Remek on the steps of a spaceship*): That's what I call a business trip! That guy must be *happy*!

MOTHER: Don't tease. Eat. Bon appétit.

KVIDO: Bon appétit.

FATHER: Likewise. This bread –?

MOTHER: Is five days old. None of you've been to the shop.

KVIDO: I for one couldn't have. Ever since I wrote that story, I can't even go through the shop door. I don't want to risk having a breakdown...

MOTHER (*emphatically*): You'll go there first thing in the morning, even if you have to take a diazepam!

KVIDO: Why me? Dad can go – he's got a day off...

MOTHER (*ironically, glancing towards Father*): Are you crazy? You're father's got that inlaid chessboard pattern to finish! We mustn't disturb him!

KVIDO (*scornfully*): Yeah, on the wardrobe door! God almighty! Tell me what chess player, fancying a game, would tip a wardrobe full of clothes onto the floor!

MOTHER (*clearly pleased*): But you're being too utilitarian about it. First and foremost, it's a *beautiful thing*! Like a biro with a digital clock in it. (*Father wants to say something, but is interrupted by the arrival of Paco. Paco is wearing a calfskin jerkin. Round his neck he has a leather string with a boar's tooth hanging from it and he has a chisel in his hand. He is very dirty.*)

KVIDO: I understand that some people don't like washing – but I don't see the necessity of becoming a tramp because of it.

MOTHER: Where've you been?

PACO: Finishing that totem pole...

FATHER (*spotting the chisel*): With my chisel! I'll kill you!

MOTHER: Why didn't you tell anyone where you were going? Or at least leave a message?

PACO: I *did* leave a message!

MOTHER (*suspiciously*): You did? Where?

PACO (*finds the pine bark in among the mess on the work top*): Here!

MOTHER (*examining Paco's incisions*): What is it?

PACO: A pictogram.

(*A brief pause*)

MOTHER (*resigned*): All right, Paco, but next time leave one in normal writing. Like you use in school, right? We palefaces use the Roman script. How many frankfurters do you want?

PACO: I've eaten. Bearskin roasted me a rook. (*Mother wants to say something, but is interrupted by the phone ringing. Kvido's father freezes. Kvido runs to the phone, followed by Mother.*)

KVIDO: Yes? Hi! (*Calling back to the kitchen*) Grandpa! Phoning from hospital again! (*Quietly*) What was wrong?... I see... And the prognosis?... (*He smiles*) Get away!... In

Benešov? Don't ask, I just can't fathom how Vančura could put up with that bourgeois lot... No, it's more or less okay at school – 'cept for the headmaster and those pictures in the hall, did I tell you?

FATHER (*unhappily*): Don't forget you're on the phone!

KVIDO: Paco? Fine, he's just had rook for dinner... No, I was just joking... No veggies, we had frankfurters and they were great, seriously!... No, no connection, really... honest!

MOTHER: Give him to me, please.

KVIDO: Father? No, no breakdown. He just says how everyone's betrayed him. Ate his chickens and emigrated.

FATHER: Are you crazy? I've said, you're on the phone!

MOTHER: Give him to me.

KVIDO: ...Father? No, he's given up driving again... No... He says he doesn't want to get done for manslaughter. He says it's just what the secret police are waiting for –

FATHER (*shouting*): Take it from him, or I'll whip it out of the wall!!!

KVIDO: ...No, that was Father... Mother wants you... Okay, see you Sunday. Bye.

VIII.

1. Kvido's mother had already had plenty of problems with the post office in Sázava. Apart from a number of foreign stamps that had been peeled off, though that didn't bother her much, whole letters had gone missing and even one or two books that she'd ordered through the Book Club; and registered letters addressed to her at work, were needlessly kept at the post office, where she had to go and pick them up in person. Mostly, however, she just brushed it aside.

But as she stood that Sunday afternoon in the corridor of the Bulovka hospital in Prague, with all those hopelessly pointless family photos, a jar of cling peaches and a new book on the history of Prague, while the telegram about her father's death, sent from the hospital at 11.35 a.m. the previous day, was still behind the post office counter somewhere, she swore she wasn't going to let it pass this time.

Having discovered, however, after two sleepless nights, that she didn't have the strength to go to the post office and accuse someone there herself, though she was within her rights, she asked Kvido's father to do it for her. He, though he had considerately taken upon himself all the business of the funeral arrangements, resisted at this point. He maintained that it was pointless to take on one more problem *right now* and so do further damage to their already frazzled nerves.

"Let's leave it for now," he begged her.

Kvido spotted, quite rightly, that something else lurked behind his reluctance – that familiar fear of the slightest of confrontations, which, ever since the incident with Kohout, had grown to pathological dimensions. This exasperated him.

"Certainly not!" he said. "If you're afraid to go, I'll do it."

His mother pushed his hair back off his forehead. She had to stretch a little to do so.

"You'd know what to do?"

Kvido hesitated, but the awareness that right was firmly on their side fortified him.

"I think so," he said.

Thanks to its dark furniture and Bordeaux carpet, the postmaster's office, to which he had himself taken that very day, looked grander than Kvido would have expected of such a small post office.

"Take a seat," the postmaster bade him amiably, but Kvido remained standing. The man smiled.

"I can guess what brings you here," he said. "But first let me express my truly sincere condolences."

Kvido gave a barely perceptible smirk, but he did accept the proffered hand.

"I can understand your embarrassment," the man said. "We are truly sorry for what has happened. Yet at the same time we shouldn't allow emotions to cloud our reason. That could end badly…"

"What do you mean?"

"The thing is, I'm not pretending that everything is as it should be at our post office. We may have made the odd mistake, and the complaint that you have raised is in some measure justified –"

"In some measure?" Kvido couldn't restrain himself. "What are you saying? We arrived to visit Grandpa – and he was dead. I was looking forward to having a chat with him – and he was dead! Can you imagine it?"

"Of course," said the postmaster. "But we've done everything in our power to ensure that it can't happen again."

"I'm glad to hear it," said Kvido sarcastically. "I've still got one left!"

His eyes briefly took in the certificates of merit on the far wall. The postmaster was trying to rattle him, but he couldn't quite put his finger on it.

"Let me tell you something," the postmaster said. "Anyone can criticise – forgive me for putting it so bluntly. It's easy to pull things down, spit on them – but concrete, realistic proposals for how to do things better, well, not many people have them. Not even you."

"Me?" Kvido couldn't believe what he was hearing. "Am I a postmaster? Do I understand how post offices work? Is it any business of mine to improve things? Isn't that *your* job?"

"There you have it!" the postmaster smiled. "You admit to not understanding the issues surrounding the post office – yet you blithely claim the right to judge it!"

Kvido was speechless. His rage grew.

"We have to have due regard to the options available to our post office," the postmaster went on. "We have too few staff and too many jobs to do, in short, there isn't the time to keep abreast of everything. Not even Rome was built in a day!"

"But please," said Kvido, barely controlling himself, "no one's asking you to build Rome! But it would be fabulous if, next time, it took you less than forty hours to deliver a telegram over a distance of less than a kilometre!"

"It's quite understandable that you're upset and can't let me finish what I was about to say," said the postmaster, smiling unpleasantly. "I meant to say that we are aware of our shortcomings, but that it would be naïve to suppose that we can overcome then at once. Only the impatience of youth – like yours – wants everything instantly. I wouldn't mind betting that that's also why you're here instead of your father."

"Maybe. But I can't agree that I want everything instantly. I don't. I needn't get my post on the instant – I'd be quite happy for it to be delivered *on time*. Especially telegrams and things sent express. As for postcards, I'd tolerate a delay of even two or three days, so they can be read by *all* your ladies, not just the ones that happen to be at work on the day – which would be unfair to the others."

"That's –"

"I don't even mind one of them peeling the odd stamp off for her husband, after all, as Goethe said, collectors are happy people, but please do make sure that in the process they only damage the less important parts of the text!"

"What you're telling me are accusations that you'd have to prove first…"

Kvido made to leave.

"I think," said the postmaster, "that every critic should begin by examining himself first. Because –"

"Good God!" Kvido blurted. "What are we talking about here?"

"What?" said the postmaster. "What? – We're talking about how you're demagogically ignoring all the good that's been done at this post office. About how you're about to blacken all those who day in, day out, do a good honest job. About…"

"Not the point," said Kvido, on the face of it wearily. "I obviously have nothing but respect for all those who daily do a good honest job. What really pissed me off was that lady comrade who probably used the telegram about my grandfather's death as a bookmark to keep her page in *Burda*!"

"The longer I listen to you," said the postmaster with a chilly smile, "the more I realise how much you have still to learn to enter this kind of debate. Especially –" he glanced at Kvido reproachfully, "the kind of language to use. But let me try to put it another way: have you ever sent, from this office, an express letter, a telegram of congratulations, a parcel, a money transfer?"

"Of course," said Kvido, vainly pondering what mental leap was coming next.

"In other words," the man said meaningfully, "you have used our services on a fairly regular basis. We regularly accommodate all your and your family's requirements – and you think that's normal…"

"Not the point!" said Kvido furiously. "You're missing the point again. We don't *think* it's normal, it simply *is* normal. None of the services you've mentioned goes beyond what are your normal everyday duties. Post offices exist precisely to enable people to send parcels, telegrams or money – so kindly stop trying to make me think I should shit myself with sheer gratitude for you bringing me a registered letter!"

"And that our comrade postwoman willingly tames your dog, which you yourselves can't control – is that also 'normal'?"

That question found Kvido unprepared.

"And that in these times the pettiest of little porters wants to make a complaint – that's also normal?"

The insult hit Kvido so hard that it briefly took his breath away.

The postmaster, red-faced in his rancour, looked at him with unconcealed disdain and loathing:

"Or his clever-clogs of a brat?"

He shoved at Kvido with his paunch.

"Get out!" he bellowed.

He pushed Kvido out into the corridor and slammed the door behind him.

Kvido aimed a few frenzied kicks at it.

It flung open again.

"And mind who you call a brat!" screamed Kvido as he beat a speedy retreat.

2. Kvido's mother could never have claimed with absolute certainty that the torn-out page with Shakespeare's Sonnet No. 66 on it, which she'd found in the bundle of Grandpa's effects, actually conveyed his wishes as regards a suitable quotation to adorn his death notice, but because she knew her father well and so knew that he would never have abused a book in such a way without some extraordinarily good reason, she believed it at once. She read the sonnet over and over and despite the pain that permeated her entire being, and was happy in the thought that if she headed the notice with it, she would be affording her father one final opportunity to speak to his nearest, dearest and friends of longstanding in words that he perhaps had felt deeply on his deathbed, when they must have gained a particular significance.

"She was out of luck," Kvido told the editor.

Kvido's mother got the point when her husband returned from the firm of undertakers in Uhlířské Janovice. Hardly had he come through the door and she saw the expression on his face, and everything was suddenly clear – and for a split second her mind even registered some surprise that she could have been so naïve.

"It can't be done!" she said.

Kvido looked quizzically towards his father.

"No, it can't," his father said.

Kvido's mother returned to the table, enfolded her tea-cup in her hands, but in the end she didn't take a sip.

"It can't be done," she repeated contemplatively.

"I did what I could, but I couldn't get through to them. That quotation isn't on their list, so that's that."

"*List?*"

"The list of *permitted* quotations," Kvido's father was more specific.

"Permitted quotations? Shakespeare's banned? It's not as if I was asking for a bit of Mussolini! Did you even say it was from Shakespeare?"

"Of course."

Kvido's mother bent over her cup.

"Oh dear, oh dear," she said.

"I can't help it, honestly," he said. "I tried to give the chap all 400 crowns I had on me –"

"And?"

"He said he'd never met anyone prepared to go to jail over 400."

"Not permit Shakespeare!" Kvido's mother shook her head. "Is there anything they won't ban now?"

"And the music," his father said with immense reluctance, "they wouldn't have the music either. But they did have some Mahler."

"How vile can you get!" said Kvido. "Vile, vile, vile!"

"Like I said," his mother laughed bitterly. "Tomorrow they'll ban us from living."

Kvido's father put his arm round her.

"And we don't even have the freedom to die as we'd like!" his mother exclaimed.

"I told him as much," his father rejoined. "And he said: Dear sir, as we live, so too do we die."

"And how very true."

3. At the funeral, Kvido didn't shed a single tear. He stared blankly at the coffin drowning in flowers and wreaths, and clamped his knees together the way he did at the dentist's. He listened angrily to the surrogate Mahler and blessed his mother for declining to have any speeches. He was thinking not just about his grandfather, but also about Grandpa's friend Frank, about Zita, about his own father – and in hushed defiance he mumbled the lines from Shakespeare.

At school he was now taciturn and irritable. He would snap not just at his classmates, but also at his friend Špála, and even at the teachers. Everywhere about him he kept finding falsehood.

"What's wrong with you?" Špála would ask him, troubled.

"Everything pisses me off," Kvido replied.

At home, it felt so unbearable following the funeral that he preferred to sign on for a Saturday potato-picking job.

They were taken off somewhere way beyond Neveklov. In late September it was fairly warm still and now and again the sun broke through the jumble of clouds, but there was also a strong wind blowing, even stronger out there in the fields. Most of the girls had scarves round their heads. There was something very feminine about that, primordial almost, like the very job itself, which – thought Kvido – in a sense hadn't changed much at all over the centuries. There were the same bent backs, the same deft female fingers. For no obvious reason it suddenly struck Kvido that in a few years' time all these crazy schoolgirls would be mothers.

The girls were in a substantial majority and Kvido and the other boys could hardly keep pace as they carried the girls' full baskets from the field to the flatbed. As luck would have it, Jarka and her class had to be on the far side of the farm track. Her baskets were being seen to by another lad this time, but Kvido couldn't care less. He just strode across the furrows and thought about the world.

At break-time he sat away from the others, resting against a crab-apple tree and watching wearily as the grey-and-white clouds rearranged themselves above the far, tree-covered horizon. He felt no hunger, though he did take a sip or two of the lemonade supplied.

"What's wrong with you?" Jarka suddenly asked.

She was wearing a black sweater that she'd knitted herself and that fitted tightly around her breasts, and some old jeans with an excessive flare, tucked into her dusty red gumboots.

"How d'you mean?" he asked her.

"Dunno," said Jarka, squatting down beside him. "But something's wrong."

She noticed his untouched lunch.

"You haven't eaten?" she asked.

"No. How can I eat when you don't love me!" Kvido mocked.

The eyes beneath her dark-blue scarf looked at him searchingly.

"What *is* the matter?"

"Nothing, dammit!" Kvido snapped back. "Do you think that if I'm not doing your fetching and carrying there must be something the matter with me?"

"Kvido!" said Jarka, surprised.

She laid a hand on his shoulder.

"What is it? Kvido?"

He closed his eyes.

"We've buried Grandpa. Among other things."

After a moment, she said:

"Why didn't you tell me?"

She was looking at him with such sincerity that Kvido had to laugh:

"Why would I have told you? You didn't even know him!"

"If not me, who else?" she asked earnestly.

In the end he told her everything: about the phone call from his grandfather, the terrible visit to the hospital, his row with the postmaster, the sonnet.

"You know the sonnet?" Jarka asked.

She was sitting next to him on her quilted jacket and looking up into the thinning crown of the apple tree. Kvido paused in surprise: he had been reciting to her for years, but this was different.

"Would you say it to me?"

"Here?"

He looked round. The wind was harrying clouds of dust. A bus passed between the lines of trees on the main road. The jagged outline of the tree-clad horizon descended gently towards the village.

Jarka took his hand. His tension slackened. His inhibition disappeared. He remembered his grandfather struggling to sit up against the pillows of his hospital bed. He began reciting, quietly, tentatively, but his voice grew ever more assured with each successive line:

"Tir'd with all these, for restful death I cry
As to behold desert a beggar born,
And needy nothing trimm'd in jollity,
And purest faith unhappily forsworn,
And gilded honour shamefully misplac'd,
And maiden virtue roughly strumpeted,
And right perfection wrongfully disgraced,
And strength by limping sway disabled,
And art made tongue-tied by authority,
And folly – doctor-like – controlling skill,
And simple truth miscall'd simplicity,
And captive good attending captain ill:
    Tir'd with all these, from these would I be gone,
    Save that, to die, I leave my love alone."

"That was lovely," said Jarka.

"Mrs Šperk would have been pleased," said Kvido, blowing his nose: "Or not. But he might have heard me."

Jarka stroked the back of his hand.

Kvido spotted the others watching them, but he didn't care.

The eyes beneath the headscarf suddenly sparkled.

"Shall we go sledging tomorrow?" Jarka asked.

So Kohout was right, thought Kvido. I've actually gone and brought her round, just like that.

IX.

1. The next spring, just before Kvido's father began whispering for all time, his mother was getting things ready for breakfast and discovered that all the glasses and glass mugs that he had once brought home from the works had disappeared. She scoured all the shelves and cupboards, but all she could find were two ancient china mugs with the handles missing and a jar that had contained apricot jam. It finally occurred to her to look in the bin. It was difficult to open and being full of broken bits, it rattled.

She summoned her husband and gave him withering, questioning look.

"Why are you looking at me like that? I'm not going to be done for economic crimes as well," he snapped.

Kvido's mother said nothing. She shook her head mournfully and poured him some tea in a rubber vessel for mixing filling plaster.

That was, incidentally, the last time his father shouted, since in the days that followed he started whispering more and more frequently, until it became his exclusive mode. This gave the impression that someone in the house spent the whole day asleep.

"Why are you whispering, for goodness' sake?" Kvido couldn't stop himself asking one day.

"Me, whispering?" his father returned in surprise.

"Yes! You whisper. All the time you just whisper. Mum, you tell him he whispers!"

"You whisper," Kvido's mother confirmed. "You whisper, you go smashing the glassware and you've hidden our books and photos somewhere."

"Why do you do it?" said Kvido, his voice rising.

"Unless you've gone and burnt them," his mother added. "Like some real *agent*."

His father looked at her enquiringly and turned a tap full on.

Kvido hissed in derision.

"I whisper because I have certain concerns," his father said hoarsely.

"What about?" Kvido exploded. "Losing your job as a porter?"

"About us," said his father. "They can do anything they like. Don't you get it?"

The next day, after lunch, and without a word, he took Kvido and his wife to the bedroom window and cautiously pulled the curtain back a little.

"Look – if you don't believe me...," he whispered.

Kvido and his mother looked in the direction in which he was pointing. Among the trees by the bend in the railway, directly below Lark Hill, stood a white portable cabin that had been brought there a couple of days previously as a temporary home for a number of track maintenance men, who were engaged in injecting concrete into cracks in the tunnel beyond the bend. Three men were sitting by the cabin.

"And what are you thinking it is?" Kvido's mother asked. "A KGB bunker?"

The whole farce was getting to be more than she could take.

"Notice the aerial," Kvido's father pointed out.

"Father," said Kvido is near-disbelief, "That's a TV aerial."

"I've been watching them for some time now," said his father, ignoring his son's comment. "There are six them all told. They regularly take turns, but what's interesting is that one of them stays inside *every time*."

"Father!" Kvido shouted. "They're there to repair the *tunnel*! Anyone will tell you that!"

His father looked at him compassionately.

"The tunnel," he whispered. "You think *they* can be bothered with some stupid tunnel?"

He was getting the family worried. He'd almost stopped reading, he just shuffled to and fro between the workshop and the dining room, and he kept bringing up his food like a baby.

"That was evidently the first phase in his psychosis," Dr Liehr later told Kvido's mother. "Though his imaginings – they're not delusions in the true sense of the word. The secret police aren't phantoms."

In the circumspection with which Kvido's father would, back then, lift the edge of the curtain there was something that his wife just couldn't stand. She used to read in the bedroom, but now, whenever he entered, she couldn't remain there with him for even a minute; she would rush out, slamming the door behind her. She no longer saw the funny side of Kvido's father's once notorious tale about his uncle, who had spent a lifetime as an assistant in an ironmonger's shop, believing throughout that he was a lady at the court of Louis XIV. The spectre of insanity began floating over the household.

One day, Kvido's father having spent longer than usual by the bedroom window, her nerves failed. She removed her apron and dashed into the bedroom.

"Now, you just sit there and watch!" she commanded.

Quickly she put her shoes on, stubbed her cigarette out and paused for five seconds in front of the mirror in the hall to straighten her hair. There was something menacing about her haste.

"Unless they've got a dog, you'll see something!" she called up to her husband and banged the front door behind her.

Kvido's father turned towards his son as if expecting some kind of explanation, but Kvido just gave a disobliging shrug. They watched from the window. Kvido's mother's tiny form was heading unswervingly for the white cabin. She turned off the road along the path that would bring her to the railway. Then, as she had to adjust her stride to the distance between the sleepers, her gait changed visibly. Kvido's father rose and gulped awkwardly several times.

"If you throw up again, it'll be you to clear it up," Kvido warned him drily, without taking his eyes off his mother.

She was now less than twenty metres from the workmen's cabin. She appeared to have called to the two men sitting outside it since they both looked up simultaneously. One of them seemed to take two or three steps towards her. Kvido noted that he was stripped to the waist. The three of them spoke for several minutes before disappearing inside the cabin.

"I'm going to take a look," said Kvido when, forty minutes later, she still hadn't reappeared. In spite of himself, his father's crazy fears were beginning to affect him as well.

"No, you're not!" yelled his father, who in that space of forty minutes had been twenty times up and down the stairs to the workshop and had completely forgotten to whisper. "I don't intend to lose my son as well!"

"Father, stop that!" said Kvido. "Take an oxazepam and calm down."

"I won't let you go!" his father cried in anguish. "What do you know about it all? The executions? The mass deportations?"

"You're mad!" screamed Kvido and fled the house.

The more worried he was for his mother, the greater his irritation at his father. As soon as he hit the road, he broke into a trot without realising. He almost twisted his ankle on the blackened ballast between the rails. But when, panting, he reached the suspect little building, all he found were two soldiers, barely a year older than himself. They were lying on sleeping bags and taking turns at a half-empty bottle. They looked him up and down mistrustfully.

"If you're looking for your mum, they've left," one of them said with a grin.

"Where?" Kvido yelped.

The soldier shrugged.

"Why?" Kvido shrieked, beginning to get frantic.

"Stop shouting," the other soldier said, adding in pure Bratislava Slovak: "And take it easy. I'm not the cops."

"That's all right then," said Kvido before trotting back home.

He first caught sight of his mother as she came strolling back across the garden towards the house, accompanied by another three soldiers. She was laughing tipsily and her diction had softened in that old familiar way.

"I've had a ride on a track inspection trolley!" she boasted to her son.

Wearing an uncertain smile, Kvido's father came out onto the veranda.

"Sergeant Miga, railway construction and maintenance corps, Prague," the commander introduced himself somewhat laboriously, likewise in Slovak. "If you really don't believe us, sir, I'll happily sign a piece of paper saying that Gustáv Husák is a prick!"

"That's all right, then," said Kvido's father.

2. Not even this clear evidence could quell his sense of some unknown threat. He continued to be anxious, touchy, with a constant, irrational tendency to self-incrimination. If Kvido or his mother passed him in the house, he would avert his gaze. But Kvido's mother wasn't giving up. I'll pull him through it, she determined. Instinct told her that a change of environment might do him good. She phoned round a number of company holiday facilities and finally succeeded in booking a small room for four in a chalet in the Giant Mountains for the first fortnight of the summer holidays.

At first, it really did look as if the stay in the mountains was having a positive effect. Kvido's father admittedly spent endless hours in a lonely search for suitable materials for carving or potentially decorative bits of roots and branches, but in the process he also found a few fine specimens of orange birch boletus and it began to look as if, for the first time in ages, something had given him pleasure. He went with the family on a few short outings, did a spot of jogging after dinner and began to read more. To his wife's delight, he also started eating better and at the Kolín Bothy he even managed over half of a large ice-cream sundae with whipped cream on top. Then when he and Paco immersed themselves up to their necks in an ice-cold stream, Kvido's mother began to take his imminent recovery for granted – and Kvido tried in vain to dampen her enthusiasm.

Unquestionably, the one who got the most out of the family holiday was Paco. He rebelled against the petty-bourgeois idea of sleeping inside the chalet and instead soon built himself a kind of suspended bed amid the jumbled branches of a contorted birch tree and there spent all the following nights. During the day he learned how to tie various knots, did a spot of rock-climbing and practised knife-throwing.

> "The lasso's loop whizzed through the air
> the graceful sorrel flicked his tail so long,
> the cowboy shook the dust from his hair
> and all the while he sang his favourite sooooong."

Kvido sang his parody of a campfire song when his little brother, filthy and suntanned, made a rare appearance at the door – this was usually for his mother to remove a tick or ticks.

"So?" Paco would respond defiantly.

Kvido was also content: he wrote several stories, which he even had time to rewrite – and from the sentences he finally rejected he always constructed a letter for Jarka.

One afternoon, Kvido's father and little brother set off into the forest above the chalet to track game. But barely twenty minutes had passed when his mother spotted them from the window as they made their way back across the meadow.

"That's not a stag," she called out to them. "You're tracking my hiking boots!"

Paco gestured scornfully towards his father.

"It's no use with him," he said.

"What's wrong," his mother asked with some disquiet.

"I need to check up on something," said Kvido's father.

When he came upstairs to their room, he asked his wife if

she'd mind reminding him of all the differences between the terms *supplying an explanation* and *witness statement*.

Kvido's mother's hands dithered ever so briefly on the board on which she had some mushrooms drying, but she quickly came to and rebuffed her husband with some jocular response. But he persisted with his question.

So she just shrugged and explained to him, quite amiably, not just the differences between them, but also the legal consequences that flowed from them. She spoke slowly, because her husband, as on every previous occasion, was making notes in writing. When she reached the end, he contemplated these a moment longer.

"If I understand it rightly, a false statement made while supplying an explanation can get you a fine, but can't lead to criminal proceedings. Is that so?" he asked finally.

"Yes," said Kvido's mother. "You've got it. But then you do have a university education and, when all's said and done, you're not hearing it for the first time."

Enter Kvido.

"Oh, no," he said. "Another training session?"

"Without exception?" his father asked.

"Without exception," his mother sighed.

His father shoved his notes in his breast pocket.

"Wait, wait," said Kvido. "Shouldn't you be eating that paper? Or at least shoving it up your anus? Have you any idea of the dangers you're exposing your family to? Haven't you heard about mass deportations on inspection trolleys?"

"Stop teasing," said his mother. "Have you written to your

grandma yet?"

"Yep," said Kvido, grinning.

"Show me!" his mother said suspiciously.

Kvido took a black-and-white postcard from his book.

"Where did you get that?" she smiled. She turned it over and read:

"In the forest, in a cottage,
 to the table's borne a pottage.
 We shall have no abstinence
 and so no signs of flatulence."

"Brilliant!" Kvido's father approved heartily.

The next day, Kvido and the others woke to a glorious morning.

"A beautiful morning rose over a deep valley at the eastern end of the Giant Mountains. Dark firs and pines stood about the mountains all clad in dew," Kvido's mother recited.

They enjoyed a substantial breakfast, his father prepared packed lunches for everyone and put them in a little rucksack, and off they went for another outing. They walked down to Pec and continued on into Giant Valley, along which they – sometimes grasping the iron chains – scrambled up to the foot of Snowy Mount. From there they meant to follow the Czechoslovak-Polish Friendship Trail to the Špindler Bothy to return finally along the White Elbe – except that Kvido's father didn't want to. His main reason seemed to be that the trail went partly across Polish territory.

"So what?" Kvido was puzzled.

"Nothing," said his father. "I don't want to go that way. I'm not one for such demonstrative gestures."

"What gestures, for God's sake?"

"I don't need to exhibit some kind of dubious courage by taking thirty paces beyond the border marker."

"You'll drive me mad," said Kvido.

"Stop it now," his mother chipped in quickly. "No more talk and let's get going!"

She took her husband's hand, but he slipped from her grip with incomprehensible obstinacy.

"Like I said, I'm not going that way!"

"But why not?" his wife asked dolefully.

"Why not? Because it strikes me as pointless to go exposing ourselves like that when all we'll achieve is to provoke the frontier guards, and there are other routes back anyway!"

"What the hell do you mean, provoke?" Kvido's voice rose. "That trail is open to the public, like any other. We wouldn't be breaking any laws!"

Some passing tourists looked back in some surprise. Kvido's father lowered his gaze.

"Everybody goes that way – look!" his mother argued.

His father stubbornly shook his head.

His lips were clamped together.

He was having trouble breathing.

"It's useless with him," said Paco.

"Look here, Father," said Kvido with an emphasis smacking of despair. "Look about you: every ten minutes, at least a hundred people follow the trail *before the very eyes of the border guards*!"

For some reason, it seemed desperately important for him to convince his father. Some of the resolution had gone from the latter's face, leaving him looking more desolate than just obstinate, but he carried on shaking his head.

"I don't like those binoculars at my back," he whispered. "I can't bear the thought that someone will demand to see my ID ever again. Don't you get it? You really can't see my point?"

He looked beseechingly at his wife.

"I don't believe it," said Kvido. "Our father's gone mad."

"Yes, we can," said Kvido's mother with sudden determination. "We'll go another way."

"He's just playing games," Paco whispered to Kvido. "Poland's not good enough for him, our man of the world!"

3. Early in September, Kvido's mother finally decided to find her husband a shrink, because she had to concede – if reluctantly – that her own intuition just wasn't up to dealing with his odd neurosis.

But she was troubled by the plainly political background to his mania and she was by no means certain how an outside doctor would react. On Radio Free Europe, she had heard a programme about the abuse of psychiatry for political ends, and although this was in the Soviet context, it was still bugging her.

So she went to Prague to see Zita and seek her advice. The

cinema was packed – they were showing *Jaws*, an American film – but the weather was still warm, so Zita didn't have much to do in her cloakroom.

"It's quite gripping – the audience is completely silent," she told Kvido's mother. "It's a real blockbuster. We're into our fifth week of showing it – do you fancy going in?"

"Not really. What's it about?"

"Not sure, lass. Divers maybe?" said Zita, unsure of herself. "I haven't seen it yet – but I intend to!" she insisted.

Kvido's mother stroked the dark-blue sleeve of Zita's smock.

"It'll be best if you go and see young Liehr," Zita finally suggested. "His father was a brilliant psychiatrist."

"What do you mean by young?" said Kvido's mother with a hint of doubt.

"Older than you," Zita reassured her. "They say he's good. In America they gave him a studentship."

"Do you know him personally?"

"I was the first in the world to see him."

"Seriously?" Kvido's mother smiled. "And where's he working now?"

Zita jabbed the air with her finger.

"At the Blaník," she said. "He's their boilerman."

4. Thus, in October, did Kvido's father start going to see Dr Liehr in the boiler-room of the Blaník cinema. This brought about a change in Kvido's attitude to his father: he conceded for the first time that the latter's strange behaviour and his bouts of defeatism could be signs that he was genuinely sick; moreover, the psychiatrist, allegedly a very able one, would surely be able to tell whether he was feigning illness or not, Kvido thought. So he began to show more consideration for his father – which did wonders for their relationship.

As Kvido's school leaving exams approached, they would often revise together: they would sit at the kitchen table by the pleasant light of a wickerwork lamp, doing sums. By tradition, Kvido wasn't much good at maths, but his father – unlike in times past – now bore his son's inability with fortitude and calmly and patiently went over, time and again, whatever was required.

"Does the doctor give him any pills?" Kvido once asked his mother, seeking at least some kind of explanation.

"No," his mother replied. "I made that a condition."

"Well, I'm not so sure," said Kvido, remembering how his father, during one such maths session, had banged the calculator down on the table so hard that its red plastic keys flew all over the kitchen.

Sometimes, when maths had left Kvido worn out, they would discuss economics: his father, quietly nostalgic, talked about some of the theories current in the 1960s with which he had sympathised and which – as it transpired – he was still loath to give up on. Now and again, Kvido's mother would let her gaze rest on them: Kvido scratching his head, his father filling whole notebooks with diagrams of the movement of goods and shedding microscopic bits of sawdust onto the white pages from the hairs on his wrist.

As time passed, Kvido learned quite a bit about economics, which enabled him to voice, among his classmates, all manner of sarcastic comments at the expense of the country's economy.

"He's our economist," they would say of him.

Kvido would have preferred to hear said of him that he was a writer, but this was better than nothing. To his father's surprisingly diffident suggestion that he might care to apply to study at the Prague School of Economics, he willingly acceded.

"My decision was driven by three key things," Kvido explained later. "Gratitude for the care lavished on me back then by my ailing father, the infantile desire to come back from a business trip abroad bearing a microwave oven for my parents, and the Yugoslav song *Procvale su rože i vijole.*"

X.

1. One warm evening during the summer holidays, when the bend in the river glinted with the reflection of the pale moonlight, Kvido asked Jarka to show him her privates. But Jarka was reluctant: she shook her head, stared into the dark, damp grass, and whenever Kvido made to speak, she clapped her red-hot hand to his mouth.

The last day before Kvido left for Prague to start at university, they undressed in the woods beneath White Rock. They stood in their stocking feet on a bed of pine needles and felt embarrassed. Kvido, who could barely see a thing, recalled his father's night-blindness. Jarka, tired of standing there, curled up on the pile of her clothes. Kvido knelt down awkwardly beside her, vainly reminiscing on the happily uninhibited way in which she had exposed herself to him in their childhood and the calm fascination of a bespectacled researcher with which he had himself contemplated what he was seeing. Neither of them knew what to do next.

"Let's get dressed," Jarka whispered.

Kvido reached into the darkness before him and jumped when he encountered her breasts. Jarka pressed herself against him, not knowing what else to do. Kvido bit his lips, groaned with pain and doused her belly in the viscous outpouring of his rapture.

"Never mind," Jarka whispered.

Seeing it in films had taught her that much.

Even after eighteen months, at the end of his third semester, Kvido had only had a dozen or so similarly unsuccessful trials. It irked him. Nothing on earth irked him more.

"My problems weren't a consequence of any theoretical inadequacy. On the contrary, they arose from knowing too much about sex," Kvido explained later. "I'd read all there was to read about deflowering: I knew the recommended positions, the optimum angle of inclination, blood pressure and temperature, plenty of psychological and technical niceties, I knew what to avoid, and I would even have been able to give first aid to a pale, fainting girl who had just become a woman – except that, even today, I still don't know how to put it all together. Even now it's not entirely clear to me how you can be 'confident, tender and natural' at the same time as moisturising a condom with petroleum jelly.

Kvido's problems were only compounded by Jarka's: besides her inexperience, the main problem was her allergy to all manner of flowers and grasses, whose pollen caused her face to go quite puffy and brought on bouts of coughing that nearly choked her. Neither had a room of their own where they might meet undisturbed, so they always met up somewhere outdoors – so Jarka's 'Not here!' usually meant 'Not in the hay!', 'Not in the wild thyme!' or 'Not near those ox-eye daisies!'. This didn't make Kvido's task any easier, obviously.

"Finding a natural fault in the landscape anywhere around Sázava – one with an angle that, according to the handbooks, would best facilitate deflowering – isn't very difficult. But finding one that is both easy of access and hidden from the gaze of passers-by is considerably harder," Kvido described the situation later. "But finding one that is concealed, accessible and has the right angle of inclination, but at the same time has none of some sixty common species of plant growing on it – that is well-nigh impossible. Believe me! The only such place within a radius of three kilometres is the sloping access road to the fire service reservoir – though even there you first have to winkle out all the pineapple weed running along the gaps between the concrete panels..."

So for Kvido and Jarka, making love, that joyous game for two bodies, became, with the passage of time, an irksome task carried out to a fixed timetable. When Kvido arrived on a Friday evening from Prague, they would go off, holding hands, to perform the task, in silence, slightly glumly, like two people going on night shift – and the awareness of their previous failures rather crippled them in advance. They were awkward, frantic and despairing. The only dates on which they could be carefree, laughing and joking the whole time, happened to coincide miraculously with Jarka's periods. They might reminisce about how they used to go sledging or spend time wondering what had come between them in the intervening years.

Once Kvido set Jarka a strange riddle:

"A horse has come all black as tar and done the dirty in our yard – what is it?"

"I don't know," said Jarka, puzzled.

"Sex," said Kvido, dismally.

Books had also taught him what the proper procedure was in such cases: the sex therapist at the clinic issues the non-achieving couple with a kind of temporary ban on attempting to have intercourse, and then the couple, liberated thus from a duty that is so traumatic to them, will, at the first opportunity, break the ban, spontaneously and successfully – but paradoxically, it was Kvido's very knowledge of this method that prevented him from applying it.

"Such is the lot of the intellectual," Kvido lamented bitterly. "Such is the role of all knowledge."

2. If Kvido hadn't been a virgin and if he hadn't spent so much time worrying about it, his lack of interest in the study of economics, which he started to sense quite early in the course, might have led him down the familiar path of the errant son at college.

"I could have idled the time away in coffee houses and made

love to chorus girls," he expounded. "As it was, I just idled the time away in coffee houses."

This was an exaggeration: he also went to the cinema and the theatre and was quite selective about what he went to see. He did actually spend a while in the coffee shop in Municipal House on a daily basis, but not to idle: over time he wrote some twenty stories, three of which he sent to *Mladý svět*. Of course, he spent his evenings much, much more reputably than he would have liked – with his Grandma Vera and Grandpa Josef. His grandfather would listen to Radio Free Europe and the Voice of America.

"Ah, got it!" he would cry having successfully tuned in. "Now, hold on to your hats, Bolshies!"

Grandma Vera sighed as she trundled round the fur coat on her stand with her mouth full of pins.

Fortunately, they went to bed quite early. Kvido would help with making the beds up. He had to pile the mattresses from the sofa on the kitchen table in such a way that the light wouldn't disturb his grandfather. Then he crawled between the mattresses himself, flicked any scattered bird seed away and read late into the night, propping his book against the crap-covered birdcage. Sometimes he wrote a letter to Jarka or another story, but he hardly ever did any studying, subsequently none at all.

Kvido grew ever more disillusioned with his studies. He learned how to compute integrals, decline Russian nouns and extend an evolution graph of the consumption of artificial leathers into the next century – with no sense at all as to what good it would be. They explained to him that the proletariat had become organised a hundred years previously, how cork oaks were cultivated in Portugal, and where to put blue cheeses in the nomenclature of commodities – but no one ever explained to him *why* they were explaining it all to him. Kvido waited for his timetable of lectures to contain some key, fundamental subject that would bring all these diverse things together and make some sense of them – like, say, a house ultimately makes sense of the initial piles of sand, timber and pipes – but he waited in vain. For hours on end they told him about the founding and disbanding of sundry labour organisations of bygone days, but told him nothing about the people of his own times. He had some sense of what was wrong with a certain Mr Dühring, but none at all of what was wrong with him himself. He didn't know how to conceive a child, but he did know how to order lathes in German.

"And nobody cared," Kvido explained. "They appropriated me like those capitalists – with no compensation."

His lecture notes – to the extent that he still attended occasionally – grew more and more slipshod and casual. In the end he even stopped numbering the sheets or putting headings to them, so that by the end of the third semester all that remained was a jumble of papers that no one could have made their way through.

"So I don't know what's going to come of that microwave oven," he mused. He threw his notes away.

And yet he did pass the exams, mostly at the first attempt. He opened the relevant course book the evening before a given exam and flicked through it with distaste. The following day he would annoy his classmates with the peculiar apathy that they apparently mistook for a pose. He always said something to the examiner (the exams being conducted orally), but he himself found it woefully inadequate. He couldn't understand why they didn't fail him. Sometimes he wished they would. The technical language of the various types of textbook, which left little room for man and real life, seemed to stifle him. If, of an evening he brought home some good novel or novella, he felt like a fish returned to the ocean. He stretched out hedonistically.

3. That spring, his Prague grandparents went to Sázava for a week, leaving Kvido alone in their tiny flat. He bumbled about the room, thinking about how he was going to be twenty in the summer. When at one moment he caught himself with hands clasped to the breasts of his grandmother's tailor's dummy, he realised that things couldn't go on like that.

He washed the dishes, hoovered, dusted and put polythene bags over all the house plants. Then he got on a train and left for Benešov to fetch Jarka. She said she'd have to ask at home and would come in the evening. He set off ahead alone.

She arrived in a cream-coloured white jumper that betrayed not only her nipples, but also the naïve advice of some girlfriend or other. Kvido smiled a gloomy smile.

They had some dinner and drank a glass of wine each.

They ate an ice-cream cake and drank a cup of coffee.

They went into the other room and put on a Louis Armstrong record.

Kvido laid his head in Jarka's lap.

He closed his eyes.

"Let's go and lie down," he said.

"There's no geological fault here," she said gravely.

"Never mind," said Kvido.

They undressed and lay down together.

Neither spoke.

"Let's get things clear!" said Kvido, reaching across to the table for a black felt-tip.

"We're not making love, we're performing a task," he wrote on Jarka's belly in block capitals.

It tickled her, but she didn't try to stop him.

"Who set us the task? Not us!" Kvido carried on writing.

He felt that he was getting to the bottom of something important.

"If I think, I do not love," he wrote excitedly.

"You'll have to wash it off," said Jarka, but Kvido took no notice.

"I love not -- and yet I am!" he wrote triumphantly close to the edge of her pubes.

He was liberated. He kissed Jarka passionately. Suddenly he felt an intense desire.

"Kvido?" she said questioningly. "What are you doing?"

Kvido achieved it.

He woke before seven. Jarka was still asleep. The soft yellow sunlight struggled into the room from behind the blind. He dressed quietly, scribbled a note to Jarka and stole out of the flat into the street. The trams joyfully rang their bells. A bed of pansies was in full bloom in the little park on the square. A pregnant Gipsy woman came out of the pharmacy. Outside the hardware store they were unloading enamelled baths from a lorry. Some pigeons took off from the roof of the milk bar. Kvido strolled past the shops, scrutinising the pictures, coffee machines, suits, pork, rings and deckchairs. Life is wonderful, he mused. He bought six bread rolls, some butter, ham, eggs, oranges, bath foam, condoms and *Mladý svět*. As he leafed through it abstractedly, he spotted his name in bold print on the back page; beneath it they'd printed his story, *The Fair*.

"I'll quit my studies," he said out loud.

"I'll quit my studies and make love to Jarka and write stories," he repeated.

Several passers-by look round.

"And he did just that," Kvido explained.

XI.

1. "Why porter, for God's sake?" Kvido's mother screeched at him when he came back to Sázava that Friday and told her that he'd given up his studies and was going to get a job as night porter at the glassworks. "Have you all gone mad?"

"It'll give me plenty of time for writing and reading," said Kvido.

That fabulous liberating sensation of the last few days vanished into thin air; now what he felt was more like guilt. He was quite put out that his mother refused to understand him: he'd said quite clearly that it was "an epiphany, the start of something new" – while she kept going on about "surrender" and "the end". She decided not to go to her class reunion the following day.

"You know I'm not one for showing off," she said ill-temperedly, "but to have to deny one's entire family – that really is asking a bit much!"

"I don't think you've anything to be ashamed of," said Kvido, offended. "No?" she laughed unappealingly. "One cowboy doing pretty badly at school, one porter with a great past and another –," she glanced with disdain at the copy of *Mladý svět*, "with a great future!"

"All beginnings are hard," Kvido philosophised later, "but some beginnings are bloody dreadful."

If her son's unexpected life-changing decision had come as a bit of a shock to his mother, to his father it was literally a fatal blow: Kvido was the last living being in whom he placed some hope; he couldn't count much on Paco, at least not for now, since he seemed not to understand anything beyond folk music and sleeping outdoors. His only dream had suddenly collapsed.

Now he never surfaced from his workshop in the cellar. He slept there and his wife even took his meals down to him. Each time, she would spend about half an hour with him. As she came back up the stairs, Kvido would avoid her gaze.

In recent months Kvido's father had focussed most on treating the surface of wood, not just classic ways of staining and waxing, but also the long maligned process of shellacking, because he increasingly saw that the time that that good old method consumed was actually no bad thing. He also took a liking to patinating, making wood look old by means of powder paint. But presently, the house often echoed to the whine of his milling cutter.

"I wonder what he's making now?" Kvido asked Paco, not feeling bold enough to ask his mother directly.

"A Little Otík, most likely," Paco smirked. "He's probably fed up of us two."

"A wooden manager!" Kvido laughed.

In his current loneliness, Kvido was glad to have Paco as an ally and sometimes he pandered to him ever so slightly.

The night from Sunday to Monday was Kvido's first on duty.

As the afternoon faded into evening, he tipped two portions of ground coffee into a glass that had contained a fruit-based snack and spread two slices of bread with butter and honey. The days when his mother would bake cakes and tarts seemed to be firmly in the past.

"Coffee contains horrendous quantities of mercury," Grandma Líba informed him as she watched his preparations.

"That doesn't matter," said Paco. "Tea's full of strontium."

"How awful!" she exclaimed. "I'd no idea..."

"So keep a good watch on things," said Paco, sensing that his brother wasn't quite himself.

"Sure," said Kvido.

His mother said nothing.

Kvido opened the door to the cellar.

"'Bye, Dad!" he called down. "I'm off!"

Only cold air and silence rose up from the cellar.

Kvido just gave a shrug and left. Kvido's mother went and stood by the kitchen window, tweaked the curtain and followed her son with a long, long look.

Outside the porter's lodge at the glassworks Kvido found Jarka waiting for him. She was wearing a white top of her own making and she was holding two summer apples and a bar of chocolate. It was to be years before he fully appreciated the irrational courage, or faith, with which she stood by him at that time, though she knew that for the foreseeable future he could offer her nothing that might be called a prospect: he had neither education, nor a flat, he was penniless and military service was looming.

Kvido flung himself towards her as cheerily as he could so as to drown out the anxiety lurking within him.

"My girl," he whispered and covered her bare shoulders with strangely urgent kisses.

"Kvido!" she cautioned him. "People can see us!"

"Let 'em!" he said, clasping her to him.

"Wait, Kvido, there's something I need to tell you."

Kvido stepped back, alarmed.

"Something awful's happened," said Jarka.

Kvido felt a strange new prickling sensation somewhere beneath his breastbone.

"What?" he asked uneasily.

Jarka looked about her, stepped closer to him and shyly lifted her white top.

"We're not making love, we're performing a task," Kvido read the large, red-rimmed letters on the skin of Jarka's belly. He couldn't read any further – she quickly pulled her top back down.

"It's come up all inflamed," she said almost tearfully. "I'm allergic to felt-tips."

2. When Kvido came in from his night shift on Monday morning, he found his mother at the kitchen table. She looked as if she hadn't slept. The ash-tray in front of her was full to overflowing.

"Haven't you slept?" he asked solicitously.

"Sh!" she said. "Your father's asleep. What was it like?"

Her expression didn't suggest any particular interest, but Kvido was glad that she'd asked.

"Piece o' cake really," he said.

He told her about his first round: he'd been right up onto the roof of the admin building.

"Tonight at ten, I'll wave to you," he said. "Be sure to be on the lookout."

"Did you sleep?" she asked.

"I asked *you* that."

"Yes, I did – but I was up very early," she said reluctantly. "And you?"

Kvido's eyes sparkled:

"Guess where!"

For the first time that morning his mother's face showed a glimmer of a smile:

"In my office?"

Kvido nodded brightly.

"I'll fix you another blanket," his mother said. "Your dad sleeps there as well."

Paco came in.

"Why aren't you two asleep?" he asked, bleary-eyed.

"Hi, Falcon Feather!" said Kvido. "We're having eggs, d'you want some?"

"Keep you voices down!" their mother urged again. She was back to looking serious. "I've told you, your father's asleep."

"We, I mean Paco and I, we'll have a go at the garden this afternoon," Kvido promised.

"Not on your life," said Paco scornfully with his mouth full. "I couldn't care less about your petty-bourgeois *greensward*!"

Their mother stood up with unexpected vigour.

"I have to show you something – come with me," she bade them.

She went out of the kitchen and down the steps to the cellar. Bewildered, Kvido and Paco followed her.

The workshop welcomed them with the familiar scent of wood and glue. It was obvious at once that everything remained absolutely ship-shape: small finished items lay along one wall, unworked timber along the other. On the tool shelf not a single chisel, file or saw was missing. The shelf beneath the window bore a neat row of tins of varnish and used brushes in jars of solvent. The floor had been swept. On the bench in the middle there were several long pieces of wood, already processed.

With resolute concentration, Kvido's mother began assembling them together. Kvido and Paco exchanged puzzled glances. In their mother's hands something was taking shape – something between a huge flower box and a bedding chest.

But as she turned the last piece over, they were startled to see on it a precision-turned cross.

"Your father," their mother said, her voice breaking, "is making himself a coffin."

Kvido's mother decided that that very day she would phone Dr Liehr from work.

"Well?" Kvido enquired when she came in.

The sight of her son, who seemed likely to be the prime cause of the latest development in his father's psychosis, got the better of her:

"Nothing!" she snapped back.

"What do you mean – nothing?"

"I'm to go and see him tomorrow," she said with a sigh. "For now we've got to make sure your father doesn't actually climb into it."

"Brilliant!" Kvido exclaimed. "How does he suppose we do that? Am I expected to stick with him all the time?"

His mother looked daggers at him.

"All right," said Kvido. "So I'll keep checking on him through the skylight."

Hardly had he said it when their father passed them as if sleepwalking, with a small, freshly gloss-painted length of wood held firm between his two index fingers: he went outside the front door to check, in the natural light, whether the raven black was intense enough. Kvido didn't know whether to bash his father on the head with something – or fall at his feet.

"There you have it," his mother said.

From that day onwards, the atmosphere in the home had something acutely depressive about it. It struck Kvido that the air of depression emanated straight from those pieces of wood and was permeating the entire house. He tried in vain to make light of it, he tried in vain to focus everyone's attention on something else. Conversation dried up and spirits flagged.

"It's difficult to share a joke with someone who sits down to dinner with his hands full of splinters from his own coffin," Kvido explained later. "That coffin – it was a masterstroke of *autopatination*."

3. "Identity? But we all lose it," Dr Liehr told Kvido's mother the next day. Kvido's father had gone to Nusle to his parents' and she had meanwhile brought Dr Liehr out for a coffee. They were sitting in the Luxor café.

"Yourself, for instance," Liehr went on. "You say you couldn't live without Prague – yet you stayed in the country anyway. You longed to go on the stage, or at least be around the theatre somehow – and now you watch television. You suffer from dog phobia – and you go and buy an Alsatian. So tell me, which is the real you?"

Kvido's mother pursed her lips. She liked Dr Liehr. She gazed at his fine broad beard and felt slightly envious of her husband: she'd always wanted a psychiatrist of her own. It struck her that her own problems would be at least as interesting to him as her husband's. Then she had a sudden image of her husband re-measuring the foot end of his coffin – and she squirmed.

"Incidentally, he painted some very nice pictures for me," said the doctor. "*Dinky little flower* pictures, I'd call them."

"Yes?" said Kvido's mother uncertainly. The doctor had put it oddly.

"And he's shown a lively interest in music therapy…"

"Do you mean he –"

"– he's been playing games. Trying to pull my leg…"

"But why?"

"He's probably afraid of me. He doesn't trust me. The fact that I hold my consultations in a boiler-room isn't evidence enough for him."

"Doctor," said Kvido's mother after a pause, "is there anything that might really help him?"

"Some kind of successful counter-revolution," the doctor replied without hesitation.

Kvido's mother smiled sadly.

"Until such time," the doctor added cheerily, "we have to keep him entertained!"

4. Kvido did his inspection rounds rather more briskly than his much older colleagues, and that always saved him a half-hour that he could spend somewhere in peace, without being missed. Now, in the summertime, he mostly spent it on the roof of the admin building. He soon got so used to it that he couldn't wait to leave the stifling offices behind, climb the iron ladder, open the heavy trapdoor – and then just inhale the mighty gush of fresh night air.

He usually sat on the tubular-steel construction that supported the massive neon light bearing the legend HAIL TO COMMUNISM, which Comrade Šperk had had installed several years previously and which they, the porters, had to switch on at nightfall. The letters, each one taller than Kvido himself, couldn't fail to draw whole clouds of midges and moths, which could be irksome, though by contrast the view out over the whole town was truly something else: there was the darkened river valley with the silvery shimmer of the water, the silhouette of the monastery, and the dozing housing estates. You could also see Šperk's house with the lower outbuilding housing the kennels, and the abandoned villa of Pavel Kohout, recognisable from its little water tower.

At one minute to ten, Kvido would hop up onto the steel pole supporting the letter I, which, thanks to its shape, afforded the best conditions for temporary concealment, stood astride it and flattened himself against the I. At the same moment, Kvido's mother was standing ready at the kitchen window, one hand on the light switch – and when she saw the letter on the distant neon sign go out, she flashed the light on and off a few times. The kitchen had two windows, and from that angle it looked to Kvido as if the house was winking at him.

The ritual took hold so firmly that Kvido's mother (and, later, Jarka as well) performed it not so much with indifference, but quite automatically, as if subconsciously. Visitors were often bewildered by the utterly matter-of-fact manner in which they would glance at the clock as the hour of ten approached – even in the middle of a conversation – and then go and stand by the window, their eyes fixed on the Communist slogan shining in the far distance. Given the irregular pattern of Kvido's shifts, it could happen that his mother would be staring, perplexed, at the neon text in all its inviolate perfection while Kvido was standing behind her, tickled pink. But then, not even he treated the arrangement with unalloyed reverence, the more so that his part in it was considerably more arduous; in inclement weather he would raise the trap with the greatest reluctance and when, lashed by rain or snow, he flattened himself against the sign, he would berate himself, his mother and, later, Jarka, with quite savage maledictions.

One day, in one corner of the roof, Kvido found an old roll of bitumen roofing felt and he conceived an idea that only cost him about twenty minutes and stubbornly black finger nails: he covered a couple of the letters in the roofing felt so that when his mother looked out on the stroke of ten, she read this rather dismissive interjection, though it lacked an exclamation mark:

HA TO COMMUNISM

"Has he gone mad?" she squawked in horror, then looked back to check that Kvido's father wasn't in the room; the sight would undoubtedly have meant his instant demise. When she looked back towards the horizon, there was no further sign of the sign.

5. "We're living a lie," Kvido would repeat after Kafka, and not only as he stood beneath the neon lights on the roof. He would think it as he earwigged outside meeting rooms, as he read the papers, as he was speaking to people.

The following Monday, the porters were summoned by the company director to a brief meeting so that he could go over the new system for locking the various floors of the admin building with them. Speaking of the machine room of the lifts, which was on the eleventh floor, he inexplicably got it wrong and kept referring to the twelfth floor. Someone soon corrected him automatically. However, something took root in Kvido's memory – without his even realising it yet – that would soon bring dividends: two nights later, as he settled down in his mother's office for his traditional three-hour nap, he had an instant's vision of the exact subject of his first novella, based on precisely such a mistake.

He sprang up, switched the desk lamp on and settled down at the desk. Acknowledging to himself that it was a bit silly, he nevertheless moved with extreme caution perhaps so as not to spook the fragile, immaterial substance that hung there before his eyes. Yet it transpired that there was nothing simpler than to get it down on his mother's office paper, except that the idea unfolded more quickly than his writing speed. What was coming to life beneath his hand was an absurd, but oh so familiar world – a world of falsehood tolerated in silence.

The novella's *sujet* was as follows: the director of a large enterprise puts his own man in charge of security. The latter is mentally disordered – a paranoiac – but that doesn't worry the director; the only thing that concerns him is that the new security chief does exactly as bidden – without asking questions. From the outset, the security chief is obsessed with all sorts of strange ideas: some just funny, others that could put people in danger. One of his delusions is that the company's eleven-storey building has twelve floors. Hence, he makes all those under him patrol even the non-existent one, or *pretend* to do so. With the director's tacit acquiescence, anyone who refuses has his bonuses cut and suffers all manner of persecution. There is no way of appealing to their rights or to common sense; those who are supposed to oversee the employees' rights are afraid of the director. So in their reports, the porters begin to record their rounds of the twelfth floor as well; some find it funny, others fume. But for a report to appear credible, it has to find all the usual problems on the twelfth floor as well, that is: broken locks, leaking taps, bulges in the lino, malfunctions in the drinks machine… The reports then get sent on through the customary bureaucratic channels – to the services and supplies department, the maintenance team and the cleaners. Thus, in their turn the maintenance men, jeering and sneering, report fictitious repairs or fictitious equipment. The cleaners, tapping their foreheads, make a pretence of sweeping fictitious corridors. The window cleaners happily submit invoices for cleaning non-existent windows. Once a crazy chain of falsehood begins, it drags everyone along with it. The abnormal is elevated to the normal.

It took Kvido just over three weeks to write his debut novella, *The Case of the Twelfth Floor*. On the last Sunday in August, he packed his manuscript up and on the Monday morning he despatched it express to the Prague publishing house whose editor had read his first short stories. "Czech literature," Kvido remarked on the occasion, "can wait no longer."

6. "My dear, young friend," the editor addressed Kvido the first time they met in person. "You're so deliciously naïve!"

Kvido was startled at the thought that the manuscript should contain anything indicative of his naivety. So he just looked mildly apologetic.

"Surely we can't go claiming that a first work is literature! You can't mean that it's a normal, proper book, can you?" the editor asked.

"Are you suggesting it isn't?" Kvido asked artlessly.

"Of course it isn't!" the editor guffawed. "It's a practice run, a trial or warm-up, call it what you will – but first and foremost, above all else, it isn't literature: a 'first work' is a common-or-garden test of political reliability!"

"Political reliability?" Kvido was genuinely puzzled.

He felt unforgivably wet behind the ears.

"Of course!" the editor was still laughing. "You really didn't know? – By the way, do you know what's completely missing? A character who's a *worker*."

"Worker?" said Kvido.

"Man," said the editor, "you can't get by without a worker. Who creates anything of worth? A worker! Not a porter."

"I don't know any," Kvido objected.

"Then get to know some!" the editor enjoined him.

XII.

1. All that winter, Kvido's mother wondered how she should distract her husband and stop him thinking about death. The coffin was nearly finished and she was mortified at what might come next.

One day, as their father was lining his dismal artefact with densely gathered satin, she summoned her two sons.

"Shut that dog away somewhere," she commanded them. "I want to tell you something important."

Paco locked Sweetie in the living room and sat down with Kvido and their mother at the kitchen table. For a moment she observed them in silence.

"I think there's only one way to snap him out of it," she said. "A baby. I'm sure a baby would do the trick."

"A baby?" Paco exclaimed, looking at Kvido.

The thought that the household, with its mysticism-obsessed grandmother and half-crazed father, should now have a baby visited upon it left the boys feeling awkward – to put it mildly. Their mother was now forty.

"Your baby," she clarified, looking at Kvido with great solemnity.

"What!!" Kvido yelped. "Am I hearing right? Whose daft idea is that?"

"It's the only solution," his mother said. "You have to do it, for him."

"I must be dreaming!" Kvido clasped his head in his hands. "My own mother trying to persuade me to get a girl in trouble! Wasn't it enough that you made me take my driving test? You always do the opposite of what you should. Normal mothers tell their sons to be careful! Next you'll be wanting me to catch the clap!"

His mother looked at him reproachfully.

"I'm sorry," said Kvido. "You're psyching me out. Why the hell can't that fancy doctor help him?"

"Because your father's scared of him," his mother said bluntly. "He's taken it into his head he's from the Ministry of the Interior…"

"He could be," said Paco.

"You stay out of things you don't understand," his mother scolded him. Then she gave a colourful account of the magical metamorphosis that would be wrought by the arrival of a tiny baby in the household.

"Can anyone remain indifferent to tiny hands stretched out beseechingly towards them?" she asked. "Can anyone remain indifferent to a wide-eyed little mite watching them in wonderment?"

"Right," said Paco. "Next thing he'll be converting the coffin into a cradle."

"Stop it. That's not funny!" his mother exploded.

"Let Paco bring a baby from the forest," Kvido suggested. "I bet he's got one there anyway."

"Kvido," said his mother. "I'm being serious. This way, you make amends."

"Amends for what?" Kvido shrieked. "Can't that doctor give him some pills? I can't understand why you're so against it."

"I'll say it again," said his mother, "the pills that don't have side-effects didn't work on your father. I don't want to try the others because I don't want to live with someone who isn't the one I married."

"Oh my God," Kvido sighed. "What about his Yugoslav mistress?" he asked cautiously. "Has anyone spoken to her?"

"Now then," said his mother calmly. "I'll let that pass; I wanted to do the very thing. I'm assuming she can't afford the time."

"No she can't," Kvido agreed. "How did you know?"

"I've seen the phone bill."

"Are my ears deceiving me?" Paco exclaimed. "And you can talk about it just like that? Disgusting!"

"That's life, Paco," said his mother.

Kvido avoided her eyes.

"I'm relying on you," she said once she caught his.

"So," said Kvido next day to Jarka, "if you want to marry me and have a baby with me, why not do it now, especially if it would help my father, allegedly?"

Jarka was – how could she not be – slightly taken aback, but then she agreed, almost eagerly.

Kvido, who had been expecting a reasonable period of indecision, was pleased, but equally somewhat mystified.

"Why should a beautiful girl of twenty decide out of the blue to have a baby for the benefit of two porters?" his surprise led him to ask.

"Because she wants to escape from the boring job of being a computer programmer into motherhood!" Jarka repeated crossly the notion that he had ventured the day before.

"So why then?"

"For goodness' sake!" she exclaimed. "D'you mean you haven't noticed that she loves you?"

Anticipation of a mission that was by its very nature an assignment had, as per tradition, a traumatic effect on Kvido. Hitherto, he had gone into lovemaking *voluntarily*, and so with relish, but the thought of that evening when, at his mother's behest, he would launch at Jarka's waiting ovum several million of his own sperm, depressed him.

"If we catch it this month, your dad can have the baby for his birthday," Jarka said with a smile.

"Don't rush me," said Kvido. "If the worst comes to the worst he can have his present late."

Jarka sensed at once (she was well used to it by now) how nervous he was getting. She didn't mind him writing all over her belly, or even her back – she'd got hold of some allergy pills that worked – but intuitively, and rightly, she was worried whether the same trick would work a second time. It was nagging at her. Discounting the bilberry tart, the baby proposition was the first job her future mother-in-law had entrusted to her – hence her desire to make a good go of it. It was on her mind day in and day out, until finally chance came to her aid. One evening, as she was watching television, she remembered how Kvido had once made her laugh with his tale of the eager anticipation with which he had waited to see a certain X-rated film that had been denied him for many long years, and she had a crazy idea.

On that memorable day, she invited Kvido to her girlfriend's flat. The table was already laden with open sandwiches, a bottle of bubbly and roasted almonds, but Kvido wasn't at ease in this alien milieu. He began to appreciate how great is the responsibility of the man assigned to take a penalty, as his father had once explained to him. Several times over, he checked the curtains, but couldn't rid himself of the notion that he was being watched, the eyes focussed right on his crotch. By the time Jarka finally disappeared through the bedroom door, he was utterly downcast.

"I'll call you when I'm ready," she told him.

Said the hangman, Kvido thought to himself.

Meanwhile Jarka stuck a large X in the lower left-hand corner of the glass door panel; she'd cut it out of a sheet of sturdy drawing paper. Then she covered the bedside lamp with a blue scarf she had ready for the purpose and switched the lamp on.

"Ready!" she called.

Kvido looked gloomily at the door and got up in surprise. The points of the X on the giant screen of the door promised things so unsuitable for children that he gulped with the thrill of it. Titillating shadows were outlined in the bluish half-light and there was no one in the offing who could switch the programme off. He felt a stunning erection coming on.

"Come on!" said Jarka.

2. At the beginning of April Jarka and Kvido went to the cinema, the Yalta in Prague. They arrived shortly before six, so the show had already started – an American film, *Planet of the Apes*. Kvido bought a ticket though without expecting to see the film through to the end, and Zita and Jarka, with the manager's consent, locked themselves in the office.

Kvido was instantly so caught up by the speed of the action that when, twenty minutes later, a torch was shone in his face, it came as an unwelcome intrusion.

"Come!" said the usherette.

"Already?" said Kvido.

"Quiet!" someone commanded.

Zita and Jarka were already in the foyer. Jarka was flushed.

"It's for real, Kvido!" said Zita with a smile.

"Seriously?" Kvido replied. "Is it certain?"

"Don't forget she's a consultant; she's never been wrong

before!" Zita's colleague assured him.

The manager came to congratulate the young couple; the usherettes and cloakroom attendants all formed an orderly queue to follow suit.

"Thank you, thank you," Kvido responded, feeling rather awkward.

"And remember me to your parents," said Zita.

"I've got something to tell you," Kvido told them over dinner.

"On the subject of...?" his mother asked cautiously, given that more and more subjects had become taboo.

"Babies," he said, giving his mother a piercing look.

His mother was interested and lay down her knife and fork.

"We're all listening," she said with a fleeting glance in the direction of her husband. He was rolling the last bite round in his mouth and staring into his plate.

Paco was grinning. Grandma Líba accidentally took a sip of her acidophilic milk through the damp cloth she kept over her mouth, leaving a thick, white nimbus on it.

"I'm expecting one," said Kvido. "A baby."

"A baby?" his mother exclaimed joyfully. "Really? Is it definite?"

Kvido showed her his cinema ticket as if it were proof of his pregnancy.

"Brilliant!" his mother was jubilant. "Isn't that wonderful? We're going to have a baby in the house! Can't you just imagine the little thing looking at us wide-eyed for the first time? Stretching out its tiny arms to us? Pursing its little lips?

Or babbling all those first words?"

She bent down to give Kvido a kiss.

"You're up for an Oscar," she whispered.

Her eyes shining bright, she scanned the others at the table. Except for Paco, who was plainly enjoying the fun, they seemed not to share her enthusiasm.

"Well, what do you say to that then?" she prompted Kvido's father into offering a view.

"He's not got a shred of responsibility," he said mutedly.

"Why so?" his mother dissented. "He's grown-up, got a job, publishes stories…"

"You'd have to be crazy to have a child in times like these!" his father said in a whisper.

With a happy sigh his mother just shrugged.

There you have it, Kvido's body language told his mother.

It'll change, her eyes declared optimistically.

"And what will you call him if it's a boy?" she was curious to know.

"Diazepam," said Kvido. "After his granddad."

"And will they be having the kids' room?" Grandma Líba enquired suspiciously.

"You'll have that," Kvido's mother rejoined. "They'll go up in the garret."

"And what about me?" Paco asked.

"Since when have you been keen to sleep indoors?"

3. "Marry in May, rue the day," Grandma Líba warned Kvido malevolently.

So the marriage had to be in April, and the only date available at the hall of ceremonies in Sázava's erstwhile monastery was on Saturday the thirtieth.

"Can't do the thirtieth," Kvido's father said with a shake of his head. "I've got a wreath-laying with the football club."

"Wreaths are laid in the evening," Kvido's mother could not acknowledge his argument. "The wedding's at eleven in the morning."

"I'll have to miss half the wedding breakfast," he objected.

"Since when were you a big eater?" his wife asked. "You'll only throw it all up anyway! Incidentally, you'll have to drive," she now remembered. "There won't be enough drivers."

"Are you crazy?" he shouted. "How can I drive a car in my condition?"

"As far as I'm aware, no one's issued you with a driving ban."

"You're expecting me to weave a car through hundreds of bystanders? Suppose I kill someone? You haven't thought of that, have you?"

"Hundreds of bystanders," Kvido's mother derided. "Pull yourself together. This isn't Robert Redford getting married! You don't need to worry: if we meet anyone on the way, I'll warn you in time."

"But I'm half-blind!" he cried.

"If you can cross the Alps and get as far as Yugoslavia, you can drive one kilometre on the flat," she assured him. "And since it's you, I'll personally shoo any deer away."

"So you want a wedding-day blood-bath!" he shouted. "All right, then!"

The wedding preparations, which had to be expedited because of the April date, fell in practice to Kvido's mother. Grandma Líba went off with her friends on a cut-price, low-season tour to Szolnok in Hungary, Paco, as spring progressed, spent more and more time in the woods, and his father, when not in his porter's lodge or workshop, spent an eternity poring over his home-drawn maps of all three crossroads that awaited him on the way to the monastery. Kvido beavered away at the text of his novella.

"I've already done my bit," he would say loftily, his gaze fixed on Jarka's slowly ballooning smock.

The most urgent matter was the compilation of the guest list so that the invitations could be sent out in timely fashion. Jarka's family was not numerous and from the column of names that Kvido's mother had drawn up as a preliminary, his father crossed out all her Prague friends, dismissing them as political stuntwomen, so it looked like being quite a small wedding. But everything could yet be changed by Grandma Líba, whose latest poem, on a black-and-white postcard from Szolnok, twice referred to their lovely, elderly guide, his wife and children as "the most fantastic family she'd ever met".

"It'll be all right on the day," Kvido's mother tried with a smile to reassure Jarka, who alone came over to help quite often. The practical nature of the preparations quickly brought them close – and when Kvido found them laughing together, the tears rolling down their cheeks and their arms all intertwined as they tried in vain to make sense of the ribbon to tie the myrtle with, he felt for the first time that marvellous, comforting sense of the profoundest security possible.

"It's hard to describe accurately," Kvido explained, "but try imagining you're out in the rain in a perfectly passable raincoat and suddenly you get an umbrella as well."

XIII.

1. Several days before the wedding, Kvido's father decided once and for all that he would drive the roughly eleven hundred metres from his garage to the ceremony, *taking no chances*, as the saying goes. He duly fulfilled his resolution to the letter, though the speed he selected would have been better suited to a funeral. He ignored the uncomprehending horns tooting behind him and the ever lengthening gap ahead of him, gripped the steering wheel tightly and maintained a cool, collected concentration.

The wedding party having alighted from the cars, lined up in due form and set out for the gravelled courtyard outside the monastery, a first surprise awaited them in the form of a double row of eight uniformed members of the glassworks security squad, having an average age of sixty-seven.

"Honour guard: 'ten-*tion*!" their commander commanded in his geriatric voice. Kvido had suspected something of the kind, because several times recently, as he came back from his rounds, the other porters had fallen silent, smiling slyly. But now, as he saw all those puffy, wrinkly, rheumaticky hands, shaking with the heroic effort of sustaining a salute, at least briefly, he had to fight back an unexpected surge of emotion.

"Stand easy!" he cried in a strangled voice.

Surprise No. 2, if it's not actually to be described as a minor sensation, was provided by Comrade Mrs Šperk, who for the benefit of her former star recitationists had brought to the hall of ceremonies two of her current charges, also a boy and a girl, in their Young Pioneer outfits.

"How very nice!" said Grandpa Josef. "Pioneers!"

"Stop that!" Grandma Vera whispered angrily.

Kvido's mother's expression was neutral.

To Kvido's father's horror, the person who appeared beneath the state coat of arms next to the velvet curtain, was Comrade Šperk. He wore a smile.

"That's him," Kvido's mother whispered to Dr Liehr. "Look at him grinning."

"Him?" the psychiatrist expressed some surprise.

"Stop that!" Kvido's father snarled.

It was nearly time for the recitation. The Young Pioneer took his partner's hand and began. Comrade Mrs Šperk winked at Jarka.

"This land is beauteous as a bride,
  no other is so pretty.
  How happy wouldst thou there reside!
  'Tis the land of liberty."

the boy recited. Reaching the words "happy wouldst thou there reside", he turned his face quickly towards the girl. Comrade Mrs Šperk nodded. Kvido glanced at Jarka. He noticed her lips moving beneath her veil.

"The rivulet clears itself a way
  and then o'erspills its wall.
  Our peace of mind and all our joy
  is in the happiness of all,"

the young performers ended in unison.
"God almighty!" Paco muttered sotto voce.
"We thank the Pioneers for such a nice curtain-raiser," said Comrade Šperk and nodded benignly to the registrar.

2. For reasons of economy the wedding breakfast was held at home, on three tables pushed together on the patio. It wasn't remotely extravagant.

"As a porter, you can't expect miracles." Kvido's mother didn't mince her words.

The meal consisted of schnitzels with potato salad. With beer to drink.

"No beer for him!" Grandma Vera insisted, covering her husband's glass with one hand.

"Did you hear that?" he asked, appealing for sympathy from the others. He stood up abruptly and went for a walk in the garden.

"To the table!" Kvido's father called with a nervous, if radiant smile.

Paco brought a tape-recorder.

"You might listen to that tape now – since we've got that Commie ritual behind us," he implored his brother. "You've been promising me for a week at least!"

"Forget that now!" his father begged.

"Spare me, bro! Isn't it enough that I'm getting married? Do I have to listen to your campfire songs as well?"

"They're not campfire songs!" Paco protested and to prove his point he pressed the start button – the shady, arched veranda swelled at once to the voice of Karel Kryl.

"For God's sake, turn it off!" his mother ordered. "We'd like to eat in peace."

"Later, Paco," Kvido reassured his brother.

"I wonder…"

"Salami in a *potato salad*!" Grandma Líba was suddenly horrified. "And the carrots – they're from the shop!"

"Indeed so," said Kvido's mother defiantly.

"*Shop* carrots!" her mother wailed. "Do you know how many micrograms of nitrates are permitted per litre of urine?"

No one replied.

"More beer?" Kvido asked his slightly awestruck

mother-in-law.

"Thank you."

"Do you?" Grandma Líba repeated.

"How many?" Dr Liehr had to ask.

"Eighty. And do you know how many we have on average?"

"How many?"

"*Seven hundred and thirty!*" Grandma Líba shrieked in triumph. "And she blithely gets her carrots *from the shop*."

"Last year, I had five whole beds of carrots," Kvido's mother explained sedately to the doctor. "And in a single month she used up the whole lot on carrot fritters."

The psychiatrist shot Kvido's father a look of commiseration, brimming with masculine solidarity.

"Excuse me a moment," Kvido's father apologised, getting up.

"Where are you going?" his mother asked. "You're not laying those wreaths till eight."

"Don't worry," his father said somewhat mysteriously.

A minute later the plaintive whine of the broach cutter rose from the bowels of the house.

"Doctor Liehr," said Kvido's mother. "Would you mind pouring me some of that bottle?"

3. Kvido's father rejoined the wedding meal only as it was approaching nine o'clock. He was in a red tracksuit and was quite bathed in sweat. In his left hand he held a flaming torch.

Mr Zvára, who arrived with him, was dressed normally; he was carrying a funeral wreath with a red ribbon and the legend Sports Club picked out in gold.

"I didn't have time to put it out," said Kvido's father, panting. He glanced at the wreath. "The idiots ordered two of them," he added by way of explanation.

"Never mind," said Kvido's mother with a smile and an oddly soft diction. "You'll find a way to deal with it!"

"There he was singing the *Internationale* instead of singing for his son's wedding," said Mr Zvára, laughing. "So I thought I'd better bring him home."

"Mr Zvára," Paco was struggling with his words. "Answer me one question –"

"No questions!" Kvido was exasperated. "Who let him have beer?"

His father tossed the torch into the rainwater barrel. There was a loud hiss.

"Are you a member of the Communist Party?" Paco called out.

"A good question," said Liehr. "The boy's got talent."

"How would you fancy a trip in a submarine, Doctor?" Kvido's mother asked merrily. "I mean with me?"

"That's not so straightforward, lad," said Zvára with an unpleasant smile.

"My husband sank our canoe!"

"Clear off, then! We're no red vanguard here!" Paco roared hoarsely.

From the bend in the road came the sound of a brass band approaching.

"The procession's coming!" Kvido's father cried angrily.

"Come on inside!"

"Ignore it," Kvido said to Zvára. "He's pissed…"

"I adore processions!" Kvido's mother whooped. "Don't you, Doctor?"

"What's he to ignore?" screamed Paco. "The truth? Honour? Conscience?"

"Not really," said the doctor. "But I do like lantern parades."

"You little warrior of ours!" said Kvido to Paco. "Get off to bed!"

"They're here!" their father called out anxiously. "Inside, all of you, quickly!"

"Bring them in," their mother demanded. "I've got the urge to dance with your doctor! What do you think, Jarka, shall we have a dance?"

"Yes!" Jarka enthused.

In the half-light above the road, the musicians' instruments glinted. Behind them you could just see the first little yellow-coloured lights."

"I'll fetch them!" said Mr Zvára, hoping to escape Paco's questions.

A few minutes later, the whole band, followed by part of the lantern parade, were standing round the veranda. Jarka went from one to the next bearing a tray full of glasses.

"To the bride and groom!" said the bandleader.

"A solo for the newlyweds!" someone shouted out.

The bandsmen placed their glasses back on the tray and gladly abandoned their revolutionary repertoire. A gliding waltz rang out into the warm air of evening. Kvido's heels sank into the soft grass on the lawn. Jarka was radiant; as her back brushed against the drooping branches of the nearest apple tree, the shoulders of her wedding dress were showered with pinkish-white petals.

"Sod the band!" Paco shouted, but fortunately nobody understood him. The next tune was for everybody. More than ten couples took to the lawn. Kvido and Jarka left to replenish their glasses. In the kitchen they ran into several children who were quite unknown to them.

"Hi, kids!" said Kvido.

"Hello," said the children. "We're thirsty."

"This is going to ruin the May Day celebrations," Kvido's father whispered to Mr Zvára. "There'll be hell to pay!"

"Don't let it get to you, man!" Zvára retorted.

Kvido's father disappeared down the cellar steps. Jarka did another round of the musicians and clinked glasses with the bandleader.

"Cheers, Mr Porter," one lad said to Kvido. "I'm Míla."

"Hi, Míla!" said Kvido.

A kind of inebriated fraternising broke out in the garden.

"I'd like to live in the country," Dr Liehr said to Kvido's mother.

"Don't be daft," she returned. "Can you tango?"

"There's nothing to drink," Míla said to Kvido. He turned an empty bottle upside down.

"You come with me," Kvido said. "We'll find something."

On the cellar steps they met an elderly man.

"*Good evening, sir,*" said Kvido with a smile.

"*Good evening,*" the man smiled back.

"Who was that?" Míla wanted to know.

"A friend of my grandma's," said Kvido. "Hungarian."

They ran into Grandma Líba. She was carrying a cardboard box.

"*Hallo!*" said Kvido.

"Hungarian?" Míla asked.

"Grandma," said Kvido. "Stealing salamis."

"That's brill!" said Míla.

"D'you want some salami?" Kvido asked.

They glanced into the workshop and Míla jumped back, aghast.

"What's that?" he shrieked.

"My father. Trying out his coffin."

"That's brill," said Míla. "What a great family you are."

"What do *you* do, Míla?" Kvido asked.

"Me?" said Míla. "I'm a worker."

"That's brill," said Kvido. "You've no idea how long I've been looking for you."

XIV.

1. A week after the wedding, Kvido met up with the editor again. This time he finally understood that any hope of seeing *The Case of the Twelfth Floor* published was practically zero, irrespective of whether or not he succeeded in implanting the character of the worker Míla into the text.

Hence he set the manuscript aside for good and started casting about for a new, less controversial subject, as the publishing house had in any case suggested he should.

He then spent many nights in his mother's darkened office thinking about possible characters for his next story – but the moment he let his gaze slip from his notes to the family photos under the glass on her desk, it came to him, time and again, that none of the characters he'd invented came within ten per cent of being as interesting, authentic and convincing as the people in the photos: his father, his mother, Paco, Grandma Líba and Grandpa Jiří. Whenever, in the course of weaving his plots, he abandoned the strangers with odd-sounding names, like Jan Hart or Florián Farský, simply to drift into thinking about Grandma Vera or Grandpa Josef, he had the acute sensation that the horizons of his imagination had gained infinitely in breadth. Kvido – like many before him – was learning that he would scarcely find a story other than his own.

"Le roman, c'est moi!" he cried.

The supposedly uncontroversial nature of the cosy story that was taking shape was, as Kvido was soon to discover, but one more grand illusion: social reality seeped through the walls of the house he was writing about from the very first pages, entirely independently, as he thought, of his will. Of course, that wasn't to the liking of the editor.

"How's it gone?" Jarka would ask in the morning, having found the lamp on Kvido's desk still on.

"Oh, you know," said Kvido and set about rubbing cream into the tightening skin on her bulge, as the handbooks dictated. "It's a crazy job – stitching something together out of the half-truths the editor wants in it. Like this: I'm allowed to be born in the theatre, but certainly not during *Waiting for Godot*, because it's existentialist. Would the idiot have me born in *The Bartered Bride*? Jarka laughed and hauled her nightie over her head. Kvido put his nose to her, relishing her smell, and his fingers were fascinated by the starchy patches of dried milk. He looked at her. He found her dark, enlarged nipples off-putting, but the handbooks did say that they would shrink back to normal.

"You ought to get dressed," he said. "Míla will be here any minute."

"Again?" Jarka made a long face.

Kvido flung his arms wide, but it was clear he was thinking about something else. He went back to the desk and glanced at the sheets covered in writing.

"I need to let those three bloody birds fly away, without bringing in Russian planes," he said. He took hold of one of the sheets.

"They might have been put to flight by a car back-firing, or by the shadow of the wings of a bird of prey that had strayed this far in from the outskirts of the city," he read sceptically. "What do you think?"

"I like it," said Jarka. "But I'm not the person to ask."

"They probably won't let me go with the bird of prey," Kvido mused out loud. "Let alone on August twenty-first…"

Jarka placed her hand lightly on the empty cot, which she and Kvido had repainted a couple of days previously. The white paint seemed to be holding.

"I probably won't be allowed to have Grandpa Jiří at all," Kvido went on. "When I asked the guy who he thought Grandma had become pregnant by, he said he'd even prefer self-fertilisation to some advocate of the Prague Spring. Excellent, I told him, but what about my other grandfather – how much do you think he should have felled in a shift? As much as he liked, the editor said, but the main thing is that he should keep his mouth shut!"

"That's awful," said Jarka sincerely.

"But I'll let him have his way!" Kvido raised his voice and his eyes shone with a strangely intense resolve. "He can have it all: I'll bury Grandpa Jiří in timely fashion, perhaps at fifty, in a car crash or something, and my other grandpa shall be a shock-worker, but without the power of speech, I'll make my mother into a jilted actress and my father… my father will be an insane, jealous woodcarver. And Grandma? A dotty herbalist! No contaminated foods!" Kvido shouted.

"Tomatoes make me bloated," said Jarka.

"You too?" said Kvido. "Míla says he'll bring us some from his allotment."

He put the paper back on the desk.

He shook his head wretchedly.

"You can't imagine it, but having to hide one's book away in a drawer is like putting your offspring in a children's home."

A stream of hot tears burst from Jarka.

"Don't be silly!" Kvido was startled.

"I'm permanently on the verge of tears," she sobbed happily.

2. However, the editor at the publishing house wasn't Kvido's only censor.

One day, he heard the postwoman lashing out at Sweetie in the hall.

"It's a good thing you're here," he called to her. "She'd got that coming – keeps jumping on the wife's belly!"

"I've got a registered letter for you," the postwoman said, catching her breath.

Sweetie tucked her bushy tail between her rear legs and crawled out of reach with a whimper.

A moment later, when Kvido opened the letter, he was surprised to find it was from his mother.

"Dear Kvido," he read, "I hope she gave the bitch a good thrashing. She was starting to jump up at me more than I could take again, and I was happy to sacrifice four crowns for the registered letter fee.

"As I expect you suspect, the essence of my letter lies elsewhere. So why am I writing to you? I need to confess something: I've gone against your wishes and last night, while you were at work, I read the unfinished chapters of your novel."

"I'll kill her!" Kvido exclaimed.

"I read them in one go, and as I got to the end around daybreak, the birds were already singing, I was all stiff and numb, but also touched and enraged at the same time. I decided to write to you at once. I know you're having a tough time even without me interfering, and I also know how you always give me that claim that the basis of autobiography is the least interesting angle from which a book can be read. Except... do others know? All those people who know us and are going to read the book? And judge us accordingly? Did you think about these people when you described the water trampled all over the house, the balls of fluff, the overflowing, putrefying rubbish bin or the toilet surround spattered with urine? Did you consider them when you wrote – quite amusingly, I agree –

about Grandma's pilfering souvenirs when she's abroad? Kvido, I do understand that a writer can't disguise his life experience in any other way than in a novel – on the other hand, I really don't wish to live to see the day when my friends develop an aversion to our toilet! And anyway – forgive such a down-to-earth question – why didn't *you* clean it? I know what you'll say – you *wrote* about it."

"Great God in Heaven!" Kvido whispered.

"Your father and I, Kvido, have always tried to make what we call a home for you," his mother's letter went on. "The times (or fate perhaps) decreed that what emerged instead of a home in the true sense of the word was a strange combination of a carpentry workshop, psychiatric hospital and old people's home. As my beloved Cordelia puts it: We are not the first who, with best meaning, have incurred the worst.

I understand what you mean. That no woman will turn into a brilliant mother merely by hoovering and cleaning the toilet; it's clear that you consider these things secondary. But again: do others know this? The snag is that you don't explicitly say as much anywhere.

I feel, Kvido, like a schoolgirl begging her teacher to give her a better mark – and here I am, your mother. My father used to use formal terms of address with my mother. No, of course, I'm not asking that of you, but couldn't you at least dispense with those urine stains? How much sharper than the adder's tooth is the ingratitude of one's own child! I tell myself with Eugene O'Neill. I don't think you're ungrateful – you say a lot of nice things about me – just a trifle unjust. You *must* see that, *objectively*, it couldn't have been me, a woman, who peed all over it.

I wish you could see me blushing as I'm obliged to write about such things – and there's nobody here to see me even. Are you really prepared to let thousands of total strangers see into my private life?

Please, dear, think about it.

Love from Mum."

"This is driving me mad!" Kvido ejaculated. "It's impossible to write anything in this country!"

3. Kvido would arrange his appointments with the editor so as to coincide with Jarka's trips to see Zita, and they would travel up to Prague together.

"You know, of course, that it was O'Neill who stipulated that his *autobiographical* play was not to appear until twenty-five years after his death," the editor said with a laugh when Kvido told him about his mother's letter. "At the time he made that stipulation, none of his family members was even alive! Your problem is that you want to publish when they're all very much alive!"

"Grandma's allegedly got cancer, and my father is building his coffin," said Kvido dryly. "So it's looking good."

"Irony's going to be your metier," the editor laughed. "I keep telling you."

"You could be right," said Kvido. "My problem remains

wanting to publish it at all. In this day and age and with you of all people."

"And yet," said the editor, "what else can thinking people and humanists do but keep groping for the right words?"

"Stop groping," said Kvido.

"So, how'd it go?" Kvido asked Jarka when they met up in the city centre.

"All okay!" Jarka reported with a smile. "Zita says hello – and how about you?"

"Me?" Kvido paused to consider how it had gone. "I'd probably call myself a high-risk pregnancy."

"I was wrong," he would explain later. "Under the care of that particular editor I was completely risk-free."

4. On Wednesday, June twentieth, Kvido was on the night shift. That afternoon the sun had peeped out between the clouds. He forced himself to go out and rake up the fallen beech leaves below the patio, as his mother wished. Shortly, he was joined by Jarka's now majestic figure, which raised a smile in him, but he wouldn't let her do any more than rake onto the fire the few leaves that the wind had blown off his heap.

"How are you feeling?" he asked.

"Good," she said.

"And how's Annie?"

"Annie? I don't know," Jarka said mischievously, "but Jimmie's good as well."

Kvido tipped the last basketful of leaves onto the fire, put his free arm round his wife's waist and so entwined they went indoors. There he got washed and changed while Jarka measured some coffee into his little tin and wrapped a few slices of the tart that she'd baked that morning. She put everything in one section of his briefcase and he filled the other with the book he was reading and the sheet of notes he was making on the Jarka character.

"I'll wave," he said automatically.

Jarka held her cheek out for a kiss.

However, when, about five hours later, Kvido scrambled up onto the load-bearing construction of the neon thing on the roof, he was troubled to discover that almost the entire house was in darkness; the only light was in the playroom. He waited in case the light in the kitchen came on, but it didn't. So he hopped back down on to the bitumen-covered roof and spent some fifteen minutes in rather gloomy contemplation. The kitchen windows remained stubbornly dark. He climbed back down the ladder to the corridor and quickly completed the rest of his rounds. He decided that once downstairs he would ask his boss for permission to pop home.

As soon as he entered the room behind the porter's lodge, he saw some full glasses on the table. All three porters were standing there, their grins laying bare their yellow-stained dentures.

"They've just phoned from Kutná Hora," the commander said. "It's a girl, you little shit!"

XV.

Visiting day at the Kutná Hora hospital. New fathers and other relatives are standing on the trampled grass outside the maternity unit. The mothers are leaning out of the third-floor window.

> JARKA (*with unfeigned delight*): Hi! You're early. That's great.
> 1ST FATHER: And why can't you sit up?
> 1ST MOTHER: Could be they sewed me up badly...?
> KVIDO (*conspicuously rapidly*): We came in the car.
> 1ST MOTHER: Or the incision was crooked...?
> JARKA (*impressed*): Really? Did you drive?
> KVIDO (*conspicuously reluctantly*): Yeah.
> JARKA (*alarmed*): What happened?
> PACO: Nothing. He ran over a dog.

JARKA (*consolingly*): That could happen to any driver, Kvido. Cheer up!

PACO: Except this one was inside its kennel…

(*Laughter; all the visitors look in astonishment at Kvido*)

KVIDO (*annoyed, to Paco*): And who kept shouting Go left! Go left! You wanted to go left, so I went left.

PACO (*explaining to Jarka*): At first I thought he'd only run over the kennel, but as I was clearing the broken planks, there was the pooch. Dead…

KVIDO'S MOTHER: Do we have to talk about dogs? (*She looks towards Annie in Jarka's arms*): Can't you see Annie rolling her lovely brown peepers?

JARKA (*apologetically, glancing at her daughter*): She's just fallen asleep…

2ND MOTHER: He's completely shredded my nipples.

2ND FATHER: Who?

2ND MOTHER: Baby Luke, silly…

KVIDO'S MOTHER: Everything's ready. Grandma's made us all some surgical masks.

JARKA (*touched*): But that's –"

KVIDO'S MOTHER: Of course, Sweetie will be wearing a muzzle… (*Glances at her husband, who is just standing there, smiling shyly*) Go on then, show her the toys…!

KVIDO'S FATHER: (*taking several wooden toys out of a bag*): I've… For the little one… (*His voice gives up the ghost*)

JARKA (*crying*): Thank you. They're really lovely! Thank you.

KVIDO (*in alarm*): Why are you crying? You're dripping

all over her!"

(*Annie wakes and starts crying*)

PACO: Now that's what I call a protest song!

KVIDO'S MOTHER: Is it wind? The best thing for that is fennel.

PACO: Long live natural healing, obscurantism and ignorance!

KVIDO'S MOTHER: Shut up and go and wash the windscreen for Kvido! (*Turning to Jarka*) And what about the swelling?

JARKA (*blowing her nose*): It turns out I'm allergic to ethacridine.

PACO: We can't go back through the same village – they'll be waiting for us with pitchforks at the ready...

KVIDO'S MOTHER: You're supposed to be washing that windscreen!

PACO: I doubt it'll help. When he rammed into that kennel, the glass was completely –

KVIDO'S MOTHER (*angrily*): Beat it! (*Turns to her husband*) Aren't you going to say something? Nobody's forcing you to start criticising our socialist health service; you could say something quite *unobjectionable* –

KVIDO (*interrupting her*): Mum!

KVIDO'S MOTHER (*ignoring his reproof*): – like how you wanted to paint the little black horse with the same paint –

KVIDO: Mum!

KVIDO'S MOTHER: – you recently used to paint your coffin with! (*General consternation among all present*)

KVIDO (*after a pause*): Well, we'd better get going.
JARKA (*choking back her tears*): Will you wave to us?
KVIDO: Of course I will.

XVI.

1. Kvido's mother's hypothesis that the addition of a baby to the household would have a dramatic impact on how his father's neurosis developed unfortunately failed to be confirmed. He did make Annie a few more wooden animals, miniature prams and a range of more or less mobile dolls, and he did play with her every day, but there was little if any change to his condition.

However, it wasn't long before something else popped up that in the years to come was to shift Kvido's father's focus away from death and at least to the fringes of living. And that was perestroika. He now spent less time on his coffin (which was, incidentally, so lavishly decorated with chip-carved detail that it had lost much of its gruesome severity and now looked more like the parts of a gingerbread house) and more on the current affairs output from the Soviet *Vremja* TV channel, most especially the speeches of Mr Gorbachev. He was inevitably at work on some occasions when they were being broadcast, so Kvido's mother would tape them on a cheap video recorder made in Hong Kong that Mr Zvára had once brought his father back from a trip to the West.

The whine of Kvido's father's woodturning lathe was now supplanted by the oddly impassioned voice of the lady who gave the running translations of Gorbachev's speeches. He seemed drawn to, if not bewitched by, the voice – just as he was apparently incapable of taking his eyes off that broad face, so unusually animated for an Eastern politician, seemingly spellbound by the mysterious birthmark on the statesman's cranium. Kvido's mother had to suppress a twinge of elation whenever she caught her husband hastily switching on his desk lamp and grabbing a notebook and pen so as to jot down this or that idea coming from the Secretary General, or when, now and again, she registered in his habitually motionless features a faint, but still detectable reflection of Mikhail Sergeyevich's frequent smiles.

"Did you see that?" she would whisper happily to Kvido.

"Our good old Slavic faith in Russia!" was Kvido's mocking response. "We can get our fingers burnt a hundred times over, yet we never learn!"

"You might not believe me," his mother said calmly, "but I'd much rather have his blind faith in Russia than see him getting the bits and bobs ready for his funeral."

"For God's sake," Kvido said in tones of derision. "It's not that long ago that was dodging back to the pavement so as not to get mown down by Soviet tanks, and now he's linking all the nation's aspirations to Russia..." He smirked. "Things won't be well for us until Boris Yeltsin fills the radiator of his Volga with water from the Vltava!"

"Look here," said his mother, "I couldn't care less if he linked the nation's aspirations to Equatorial Guinea. And I'd be grateful if you didn't go about disproving his truth. I'm glad he believes in something at least, even if blindly. His brain is full enough of disproved truths already."

"What he's got isn't a brain," said Paco. "It's a forest with all the trees blown down."

Kvido's father now spent endless hours trying to get hold of Soviet periodicals, including ones published inside Czechoslovakia, and then reading them; they had begun serving up the truth to their readers in unprecedented concentrations. He wasn't surprised so much by the truth being put about as by its being put about in the very country that everyone had held up to him as a model.

Years of ideological enslavement had suddenly turned into something positive. If they can think it, so can we, Kvido's father mused in his infantile fashion. Having read, for example, that the time had come for the intelligentsia to stop being distrusted and ordered about, he believed that the same time *had* to come in Czechoslovakia as well. He was convinced that the relevant sentence, which he copied out faithfully, was the foundation of his legal entitlement not to be distrusted and ordered about.

"It was a sorry sight," Kvido explained later, "to see my grown-up father resting all his hopes and aspirations on a handful of cuttings from *Týdeník aktualit*."

During this time, the square-cut lime and planked pine in the workshop fell under a heavy coat of dust. The casual indifference with which Kvido's father lent his finest Swedish chisels to Mr Zvára spoke volumes.

"You really don't mind lending me the Swedish ones?" Zvára could scarcely believe his luck.

"Sure," Kvido explained to him, "the ice of Communism is starting to break up..."

However, the workshop in the cellar didn't remain abandoned for long, because even Kvido's father began to see the true nature of things.

"He discovered," Kvido explained chirpily, "that Šperk and the rest of them were also saving up press cuttings – and unlike him, they were well placed enough to lay their hands on even the hard-to-get *Sputnik*."

2. Yet the Soviet Union remained a topic of conversation in the household for some time, thanks to Grandma Líba.

One Sunday, Kvido, still embittered by his editor's latest demands, turned up at the lunch table to be greeted by the unmistakable aroma of potato gnocchi.

"Aargh, gnocchi!" he said ominously. "Gnocchi again! Back to gnocchi!"

Jarka patted him on the shoulder comfortingly.

"Calm down," she whispered. "I'll cook you a lovely dinner tomorrow." Kvido sighed and kissed her on the cheek.

But then, when he saw all the leftovers on little Annie's plate, his fury rose to its previous level. He banged his knife and fork down.

"I wouldn't wish to deny these pretty yellow gnocchi – or yesterday's dumplings or the day before's pancakes – their alleged nutritional value," he declaimed into the oppressive silence, "but I suggest we consider collectively whether – especially in light of the developmental needs of this child – whether we might not from time to time buy – excuse my language – some *meat*..."

"Stop that!" said his mother.

The others – except little Annie, who was casting reproachful looks at Grandma Líba – made an exaggerated play of concentrating on their plates.

"Obviously I mean *cheap cuts from freshly slaughtered animals*," Kvido went on icily, having downed his last gnocchi, "since the household budget can't be governed by wishful thinking and subject itself to the extortions of dictatorial butchers who shamelessly charge as much as twenty-five crowns for a kilogram of braising steak, which is, as anyone can calculate for themselves, the same as half the cost of the revenue stamp charged on a customs declaration. Thank you –," and he pushed his plate determinedly aside, "that was very nice and cheap."

"She's off to Leningrad with her girls," his mother explained to him after lunch, "do try and understand."

"Please," she added.

Kvido took his mother's urging to heart and subsequently ate all the cost-saving, wartime austerity meals that traditionally preceded his grandmother's excursions, without a murmur. He appeared to have mentally forgiven her, since he let her tell him about the 'Venice of the North' from time to time, giving her the impression of a possibly melancholic, yet fairly attentive listener.

At other times, he and Paco would help themselves out with humour, which seemed to facilitate consumption of even the dreaded bread soup. Paco wondered, for instance, what Grandma would bring them back this time, his own tip being that it would be a big nesting doll, only slightly battered, containing a gold-coloured, carefully washed, but empty caviar pot, inside which there'd be a badge bearing a silhouette of the Aurora. Kvido liked betting on how much younger Grandma would get on such a long trip eastwards, *against* the progression of time.

"I wouldn't be in the least surprised," he once told Paco over a bowl of eked-out porridge, "if they nabbed the amorous young man smooching with Grandma on Nevsky Prospect and did him for sexual exploitation."

Despite all these crazy notions, a post-card came from Leningrad with the message, amazingly, in *prose*.

"Greetings to you all from Leningrad, thinking of you, Grandma," it said.

"Not a line of verse?" Paco was surprised. "Could she be having a crisis of creativity?"

"I don't know," said Kvido's mother pensively.

3. As it transpired, the first of those acute pains that she couldn't take hit Grandma Líba while still in Leningrad, in the lobby of the Druzhba hotel, where she was waiting with the other tourists for the airport coach. The doctor was with her in less than a minute; the downside of this favourable turn of events was the six silver-plated teaspoons bearing the Druzhba logo, which the doctor, to his growing surprise, hit on one by one as he struggled through the layers of her travelling garb.

"Ya tolka khatyela padgatovit' chaja,"* an embarrassed Grandma Líba explained disjointedly again and again until a new wave of fierce pain left her incapable of feeling anything else at all.

"Nichevo, babushka, nichevo,"† the doctor comforted her, anxiously feeling all over her strangely solid abdomen.

"Dear girl," said Zita to Kvido's mother a few days later, pushing her hair from her forehead. "My dear girl."

Kvido's mother closed her eyes and bit her lower lip.

Zita looked towards Paco and Kvido.

"Boys," she said, "I wonder if you know what your grandmother has brought you."

She reached into her bag and took out two heavy packets.

Kvido gulped with some effort.

---

* I only wanted to make some tea.
† Never mind, Grandma, never mind.

"This Zenit camera," said Zita with feeling, "and this magnificent videocamera."

Paco's chin quivered.

"She loved you so much," said Zita, very, very gravely.

XVII.

Grandma Líba's sudden death had actually distracted Kvido from working on his novel for only a few days, but when he returned to his manuscript after the funeral, he felt a kind of barely definable apathy and asked himself how and whether to go on with it.

One Saturday evening, after he'd spent long minutes gawping at a blank page, he had an idea, quite out of the blue, that he should perhaps replace the old straw matting on the wall behind the divan in the bedroom with a wooden fascia. He doodled absently on the blank page – but then he actually stood up and pulled the divan away from the wall experimentally. Then he went down into his father's workshop.

For a moment he surveyed the tidy piles of timber, examined the strikingly grained planks of cherry wood, weighed some blocks of oak in his hand and ran a finger over the blades of the chisels. He ended up selecting some twenty pinewood battens to cut back to the required length; he clamped the first one to the bench, relishing how beautifully smooth it was to the touch.

He began sawing.

Microscopic bits of sawdust clung to the hairs on his wrist.

He told himself he needed to get on with the job quickly so as to be able to surprise Jarka.

"Hold still, you can have the skin!" he muttered darkly to himself.

"Hold still, you can have the skin!"

Epilogue

In June 1989 Paco gained admission to the Arts Faculty of Charles University in Prague. On the heels of the November revolution, he arrived at the Sázava glassworks at the head of a student delegation. The Chairman of the Works Committee of the Communist Party of Czecho-Slovakia, Comrade Šperk, told the porters not to let the students inside. After a brief scuffle with his father, Paco and the others climbed over the fence and a discussion with the workforce took place after all (Paco's girlfriend, a first-year law student, will at this point indulgently explain to Kvido's mother the essence of civil law).

Future events unfolding in the Czecho-Slovak Federal Republic bring ever greater disappointments to Paco. He resigns from his post in the so-called Student Parliament, interrupts his course and with a sense that someone has stolen the revolution away from him, goes to America on a studentship.

On his return, he becomes active in the Anarchist Movement. His pacifist convictions go from strength to strength. In the April he receives his call-up papers; along with similarly afflicted anarchists, he stages an event to burn the papers outside the barracks on Republic Square to cries of 'Fuck the Army!'. He applies for a transfer to alternative non-military service, replying simultaneously to an advert placed by a Belgian company with a branch in Prague (requirements: knowledge of English, basic computer skills, driving license and age 28 or lower). After getting through the interviews he is employed on extraordinarily good salary terms. However, in the first month he crashes his company Ford Sierra so many times as he exits the company car park that he is dismissed on the grounds of untrustworthiness.

In the year following the Revolution, Grandpa Josef, via the pages of the advertising magazine *Annonce*, makes several pretty good deals (for example, swapping seven 100-crown notes bearing the portrait of Klement Gottwald for a full thousand crowns), but his comments on the political life of the new times grow more and more resentful. He dislikes the salary rates for members of parliament, the long hair of minister Langoš, the inclusion of ex-communists in the government and the sluggish pace of lustration.

"Hang 'em, it's no good just naming them!" he roars time and again.

"Stop it! Do you hear?" Grandma Vera ticks him off emphatically.

One evening in December 1989, at one minute to ten, Jarka looks up at the red neon light on the dark horizon and notes to her surprise that one of the letters is hidden by someone's silhouette. Kvido, standing behind her, is devastated.

"I could forgive you for finding someone else," he yelled jealously, "but I'll never forgive you for letting him do this…!" It transpires next day that the man on the roof of the admin building had been Comrade Šperk, using his own body to try to prevent a number of members of Civic Forum from dismantling it.

On December 6th the sign is removed for good. That same evening, Comrade Šperk points his hunting rifle at his right temple and pulls the trigger. However, the bullet misses and the only consequence of this attempted suicide, as the medical report later states, is temporary loss of hearing in his right ear. After a brief convalescence, Comrade Šperk purchases, at an auction held within the so-called small-scale privatisation, a restaurant called The Keeper's Lodge for the reserve price of 3,240,000 crowns.

From January 1990 onwards, Kvido's father heads up the commercial section of the Ministry of Foreign Trade. He commutes to work in his own car. In the following September he is despatched to Brazil on a contract-signing trip.

"Not bad, eh?" he often says these days with a smile.

Shortly after his return, general vettings are carried out at the ministry; he is found 'positive' and dismissed. He rejoins the glassworks, now Kavalier Sázava Co. Ltd, with responsibility for pricing.

During the months that follow, Grandma Vera's sleep is erratic. In the night from the 18th to the 19th of August 1991 she doesn't sleep at all. She cannot explain it. In the morning, she discovers that all three budgerigars have flown off again. A few minutes later, she hears on the radio that there's been a putsch in the USSR and that there are tanks on the streets of Moscow.

"A realist can never be disconcerted by miracles," is Kvido's comment on this turn of events.

Kvido's mother has no time for miracles, since she is supposed to be submitting the draft for a project called large-scale privatisation. She is also worried about the return of her husband's illness.

September 12th sees the arrival of Mirjana from Pula in Croatia, currently under threat from Serbian nationalists; Kvido's mother offers her political asylum.

On October 10th Kvido submits the manuscript of his novel, *Bliss was it in Bohemia,* to the Československý Spisovatel publishing house.

APPENDIX
of
HISTORICAL AND GEOGRAPHICAL ENTITIES MENTIONED IN THE NOVEL

Compiled by the translator for the idly curious reader, with some pointers to where s/he might find out more. The translator craves the indulgence of those readers to whom the literary, historical, social and political background to this novel is entirely familiar. I have placed at the head two quotations cited in the novel without reference to their source.

If more information were sought, then one could not be better advised than to refer to the pages on jantarpublishing.com/publications/bliss-was-it-in-bohemia

"A beautiful morning rose over a deep valley…" (p. 197): This passage recited by Kvido's actress-mother comes from Karel Hynek Mácha's (1810–36) short-story *Pouť krknošská* (A journey to the Giant Mountains, 1833). Mácha was the leading Czech Romantic poet and arguably the most important figure in the whole of Czech literature, largely on the basis of his narrative poem *Máj* (May, 1836).

"The lasso's loop whizzed through the air…" (p. 195): a rendering of the popular cowboy/campfire song *Koníčku můj* by Vladimír Rubeš and Karel Sehnoutka.

Abrhám, Josef (b. 1939): popular Czech actor (film and theatre). Appeared, *inter alia*, in the 1970 film of Vítězslav Nezval's novel *Valerie and her Week of Wonders*, and the 2006 film version of Bohumil Hrabal's *I Served the King of England*. (Both these novels have been translated into English.)

Bican, Josef (1913–2001): Austro-Czech footballer, highly regarded in both countries, nicknamed 'the cannoneer', he scored over 4,500 goals, mostly impressive. He had a minor planet named after him (as Pepibican) in 1998.

Brodský, Vlastimil (1920–2002): popular Czech actor, whose career was associated chiefly with Vinohrady Theatre, but also with a lifelong involvement in film and television, stretching from 1937 to 2001 and including, among the films perhaps best-known in Britain, *Closely Watched Trains* (1966) and *Capricious Summer* (1968).

Canada by Night (game): A (Czech?) game that requires scout (and similar) troop leaders and their assistants to enter the children's tents/chalets at night and decorate their faces and hair with face paint, various foams, whipping cream, tooth-paste etc., further tricked out with glitter etc., taking care also to smear tooth-paste on any door handles. The kids are supposed to wake up in the morning surprised at how the change has affected their appearance.

Český Šternberk: A small country town with an impressive, much visited, castle, about five miles upstream (i.e. southwards) from Sázava.

Civic Forum (*Občanské fórum*): This was the Czech political umbrella movement that sought in 1989 to bring together all the various dissident stirrings in the 'Velvet Revolution' of the dying days of Communist Czechoslovakia. Its Slovak counterpart was Public Against Violence (*Verejnosť proti násiliu*), and Ján Langoš (below) was a member.

Demínka: A popular Prague watering-hole, founded 1886 – coffee-house, restaurant, now a pub-restaurant, notable for its Art Nouveau décor and its 'celebrity' clientele in every age.

Disman Radio Ensemble: Properly the Disman Radio Children's Choir, founded by the educationist and theatre and radio director Miloslav Disman (1904–81) in 1935 and still going strong.

Erben, Karel Jaromír (1811–70): Czech revivalist poet (and archivist and translator…) best known for his collection *Kytice* (A Garland of Czech Legends; 1853, 1981), in which 'Poklad' (Treasure) is the second ballad. The book has recently (2014) become available in English translation (Jantar).

Friends of the Armed Forces: More formally known as the Union for Cooperation with the Armed Forces (and in Czech by its acronym Svazarm), this was a body that existed largely to monitor sport and leisure activities best not allowed to proliferate at random, such as dog breeding (with an eye to Alsatians), gun sports, short-wave radio, amateur flying and gliding, and motorsports (including driving schools).

Husák, Gustáv (1913–91): The unloved Slovak politician who became President of Czechoslovakia after General Svoboda (in 1975), having previously succeeded Alexander Dubček as Secretary General of the Communist Party of Czechoslovakia (1969–97). It was his period of office that came to be known as 'normalisation' following the liberal times of the Prague Spring.

Jirásek, Alois (1851–1930): prolific Czech author of largely historical novels and plays, in a distinctly nationalistic mould.

Kohout, Pavel (b. 1928): Czech verse and prose writer and dramatist, notable for starting out as an arch-Stalinist (by his own desire, he married his first wife on Stalin's birthday), sobering up during the Prague Spring and finally going into exile in the 1970s (hence his appearance in the book as an enemy of the [post-1968] regime). The play mentioned herein, *August, August, August,* is set in a circus, and the quatrain declaimed at one point by Kvido's mother ends Kohout's, some might say notorious, entry in the visitor's book of the S. K. Neumann Theatre of 19 April 1953.

Kryl, Karel (1944–94): Prolific Moravian singer-songwriter of protest songs following the stemming of the Prague Spring liberalisation period by the Soviet occupation of August 1968.

Kutná Hora: Historic city, famous for its medieval silver mines and ossuary, some ten miles east-north-east of Sazava.

Langoš, Ján (1946–2006): Slovak politician, pre-1989 dissident and post-1989 member of parliament and Interior Minister (1990–92), killed in a road accident. A google search reveals that he indeed had quite flowing locks (as complained of herein) in the early days.

Libíček, Jan (1931–74): Czech comic actor whose career began in his native Gottwaldov (today's Zlín), but who had a stint (1963–68) at the Theatre on the Balustrade, playing memorable roles in *Ubu Roi*, *Waiting for Godot* (as in this book), and Václav Havel's *The Garden Party*.

Literární noviny: A Czech weekly for literature, culture and politics which came out, with breaks, from 1927 to 1967 (relaunched in 1989/90. It was a major platform for political debate during the Prague Spring of 1968 and contributed in no small measure to the period liberalisation of Czech(oslovak) society.

Little Otík: A highly acclaimed, whimsically drastic film (also known in English as *Greedyguts*), part acted, part animation, called *Otesánek* in Czech, and about a lump of wood brought to life; it is by Jan and Eva Švankmajer and is based on Karel Jaromír Erben's eponymous 'folktale'.

Makarenko, Anton Semyonovich (1888–1939): the leading Soviet educational theorist.

Mladý svět ('Young World'): This was a hugely popular, and at its peak quite readable illustrated weekly, founded in 1959 and later becoming the official journal of the Socialist Union of Youth, though with a general, not just youthful readership. It would be a fairly obvious place for a young writer to offer short stories to. Its post-1990 successor never enjoyed the same success and effectively folded in 2005.

National Avenue: The main North-South thoroughfare in central Prague from the bottom of Wenceslas Square to the National Theatre by the river.

National Front: *Not* to be confused with any similarly named bodies in Britain or France. This was an association of the political parties and, in due course, certain other bodies, who were to have a say in running Czechoslovakia after the war. From the outset it was inevitably dominated by the Communist Party of Czechoslovakia.

normalisation: In the Czechoslovak context this refers to the period after 1969 when all the gains of the 'Prague Spring' were reversed and what some have called neo-Stalinism ensued. It is closely associated with the 'reign' of Gustáv Husák (see above).

Neumann, S[tanislav] K[ostka] (1875–1947): Czech left-wing journalist and Decadent poet, scourge of the bourgeoisie and eventually co-founder of the Communist Party of Czechoslovakia and initiator of the Czech school of Proletarian Poetry.

Paris Commune Square (*Náměstí Pařížské komuny*) – in the Nusle quarter of Prague. An often renamed square, given its present name in 1962, at the suggestion of the Institute of History of the Czechoslovak Academy of Sciences, to mark the 90th anniversary of the Paris Commune (1871).

Pavel, Ota (1930–73): Czech writer, journalist and sports reporter. His *Dukla Among the Skyscrapers* (1964) merged literature and journalism in an account of the Czechoslovak national football team's successes abroad.

Plamen: A literary journal of 1959–69, set up as a platform for the rising generation of young Czech writers. Key writers involved in running and contributing to it and perhaps most likely to be known to the present book's readers included Milan Kundera and Josef Škvorecký.

Plicka, Karel (1894–1987): A man of many parts (ethnographer, film director, photographer among much else) undoubtedly best known for his coffee-table books of photos of Prague and its Castle, which appeared in several languages.

Podolí: This lies in the west of Prague and is home to a maternity hospital seen widely, if not universally, as the city's best.

privatisation (small-scale, large-scale, following the 1989 'changes'): The Czechoslovak privatisation process was not without its critics. Again, one could not be better advised than to refer to the pages on jantarpublishing.com/publications/bliss-was-it-in-bohemia.

Proud Princess: An allusion to the eponymous 1952 Czech film, in which a snooty fairy-tale princess is brought down to earth.

Realist Theatre (*Realistické divadlo*): The main theatre in Smíchov (south-west Prague, west of the river). So named since 1945, full name from 1953 the *Zdeněk Nejedlý Realist Theatre*, from 1991 the *Labyrinth Theatre*; closed in 1998. Rebuilt and reopened in 2002 as *The Švanda Theatre in Smíchov* (named after Pavel Švanda's [1835–91] first theatre on the site, 1871).

Remek, Vladimír (b. 1948): A high-ranking Slovak officer in the Czechoslovak Air Force, much vaunted as the first Czechoslovak (and first non-Soviet European) astronaut (the Soyuz 28 mission of 1978), and in those days, therefore, a great national hero. In 2014 he was appointed Czech ambassador to Russia.

Rozvadov: A border crossing next to the German frontier, named after the nearby village. Ever the route out of Czechoslovakia when you headed West from Prague, and the crossing that everyone knew about.

St Anne's Square (*Anenské náměstí*), Prague: A small square just off the main tourist trails in Prague Old Town, named after St Anne's Dominican monastery, but universally associated with the Theatre on the Balustrade.

Schikaneder, Jakub (1855–1924): An important Czech painter known for his landscapes, some townscapes and particularly his portraits of women; he had a particular interest in the fate of women within modern civilisation.

Sixty-Eight Publishers: The largest Czech(oslovak) émigré publishing house, based in Toronto and set up in 1971 by the then expatriate writer Josef Škvorecký (1924–2012) and his wife Zdena Salivarová (b. 1933) to publish works by writers banned at home.

Skála, Ivan (1922–97): Czech communist politician and political poet, a leading 'normaliser' in the 1970s and Chairman of the Union of Czech Writers from 1982 to November 1989.

Sloup, Václav (1936–2014): Czech actor, whose career centred on all three theatres mentioned (if only obliquely) herein: Theatre on the Balustrade (1962–77), the S. K. Neumann Theatre (1977–83) and the Vinohrady Theatre (1983–98). He also appeared in a number of films.

Šik, Ota (1919–2004): A Czech communist politican and economist, remembered chiefly as architect of the economic reforms, the 'third way', instituted as part of the 'Prague Spring'. Dismissed by the Soviets as an agent of US imperialism, he emigrated to Switzerland after 1968.

Šmeral, Vladimír (1903–82): Czech actor, left-wing intellectual and communist functionary, associated throughout his career with the more experimental theatres, and from 1978 with membership of the Vinohrady Theatre, where he had already appeared frequently over the previous three decades. During the war, having refused to divorce his Jewish wife, he was deported to a concentration camp in Poland. Between 1949 and 1966 he also taught at one of the leading Prague drama schools.

Sputnik: Published in seven languages (allegedly universally appallingly translated), this was, until its closure in 1991, meant to be the Soviet counterpart to *Reader's Digest*. When *perestroika* and *glasnost* arrived, its popularity in Czechoslovakia suddenly rose as one of the few sources from which outsiders might learn what was really happening in the Soviet Union and its pages began to be filled with topics that would never have been possible previously: repression of dissidents, freedom of speech, banned films etc. etc.

Suvorov, A. V. (1729/30–1800): Russian general, a national hero undefeated in over 60 battles.

Svoboda, Ludvík (1895–1979): a Czech national hero and the popular President of the Czechoslovak Socialist Republic 1968–75, i.e. during the 'Prague Spring' and 'Years of Crisis'.

Theatre on the Balustrade (*Divadlo na zábradlí*): A major Prague theatre, avant-garde ever since its inception in 1958.

Tuchlovice: a village in the Kladno coalfield to the west of Prague with its own mine.

Týdeník aktualit: A weekly 'normalisation' newssheet notorious for its clunky translations from Russian.

Josef Kajetán Tyl (1808–56): Czech dramatist, theatre critic and an important figure in the Czech National revival, notably as translator and adaptor of over fifty plays from German, by which he sought in part to compensate for the paucity of original Czech plays in the Prague theatres. Today he is best known for a handful of his plays, rather less well known for the *ménage à trois* he lived in with his wife and her sister (he had nine children with the latter who were raised by the former).

Uhlířské Janovice: A small town approximately 30 miles west-south-west of Prague and 10 miles east of Sázava.

Valdek: Formerly a block of flats, built 1928-30, between Jugoslávská and Anglická Streets in Vinohrady, it also housed a coffee-house and cinema. Today it is a classy office block rejoicing in the (English) name of Valdek House.

Vršovice Station: A major railway station south of the central part of city.

Vyšehrad: The elevation on the right bank of the Vltava in Prague, with a history going back to the first tenth-century fort, and famed for its basilica of St Peter and St Paul, and the memorial burial ground, which has served and serves a purpose akin to that of Westminster Abbey. The site is also wreathed in legend and the pre-'history' of the Czechs.

Also available from Jantar Publishing

PRAGUE. I SEE A CITY...
by Daniela Hodrová

Translation by David Short
Foreword by Rajendra Chitnis

Originally commissioned for a French series of alternative guidebooks, Hodrová's novel is a conscious addition to the tradition of Prague literary texts by, for example, Karel Hynek Mácha, Jakub Arbes, Gustav Meyrink and Franz Kafka, who present the city as a hostile living creature or labyrinthine place of magic and mystery in which the individual human being may easily get lost.

A KINGDOM OF SOULS
by Daniela Hodrová

Translation by Véronique Firkusny and Elena Sokol
Introduction by Elena Sokol

Through playful poetic prose, imaginatively blending historical and cultural motifs with autobiographical moments, Daniela Hodrová shares her unique perception of Prague.
A Kingdom of Souls is the first volume of this author's literary journey — an unusual quest for self, for one's place in life and in the world, a world that for Hodrová is embodied in Prague.

www.jantarpublishing.com

Also available from Jantar Publishing

THREE FACES OF AN ANGEL
by Jiří Pehe

Translation by Gerald Turner
Foreword by Dr Marketa Goetz-Stankiewicz, FRSC

Three Faces of an Angel is a novel about the twentieth century that begins when time was linear and ended when the notion of progress was less well defined. The Brehmes' story guides the reader through revolution, war, the holocaust, and ultimately exile and return. A novel about what man does to man and whether God intervenes.

KYTICE
CZECH & ENGLISH BILINGUAL EDITION
by Karel Jaromír Erben

Translation and Introduction by Susan Reynolds

Kytice was inspired by Erben's love of Slavonic myth and the folklore surrounding such creatures as the Noonday Witch and the Water Goblin. First published in 1853, these poems, along with Mácha's *Máj* and Němcová's *Babička*, are the best loved and most widely read 19th century Czech classics. Published in the expanded 1861 version, the collection has moved generations of artists and composers, including Dvořák, Smetana and Janáček.

www.jantarpublishing.com